B

TO

BATTLE

THE CONFESSIONS OF SAINT ILLTYD

by

D. A. Stewart

STRAEON
Llantwit Major, Wales
2021

Illtyd's World

Illtyd's Western Europe

ILLTYD'S BRITANNIA

PROLOGUE

He called, I answered.

The sweet smell of ripening apples filled the air as my companions and I wound our way inland. Stone walls appeared through groves of trees as we approached our destination. I hurried on, eager to see my master, again. I am what I am because of him.

As my feet trod the soil of Armorica in the late afternoon sun, my mind carried me back more than twenty years. On my last voyage here, Illtyd stood with me in the prow of a grain-laden ship.

News had reached us across the sea in Britannia that the Britons of Armorica were starving. The combination of poor harvests and hostile raids had wreaked havoc; many would not survive the winter. We knew we must share what little we had. Illtyd, not content to merely share from our storehouses, travelled throughout Gorfynydd and Penychen prevailing upon the lords of the land to send grain from their harvests.

Persuasive even when not pressed, Illtyd took this need to heart. Kings gave him a hearing. Who would not in those days? They all gave … some more grudgingly than others.

A few weeks later, we set sail with seven ships full of grain and the promise of more behind us. In my mind's eye I see Illtyd with furrowed brow, his beard and hair of silver-streaked gold wildly blowing around him like the mane of a lion as he intensely prayed for wind, willing us onward, longing to ease the suffering of his beloved people.

When we arrived, the people thronged to meet us. It was a miracle they said. Illtyd had saved them.

This sweet memory filled my mind as we approached the oaken gates. My old friend Samson greeted us warmly as the gates swung open. His ample beard more grizzled than I remembered, he graciously invited us in to share his hospitality. After seeing to the rest of our party, he turned to me.

1

"It is good to see you again, Gildas. It has been too long. We both have travelled many miles since we last met. I see from your creased brow and careworn face that not all the miles have been easy. I am glad you have come. He has been asking for you. Some are already with him."

I was only too happy to follow as he led me across the cobbled courtyard through a stone arch and down a long hallway.

"Who else has come?" I asked.

"Pawl and Teilo have been here some days. Dewi arrived just yesterday. I'm not sure if the others will make it in time," he answered as he opened an iron-bound door.

I found myself ushered into a large chamber, warm and close. A fire blazed in a small hearth, and smoke from the rushes crept up the walls and floated across the vaulted ceiling. The light seemed to ripple through the room. There in the centre, on a bed surrounded by my old friends - my brothers - lay my master, Illtyd ap Bicanys.

He looked smaller than I remembered, his warrior's body ravaged and withered. His gaunt face, framed by his white beard and a crown of wild, snowy hair, broke into a gentle smile when he saw me. Warmth rose in my cheeks as he beckoned to us to gather near, those nearest helping him sit up, placing pillows behind him.

He pointed me into a chair at a small writing table near his head. I quickly took my seat as he began to speak.

~

"Come, my children, come. Come and listen to the words of your father. I am glad to have you with me once more.

"Thank you for travelling from the far-flung places God has blown you in these troubled times. Our lives are not our own, and we all go where he bids us. I seem to have come full circle. Thank you for coming to me here. I would have you hear my confession before I go. I hope my story will profit you. I know it will profit me to pour it into your loving ears.

2

"I don't know that I would have chosen this life of mine, but I suppose it is good I was not given a choice. Only God knows the end from the beginning. But I am getting ahead of myself. I should start with my beginning, not my end.

"Gildas, my fiery son, take up your pen for me. Be gentle as you record these words. Write the truth in love. I know the Spirit has put prophetic fire in your soul; but for these days be but a faithful scribe, I entreat you.

"If you will be patient with an old man, I will tell you my story. If there is any value in it, any wisdom to gain, you will be the judge. Will you indulge me?

"Here ... listen carefully and write down what bears remembering ..."

~

CHAPTER 1

My name is Illtyd. I am a Briton but not from Britannia. I was born in Armorica, in the dying days of the Roman Empire. Britons like my father answered the empire's call to fight the Huns.

They sailed to Gaul to fight for Rome and settled in Armorica, as far west as a man may go save by boat. They still believed the empire could be saved. Oh, the folly of it all! They could not see what is so clear to us now: the empire was doomed. But no one knew that then. In those troubled days Armorica became a bastion of hope and a home for many Britons … my family not the least among them.

My father, Bicanys ap Aldwr, was esteemed as a leader and feared as a warrior. Growing up, I heard little about his feats in battle. He was not a talkative man; the scars on his body and the respect he inspired told his story for him. Armorica needed strength, and my father was nothing if not strong. Together with his brother, King Budic, they formed alliances with the rulers in Britannia and defended Armorica against all threats.

As the only son of a Briton prince and doted on by all, the comings and goings of people and events sailed over my sandy-haired head like waves running up the pebbled beach only to retreat again. It seemed nothing could be amiss surrounded by love, bathing in the warmth of the fire. Everyone from our settlement and those from nearby knew they were welcome. As a prince among the Britons, my father was a river to his people. He was loved, but he was also feared.

I remember the day I came to fear him.

I couldn't have been more than five or six. Fascinated by the flames, I lay by the hearth whittling a stick and throwing the scraps in the fire, enjoying the mystery as they glowed, curled and blackened. Suddenly my father told me to leave. I don't remember how the confrontation started; I only remember my rage. I lashed out with the only weapon then at my command - my words.

"You're a stupid fool!" I shouted through my tears. As I saw his face contort, I realised my mistake. I turned to run, shouting my hasty surrender, "I'm going! I'm going!!" He was on his feet in an instant. I felt his strong hands sweep me off my feet, whirling me around to face him. My feet hung in mid-air as he drew me close enough to smell the meat and mead on his warm breath.

"You dare to speak to me in this manner?!" he hissed.

I had never seen this look in his eyes, and I was sore afraid. I had no name for that fear, no understanding then, but I have sometimes wondered how I survived that confrontation with my father. I chewed my lips and waited.

"You are wise now to hold your tongue, my son," he said as he studied my face. The veins stood out on his temple and neck. I could feel the power in his hands holding me suspended between heaven and earth, awaiting the judgement he would deliver. "If only your mind had been a bit quicker than your tongue, you could have been spared."

With that, he threw me over his shoulder like a sack of grain and strode into the night. He gave me a good thrashing that night. I remember laying abed, whimpering and running my fingers over the welts on my backside.

I would like to tell you that was the last time we battled or the last time I deserved or tasted his justice. But I was a strong-willed lad, prone to test myself against anything and everyone. Sometimes this has served me well, but often it has made my journey more difficult.

When I was a boy my father was often away; but when he was home his solid solemnity reverberated through our settlement. He seemed to change the atmosphere with his mere presence. He was a tough man with scant softness about him. He could be harsh; and in those early days I feared as much as loved him.

But oh, I do remember the way he loved my mother. When she sang, his craggy visage would melt. Sometimes tears ploughed furrows down his ruddy cheeks as she sang at the hearth.

My mother, Rheinwylydd ferch Amlawdd, was a strong and pious woman. She sang hymns and psalms of course, but she loved the old songs as well. It didn't matter what she sang; it mattered that she sang. Music lived somewhere inside her. Low and mournful or bright and cheery, it was rare that she was not singing or at least humming something throughout the day.

I do believe my earliest memories were those evenings when I lay warm and cosy in the dreamy enchantment of my mother's songs. Snuggling up in woollen blankets, I would lay as near the hearth as I could get … so near my lips dried and cracked; but I didn't mind. My body felt deliciously warm as I gnawed on a bone or a bit of bread. The hounds curled nearby, hoping for a scrap.

I see her still - a beautiful woman with masses of dark ringlets and darker eyes taking up her harp and staring into the distance as she sought inspiration. As she plucked the first note, the hall would quiet. It seemed even the hounds cocked their head to listen. Even now, I close my eyes and fancy I hear her melodious voice wafting in from somewhere nearby.

She sang of Bran the Blessed, Arawn the ruler of Annwn, and a hundred other stories, each one simple but full of hidden depth. She sang to lighten our hearts or to loosen our tears. Her songs protected and built our community nearly as much as my father's sword.

Those evenings around the fire allowed me to see the softer side of my father as well. I remember his tears and the softness of his face as she sang. I have vague but warm memories of my father's strong arms scooping me up and carrying me to my bed; roughly ruffling my hair or gruffly pulling me into his lap and clasping me tight as my mother sang songs that tied us all together.

It wasn't long before she had me singing the songs as well. Of course, I didn't know it then, but this began my education. My mother was singing the old ways into me. She took me on walks through the forest and along the coast, teaching me the names and nature of plants and animals. Creation has so much to show us if we will attend to the lessons. Soon, my childish meandering was replaced by more serious study as my tutors arrived.

Kian arrived first. He was an aged mystery of a man wrapped in a green cloak covered with whorls, and arcane symbols I later learned were runes. At the time, I was struck by his piercing blue eyes and weather-beaten features, as well as his intensity, one that matched my father's but was somehow different.

Kian was a man of great learning and insight. Although not a Christian, he taught me many things worth knowing. From Kian I learned the ancient ways of my people and more specifically my mother's people, the Silures. We are heirs to esoteric knowledge and a proud warrior tradition. Perhaps that was why my mother and father were so well suited. Although my mother was a refined and educated woman, she respected and valued all the best in a warrior ... as well she might in those troubled times.

I remember Kian saying, "A quick mind and a quick tongue will serve you well in the hall of a king or conducting diplomacy, but these virtues and occupations will do nothing against Frankish axe, Gothic sword, or Saecson treachery. There is a need for both scholar and warrior, and a time for every purpose under heaven. In chaotic times like ours, the skills and virtues of the warrior are deemed more readily useful. There can be no scholarship without safety. The warrior supports the scholar as the walls support the roof ... but which one keeps the rain off, eh?!" He ended with a knowing chortle.

Kian rarely delivered his lessons indoors. On my wandering walks with Kian I learned to value nature and the many gifts of God's good earth. He had such keen vision and attentiveness to his surroundings! He taught me to pay attention to all things. "Even the smallest movement of a bird or the wind in the trees can carry a deeper meaning. Learn to listen for the deeper truths behind the surface of things. Be curious and hold a space in yourself for questions that arise. Questions are often more important than answers, and they nearly always come first."

Kian acknowledged only a hazy distinction between the natural world and the supernatural one. "The Otherworld and this world are seamlessly intertwined," Kian said. "There are powers all around us that not all men perceive." Kian made it his goal for me to memorise and recite the names and natures of the trees and birds, fish, plants, and stones. He carried no books. Kian scoffed when I asked him why. "Books are for the feeble-minded," he answered. "Your head is the seat of your power, and you must train your mind to contain all that you will need."

This assertion went largely unchallenged until the arrival of Scapilion from Avallon. I wish you had known him, my children. Scapilion's tender but uncompromising love of God and man was a sight to behold. You would not have thought his frail frame could contain such strength, but there was iron in his spine and fire in his soul.

Where Kian was a man of knowledge, Scapilion was a man of letters. Scapilion loved books - one book in particular. Well, one book made up of many. In short, Scapilion loved the Scriptures and made it his mission to make me love them too. I am afraid I did not … not at first anyway. That came much later.

Scapilion was our priest as well as my teacher. He led us in our prayers and preached on Sundays and feast days. He also made it a point to seek the conversion of those who joined our settlement.

People came from all over. Many were on the move in those days - Roman, Briton, and barbarian. It was not uncommon for men or whole families to turn up at our gates looking for refuge. If they were willing to work and give their oath of allegiance, my father welcomed them. It didn't take long for Scapilion to discern the state of their spiritual journey, and it took him no time at all to invite the pagans among them to convert. He was not afraid to push hard for them to make a decision. "Having just pledged your loyalty to your lord, perhaps you would like to pledge yourself to the High King of Heaven?"

Scapilion showed me the shape of letters, how letters made sounds, how sounds made words, and how words expressed meaning. He taught me to write as well as to read. I do not know how many times I formed those shapes on the waxen surface of my board. Each night I would scrape the surface, melt, and pour fresh wax onto the tablet to harden in time for the next day's lessons. "Start every day with a clean slate," Scapilion would say. "You melt and pour the same wax but start fresh each day, just as we find God's mercies are eternal and yet new every morning."

Kian and Scapilion were excellent teachers, albeit of very different subject matters. They often clashed over the differences in their views on religion, but they tolerated each other for the most part. Most of my childhood I spent the morning with Kian and the afternoon with Scapilion.

Some of their instructions dovetailed nicely, such as the rules of rhetoric from Scapilion and the storytelling methods of Kian. At other times their teachings were wildly at odds, mostly when talking about God or the gods. Some found it strange to have a pagan bard and a Christian priest under the same roof. When questioned, my mother would simply reply by quoting Augustine, "Wherever truth may be found, it belongs to the Lord."

My mother made sure we were Christians. Kian was invited to share all he knew, but I was not to follow the old gods. There was much I treasure from my lessons with Kian and still find use of today, but there were darker strains among the tales - dark tales of power and blood, sacrifice and spells. I was intrigued but not drawn to these stories in the way that Myrddin was.

Myrddin ap Cynwal came to us when I was seven. He was my cousin on my mother's side, the son of Cynwal of Glywysing. Although we were kin and of similar age, we could not have been more different in appearance. He had dark eyes and hair similar to my mother's, while I had the fair hair and light skin of my father's people from Rhegin. Myrddin was short, broad, and thick of limb while I was taller and leaner. Despite our outward differences, we soon became fast friends. We shared a quick wit and a ready laugh as well as a temper.

With Myrddin came Arthwyr. My father's cousin, Meurig, married my mother's sister; so Arthwyr was my twice-born cousin. He had my length of limb but Myrddin's thickness. He shared Myrddin's swarthy skin and dark hair but had striking light green eyes. Only two years older than us, he was already a head taller than me. Arthwyr was a bear of a boy who became a dragon of a man. He seemed to carry a weight even from his childhood … a heavy sort of seriousness that marked his whole life.

The arrival of my cousins brought changes to our household. We were tasked with caring for the horses and doing other work on our holding. We shared our food and bed as well as chores. We were seldom apart in those days. When we weren't in lessons with Kian or Scapilion or attending to our duties, we were off exploring the countryside, wrestling giants or fighting the foes of our imagination. We sometimes fought each other as well, but we developed a deep bond. These were the first of many battles Arthwyr and I would share throughout our lives. Little did we know then how our paths would tangle in the coming years. Who would have predicted our fates? Ahhh … but what became of Myrddin is one of the great sadnesses of my life.

But I forget myself, we are still at the beginning of our story.

CHAPTER 2

Almost exactly a year after the arrival of Arthwyr and Myrddin, another change occurred. My father took a rather sudden and more active interest in my schooling.

One morning in the courtyard, when we had finished tending the horses, Bicanys called us. As we approached, we found two strips of ash in his hand. Handing one to Myrddin and one to me, he said, "Fight."

We looked at each other and back to him. "Fight?" I asked.

"Fight!" he sternly responded.

I turned toward Myrddin, shrugged, and quickly attacked, lunging for his chest. I thought to catch him off guard, but Myrddin quickly parried my thrust and slashed toward the side of my head. I ducked and spun, hitting him in the knee as I came around. But before I could savour my victory his stick came crashing down on the top of my head.

I found myself sitting on the ground, not entirely sure how I got there. I shook my head, and as my eyes came back into focus I saw Myrddin standing over me, smiling. I hooked the point of his heel with my toes and swept his feet out from under him. We both leapt up, boiling mad and ready to fight. But before we could do severe damage, my father grabbed us both by the back of our tunics, lifting us bodily off the ground while chuckling to himself.

"That's enough!" he commanded.

We stopped struggling.

"What do you think, Brennus?"

Only then did I notice the man standing in the doorway. He looked old to my young eyes, but I would guess that he was not beyond his thirtieth year. Grey hairs glinted from his temples as he rubbed the stubble on his chin.

"Well, it's hard to tell what the stone will yield until you take a chisel to it, but I'd say there is enough raw ore in these two to make it worth my while to try. I can already tell they have the temperament for it," he responded with a good-natured smile. He then turned his gaze to Arthwyr, seeming to measure him against a secret standard in his mind. "What about you? Ready?" Arthwyr merely nodded sombrely.

That was my first introduction to Brennus, the third of my childhood teachers. While Kian and Scapilion made sure we did not neglect our minds, Brennus worked hard to train our bodies. I had hoped it would be fun, and it was at times; but it was also gruelling work.

The very first day, he took us into the forest and showed us a sizeable brown boulder. "Which of you can move this stone?" I looked back and forth from the rock to Brennus. The rock was taller than I was! I couldn't get my arms even halfway around it. It was like the broken trunk of some ancient oak. Myrddin tried first. He set his shoulder against the rock and pushed with all his might.

Nothing.

Next, he put his back against the stone. Sinking down into a tight squat he pushed mightily, angling to topple through the stone.

Still nothing.

With a downcast expression he stepped away. Brennus gestured for me to try.

Shaking my head at this lunacy I approached the stone, rubbing my hands together in anticipation. I circled the rock, looking for the right place. I found a spot where I could brace against a root protruding from the forest floor. Coiling myself like a spring between the root and the stone, I took a deep breath and tried with all my might to straighten my back and legs. After a couple of attempts I gave up, backing away still eying my adversary.

Without any encouragement, Arthwyr stepped up to the rock. He commenced to poking and slapping the stone from all angles, wedging his toe under it and looking for some handhold to grasp. Scanning the ground, he spotted a sturdy-looking limb and moved toward it.

"No. No wood. Just flesh against stone," Brennus interjected.

Arthwyr grunted, turned, and with one fluid motion took three rapid steps, hurling himself at the rock. Despite his running leap and throwing the full weight of his body through his shoulder, Arthwyr bounced off the rock, landing with a thud on the ground. He was dusting himself off, rubbing his shoulder, and sizing up the stone for another attempt when Brennus stepped between him and his stony foe.

"That's enough of that. What you boys lack in knowledge you make up in zeal!" He motioned us to gather to him. Slapping us each on the back he said, "Nice try, lads. That was a good effort, that was. Now, the next time you try I want you to use your arms as well as your legs, like this ..." he said as he demonstrated the posture. With his left arm curled across his body and his right hand pressed against the stone he explained, "And when you push, I want you to breathe like this. Fuahh!" He forced all the air out in a rush. "You try," Brennus said, beckoning me forward.

He helped me to adjust my arms and legs. "Here ... your back should be straight like this." He moved me into position. I tried his way. But again nothing happened.

"What's the use?! It's never going to move," I complained.

"Oh, really? You have it all figured out, do you? For one so young, you have learned so much ... and so little." He approached me until our faces were but a hands breadth apart and said, "Listen well, young man. Perhaps the most important lesson you will ever learn is obedience. I am surprised you have survived so long in the household of Bicanys without mastering it." Then, fixing me with an icy glare, he added, "You don't have to understand to obey. You will push the rock because I am telling you to do so."

He grinned at us then. "Besides, you shouldn't be so easily discouraged. Ready to give up already, are you?" Brennus often issued his challenges mixed with just a hint of humour. "Would you like to try it this way?" Brennus crouched down low, wrapped his arms around the sides of the stone, and heaved upwards. "Fuahh!" I heard rather than saw it grind and shift.

"Let me try!" insisted Arthwyr. His arms didn't reach quite as far around. "Fuahh!"

Nothing. Now it was Arthwyr's turn to look dejected. Brennus ruffled his dark hair and said, "Good breathing!"

"I want you lads out here at this rock every day. First thing in the morning, every morning. And you'll be needing these for your breathing." He tossed us each a smooth stone about the size of a small apple.

"What do we do with these?" I asked.

"You practice your breathing, as I've said," he answered with a wink. "Here, lie on your back." We obeyed. "Now place the stone on your lips and force the air out." We all tried but ended up shifting more spittle than stone. "When you can push it off your face with nothing but your breath, let me know. That will be your first feat. I will teach you the twenty-four feats of the warrior, the twelve windows of the soul, the seven fractures, and the eight weapons. Once you master these, you will be ready to take your place in the war-band when called upon. And make no mistake my young friends … you will be called upon." He fixed us with his stern gaze for what seemed a long time before brightening his countenance and continuing with a smile, "But not today, lads. Not for many years yet. Now get you gone and learn your letters."

With that, our first day of training was over. Day by day we pushed the rock and practised our breathing. Brennus added new feats and exercises to our practice, eventually adding weapons training as well. We learned the traditional weapons of the legions and our people, but also the francisca. Brennus assured us we would be facing the dreaded Frankish throwing axe one day, and it would serve us well to know the weapons of our enemies.

The next four years of pushing the rock and battering each other with wooden weapons hardened our young bodies and shaped our young minds. It was in that harsh school that I learned bonding through hardship. Often we cursed Brennus under our breath as he forced us to submit to his leadership. He was given a free hand to discipline us as he saw fit.

One thing Arthwyr, Myrddin and I had in common was our heritage. As descendants of kings we already imagined ourselves princes of the realm. Brennus trained us physically, but shaping our character to obedience proved perhaps his most challenging task.

One day I threw down my sword and shield in frustration after Arthwyr bested me again.

"What are you doing!?" Brennus bellowed. "Pick up your weapons and try again."

"No, you pick them up!" I retorted.

"If I pick them up, you will not like what I do with them," Brennus responded, starting toward me.

I remember just a moment of fear, but secure in my place in my own mind I crossed my arms and assumed an air of nonchalance. "Do what you like. I'm done for today." I turned on my heel and started for home.

I heard a rush of movement behind me before the first blow fell. The back of my legs felt like they were on fire. Thwack! Thwack! Thwack! More strikes landed on my back, arms, and legs. I turned to see the enraged face of Brennus raining down blows upon me with my own weapons.

"Ow! You're hurting me! Stop!" I protested.

But Brennus did not stop. "You will learn. One way or another, you will learn." He grunted through gritted teeth as he continued to smack me with the flat of the wooden sword.

"That's enough!" I heard Arthwyr command.

Brennus looked surprised but unbowed. "Really! You would command me?! I am your battle chief, you whelp. Let us see how much you have learned in our years together. Come and stop me if you can." He aimed another blow at my shins and found his mark.

Both Myrddin and Arthwyr charged at Brennus with a scream thinking to take him by storm and eager to avenge themselves upon our tormenter and trainer.

Brennus caught Arthwyr's blow on his shield while simultaneously spinning and kicking Myrddin's legs out from under him and sending him sprawling. Then he threw all of his force through his shield into Arthwyr's. Arthwyr's size was not insubstantial, but Brennus cast him aside like a rag doll. He leapt upon Arthwyr, pinning him to the ground with his boot on his shield and his wooden sword at his throat.

"You miserable curs! You would all be dead! Dead! Do you hear me?! I would have your heads! This is not a game we are playing at!"

He stepped off of Arthwyr and backed slowly away, taking us all into his field of view before continuing, "Obedience and trust … the bonds between the commander and his men are the difference between victory and death. You must - you will - learn obedience!"

Brennus began to chuckle. "I must say though, I like the way you charged in to defend your comrade in trouble." He shook his head, wiping the tears from his eyes as he roared with laughter. "Your tactics were terrible, but I do love your hearts! You may yet be ready when the time comes … we shall see," he added as he tossed my sword toward me.

"Now, take up your weapons once more and do as I say." With that, our training resumed.

That evening, after rinsing off our grime and sweat in the river, we retired to our beds in the bunkhouse. We rubbed our aching limbs with a potion Kian had prepared for us from oil and refreshing - if pungent - herbs.

I winced and hissed as the concoction found a cut on my shin.

Arthwyr glanced at me, smiled, and shook his head, "It could have been much worse … and not just for you."

"Yeah, thanks a lot Illtyd!" Myrddin laughed. "You could have got us all killed today!"

"No doubt! What got into him today?!" I wondered.

"What got into him?! You and your mouth did! It was you who provoked him!" Myrddin spat, before shaking his head ruefully. "What were you thinking?! 'I'm done for the day!'" he added, doing his best impression of me. "You should have known better!"

"I know. I know," I admitted, painfully rubbing my calves and wincing again.

"Here, let me do your back for you," Myrddin offered, coming over to my bed.

I laid down and let him rub the smelly goo all over the welts that had risen - a small mountain range of ridges traced lines of pain from Brennus' beating. It was nearly unbearable.

"I only hope he doesn't tell my father," I said through gritted teeth.

"Or your mother," put in Arthwyr.

"I'm not sure which would be worse!" Myrddin shook his head as he considered the alternatives.

"I don't know," I pondered aloud. "My father would be furious and I might get another beating … but my mother's disapproving looks might be worse. Father's temper is like a storm that blows quick and hard but blows itself out before long. Mother quietly simmers and stews for a long time."

"Well, let's just hope that Brennus considers the matter closed," Arthwyr said as he stood, shaking out his long limbs. "We had better get moving before we get in trouble for not finishing our chores before supper. We still need to muck out the stalls," he reminded us as he headed for the door.

Myrddin laid a playful smack across the back of my head. "That's for the trouble you brought on us. You thought yourself a lion and were shown but a whelp! Come on, let's go!" he added as he sprinted out the door.

I made to sprint after him, but my head swam as I rose from the bed. I think I waddled more than ran after him to the stables, my aching body reminding me of the rough lessons of the day.

CHAPTER 3

All our tutors trained us for war - each in their way - although I'm not sure that Kian and Scapilion would have seen it that way. They had other objectives for their instruction. Kian told us tales of great warriors and master smiths who forged weapons of great power. Scapilion introduced us to the history and tactics of war from the pages of the Scriptures and Latin historians. Clearly, Brennus took an altogether more hands-on approach to our training. You might say Kian prepared our hearts, Scapilion prepared our minds, and Brennus prepared our bodies. Little did we know then how important our training would become.

We were being trained not just to fight but to lead. In times like ours, war is a necessary part of leadership; but is not an end in itself. Kian taught us the ancient ways of influence and statesmanship. He also taught us about the necessity for a lord to know about agriculture and husbandry as well as arms and tactics. "The skills that come to the fore in peace are just as important as the skills that are necessary for war. If a leader is only a warrior, he will seek only war. A man like that may be a good battle chief, but he is not fit to lead a people. A prince must be a scholar and a farmer, a shepherd and a judge. He must build and keep the peace, and that is even more difficult than winning a war."

Scapilion sought to shape our character into the likeness of Christ. We were wild and young and energetic. We trusted in the strength of our limbs and our bonds of kinship. Meekness, humility, and love held no fascination for us. The importance of these virtues would not dawn upon me for many years. Looking back, I see that Scapilion had been assigned the most challenging task.

As we grew older, my father took our scholastic troop on the road. We accompanied him as he travelled. Father consulted with Kian and Scapilion from time to time when resolving disputes or suggesting solutions. As we walked the oft-soggy roads of Armorica, we were invited to offer our observations. Many things were learned along the way which might have never found a home in us without this exposure to the world around us.

I remember riding into a small hamlet near our eastern border one morning to find twenty Frankish warriors at the well in the centre. The villagers were huddled together before them, and a cruel-looking young Frank was laughing at something that amused only him while testing his thumb on his axe.

I made a quick calculation of our forces and tactics and knew we were in trouble. Our band consisted of my father, Morgan, Llew, Rhodri, and Cai as well as Arthwyr, Myrddin, and me. I did not like our chances.

My father did not hesitate but rode straight up to the villagers. Ignoring the Franks entirely, he swung down from his horse and strode up to the village elder. "Conan, how go things here?" he asked.

Conan, looking visibly relieved to see his prince, cautiously stepped forward, gesturing around him. "Things are as you see them, my lord."

"Yes, the weather is changeable this time of year. The track here has become overgrown since my last visit. Do not worry, all will soon be set right." Then turning to face the Franks who, unsure of what was happening, shifted uneasily, he added, "And who are our guests, and why have you left them standing out here rather than offering them hospitality befitting a Briton?"

"In truth my lord, I did not even think to offer it," Conan replied hesitatingly.

"Let me begin the introductions then," he said, addressing himself to their apparent leader, his axe still in hand. "I am Bicanys ap Aldwr, and who might you be?"

"I am Clothar, son of Clovis."

That was not good news. We all knew of Clovis, the king of the Franks. If this man was his son, this was a fateful meeting indeed. But my father acted as if he had just heard he was the miller's son. My mind was racing and my heart was beating; but I tried to mimic my father's calm demeanour. I did not understand his tactics.

"Oh, really? So Clothar, what brings you onto my lands? Perhaps you were lost and asking my kinsfolk for directions?" These words were spoken casually as he gestured to the villagers, but my father's hand came to rest on his sword as he said it.

Clothar too seemed unsettled. "I was out riding with my companions when we became thirsty. When we spied this well, we decided it was a good place to water our horses and have some amusement."

"Have your horses been watered?" my father asked.

"Not yet."

"Well then, that is too bad. I am afraid our arrival has spoiled your plans. For we have other uses for our kinsman this day, as you heard me mention. The track needs seeing to, and we don't have all day to do to it. I'm sure you understand."

Clothar reddened at this and he was about to reply when my father added, "And please greet your illustrious father for me. While I have never met him, I have heard he is a great and noble leader who takes good care of his people, as all leaders must."

I could almost hear the cogs turning in Clothar's head as he ran through whatever calculations he was making. For a moment that seemed an age, no one moved; all eyes were fixed on Clothar and my father, squared off to each other beside the well.

Then a smile slowly spread on Clothar's face as he tucked his axe into his belt. "Yes, Bicanys - all lords must look after their people and their lands. Only a fool would fail to do so. I will share your kind words with my father." Then, turning to his men he said, "Come, we will enjoy Briton hospitality on a more convenient day."

In just a few minutes they were gone, and we were all breathing sighs of relief. I wondered at the bravery and power of my father. My admiration and affection for him felt almost tangible in my chest.

I remember my father's words on the ride back. "You must never be weak. Even when you are weak, you must portray strength. You must never let your vulnerability show. In this world the strong rule the weak." He paused before continuing, "Listen, boys … a strong man does not seek a quarrel nor go to blows if it can be avoided. You may not start a fight, but you must be strong enough to finish it. Be cunning and wise when you can; but you must never hesitate to vanquish your foe once it has begun."

We learned many things on those trips, some of which took me many years to unlearn.

As we surveyed our lands, listening to our people, their main concerns were food and weapons. We could no longer rely on grain or other resources from within the empire. We had to feed ourselves. Farmers and fisherfolk we had in plenty, but with a steady stream of refugees arriving we were often stretched to our limits. It was only through the active application of leadership that we managed to share what food we had among the people. One boon in this time was the cessation of Roman taxation. Without imperial taxes, we were able to keep whatever we could scrape together rather than trying to satiate the unquenchable appetite of Rome.

Weapons were another problem. We knew every able-bodied man would serve if called upon, if only to keep the terrors they had seen from touching their families again. But what we really needed were smiths. There are secrets in the cracking, burning, and melting of stone that few know and even fewer master.

Brennus carried my father's request for a smith to the surrounding realms. He returned with many regrets but no smith. It was a token of the seriousness of the situation that my father sent Brennus. I did not know it then, but Brennus' battle feats were known across Britannia as well as much of Gaul.

Brennus and my father had ridden with Riothamus, a great king of Britannia who rode to the aid of Rome some years before. He amassed thousands of warriors from Britannia to drive the barbarians from Roman Gaul. But it was not to be.

The Britons with Riothamus had been decisively beaten at the battle of Bourges. I later learned that Brennus and my father had served in the king's guard. They made their names as great warriors in that horrible defeat. Brennus killed forty men with his spear alone that day. Kian composed a song about their deeds, but my father forbade him to sing it among us.

Although grievously wounded, they fought a rearguard action to protect their chaotic retreat. The path back to the coast cut off, their only choice was to push further east and hope to be warmly received by Rome's Burgundian allies. The Burgundians welcomed the survivors and conducted them to Avallon.

In Avallon they found solace and rest at the healing springs by the river of Cure. There they learned of their betrayal and why, instead of the Roman legion they expected, they were ambushed by the massed Gothic war host. They were betrayed into the hands of the Goths as part of a power struggle between Roman patricians. Even then, the Romans could not grasp the severity of their situation … like dogs fighting over a bone while their house burned around them.

They stayed among the Burgundians for some months while they recovered. They found them to be true Christian brothers and learned to appreciate their hospitality. This German tribe had come over the Rhine with a previous wave of invaders but quickly adapted to Roman ways, including the true worship of our Lord Jesus Christ. But the Goths and so many others embraced Arius' heresy. In the years since their arrival, the Burgundians had - like the Britons before them - developed an appreciation for Roman ways. But by that time Rome itself was ruled by a German pretender, Odoacer. No hope would be found in that quarter.

The pagan Franks grew bolder each season and, as our encounter with Clothar demonstrated, they cast their hungry eyes in all directions.

The days were dark and getting darker.

CHAPTER 4

The following summer - the summer of my thirteenth year - my uncle Budic called a council. The death of Euric, king of the neighbouring Visigoths, upset the delicate balance of power in Gaul. Would his kingdom hold together? What would the Franks do without Euric to oppose them? With Euric gone, fear and uncertainty crept into every holding.

All the princes of Armorica attended the counsel, my father among them. Representatives of local kings, the remaining Roman aristocracy in Gaul, and even some kings of Britannia harkened to his call. Those were dangerous times, and it was clear it would do well for friends to know each other's strength and intentions.

The news from Britannia was grim. We heard of the raids of Picts, Scoti, and Saecsons. The Saecsons had settled on lands in the east, and their goal changed from raids to conquest.

The council of Budic reaffirmed the alliances of the Britons and the few remaining Romans in Gaul. Together, they also agreed to dispatch my father to seek an agreement with the Burgundians. Once again we turned our hopes toward Avallon, and beyond that to the King of Heaven who alone never disappoints.

As the council was ending, my father told me that I would accompany him on his mission to the Burgundians. I must admit my excitement to travel beyond our lands and see the wider world. I rushed to share my good fortune with Arthwyr and Myrddin.

"We are going to Burgundia!" I cried as I ran into the bunkhouse to share the news.

I stopped short as my eyes adjusted to the gloom of the room and found our small accommodation crowded. Arthwyr and Myrddin were there as I expected, but they were joined by Brennus and Kian. They were helping to fill the bags on their beds.

"We are not going to Avallon," Arthwyr responded. "I am summoned back to Britannia. I will ride beside my father in the Dragon's Flight." We had heard tales of Meurig's heavy cavalry and their new tactics. Arthwyr was no longer a boy. At fifteen he was already tall - as big as many men and bigger than most. Brennus' training had imbued us with strength, speed, and quickness as well as weapon skills. I feared that Arthwyr would be testing himself in battle before too long.

"I am sorry to see you go, cousin, but I suspect you are glad to be joining your father."

"Yes," Arthwyr said. "It is an honour for any man to ride by his side. I only hope I may prove worthy."

"And you?" I turned to Myrddin.

"My father is ill and bids me to his side with all haste," Myrddin said as he continued stuffing things into his bags.

"Oh, my brother!" I exclaimed as I stepped closer. Although he had not seen his father in six years, I knew their bond was strong. "So you'll be leaving soon?" I asked.

"Today," he responded.

"That soon! I thought we might have more time."

"It cannot wait. I must hurry."

"I understand," I said, putting my hand on his shoulder.

Pulling me into a rough embrace, he said, "Take care, my brother, until we meet again." Tears flowed freely down both our cheeks.

"Come now boys, do not worry; I will accompany Myrddin to his father. What evil could befall you while a bard of Britain guides you? Besides, your paths will cross again. I have foreseen it," Kian added as he gently pulled us apart.

I see him still, in my mind's eye … Myrddin walking away, Kian's guiding hand upon his shoulder as he wiped his eyes and set his heart toward the challenges awaiting him.

I was rubbing the tears from my cheeks when Brennus' hand clasped my shoulder. "We too must be going. Arthwyr and I sail with them. Fear not, young Illtyd. I'll watch over Arthwyr or he'll watch over me." He grinned into Arthwyr's face, now towering over his. "I'll be back before you know it," he added.

With a final stoic nod from Arthwyr, they pushed past me and out the door, carrying my childhood with them. The sadness of their departure was deepened by the ominous cloud hanging over us all. In uncertain times every parting seems a final one.

I did not have long to brood over their departure, as we set out the next day. There were seven in our party ... an auspicious number. In addition to my father, Scapilion, and myself, we took four of my father's warrior companions. All but Scapilion rode armed, even me ... although we anticipated no trouble and intended to spend each night in a villa or inn along the way.

"Better to be prepared for a battle that never comes, than to be unprepared when the baleful day arises," my father said.

The grim faces of my father and the warriors cast no shadow on Scapilion's sunny disposition. He was going home. Scapilion's family had lived in Gaul for generations. Long before the Burgundians had settled there, his family were prominent and wealthy leaders in the Roman administration. With the arrival of the German tribe, they quickly made arrangements to provide for the Burgundian warriors as they had previously for the legions.

"Better to pay them to use their military might to protect us than to have them take what they want by force," Scapilion explained. "We used to pay taxes to Rome for their support, and now we pay the Burgundians instead. I think we have all adjusted rather well. I don't remember what it was like before, but we have a nice arrangement now. They fight and we feed them."

We travelled for days on end that summer. I have to admit to being a little saddle sore. I was not a bad horseman, but to ride for a fortnight was a lot for my young backside. This amused the warriors with us.

"You'll have to tan that rump of yours if you're going to be any use on the battlefield, young one," they laughed.

We might have shortened the route, but my father did not want to cross Gothic territory. Deep wounds heal slowly, so we stayed on the north of the Liger River. It was beautiful country, so peaceful and warm that summer. The fields were full, and peace lay lightly upon the land. Nevertheless, our armed troop was met with furtive glances as we travelled. Scapilion's presence calmed most fears. After all, raiding parties do not usually bring a priest along.

Those long days in the saddle I heard nary a word from my father. The warriors seemed to know his mind without needing direction of any kind. Scapilion was full of information about the history of Gaul and the changes brought in the last century. He often quizzed me about Julius Caesar's Gallic Wars or the missionary travels of Paul. I passed the time answering his questions, pondering the past and wondering about the future.

Two weeks after we embarked we came to a villa on a hill overlooking a picturesque valley below. As my father dismounted, I caught just the slightest trace of a smile creasing his face. As servants appeared to take our horses, a dignified man in an elegant tunic approached us cautiously.

As my father turned to face him, I saw a flash of confusion and then recognition in his eyes. "Could it be you, Bicanys? After all these years?!"

"Yes, Vesalius, it is I! I've come back to check on your apple harvest and to soak in your springs once more!" My father positively beamed with joy as they embraced and slapped each other on the back.

"It seems you come in better spirits than our first meeting. Oh, but those were dark days ... but who is this in your wake? Can this strapping young man be your son?"

"You always were a quick one. Yes, this is my son, Illtyd. He will be studying in Avallon these next years, I would be grateful to you to keep an eye out for him."

I went from being filled with wonder at my father's lightness of heart to blinding anger in a flash.

"But father ..." I began to protest.

A quick turn and stern look from my father was all it took. I bit my tongue and looked at the ground. My anger smouldered as we made our way inside. Scapilion put a reassuring hand on my shoulder, but I roughly brushed him aside.

"So, the villa seems to have expanded, and you along with it." My father joked, pointing towards Vesalius' abundant girth. "I remember a thinner man, I believe?!"

They continued to joke back and forth, but I heard no more of it. My angry thoughts consumed me.

That night we ate with Vesalius and his household. Everyone said it was a wonderful meal, and I suppose it was; but I had no stomach for it. Most of the conversation seemed to be about people and events that I did not know, and I could not have been less interested that night. As the evening wore on, I looked for an opportunity to confront my father.

He must have known I wanted to talk with him. As his old friend excused himself to go to bed, he turned toward me across the table. "I believe you have something to say to me."

"Father, how could you do this?! How could you bring me all this way, never telling me that you were going to leave me in Avallon with people I do not know?!" I hissed, only just managing to keep my tone somewhat level.

"I am your father. You are my son. I do not answer to you for my decisions. I know what is best for you. Storms are approaching ... surely you know this, even if you are still a child."

"But I'm not a child anymore! I have been training for times like this. Arthwyr has gone to join the Dragon's Flight, and I will join your war band and fight at your side. I may not be ready yet, but I will be soon."

"You do not know war, not yet. You are still my child. I am still your father. You will not become a warrior. Don't you see? Anyone with a strong arm and a thick skull can be a warrior. It's true - I have watched you train with Arthwyr and Myrddin; you have skill and you are getting stronger every day. But you also have a head on your shoulders that is more than just a place to put your battle helm. God has given you a mind, and I promised your mother that you would become a priest. So, a priest you will be."

"A priest! That's your plan for me!?"

"Yes, a priest, like Scapilion or perhaps even like Germanus or Augustine. There are more ways to serve your people than as a warrior."

"But you are a great warrior and a prince among our people. I would be like you."

I watched as his eyes grew wider, hidden thoughts passing behind them. A slight smile crossed his lips, and he seemed to swell somehow.

"Thank you, my son. You honour me. You may yet be a prince among our people. Are not bishops like Germanus princes? My way has been the way of the sword. Your way will be the way of the mind." His words had an air of finality to them.

My head dropped to my chest as I fought back anger and tears. He reached across the table and placed his rough hand under my chin, gently forcing my head up until my eyes met his. With tears in his eyes and softness in his voice that I had seldom heard he said, "It's better this way. Trust me, my son. I know it is hard, but it is better this way." We looked into each other's eyes for a moment.

He coughed and looked away, rubbing his hands together. "Besides," he quickly added, "I'm not sending you alone; Scapilion will be with you. In fact, he will still be your teacher." He took a drink of his wine. "Now, off to bed with you!" he said, rising from the table. "We have a lot to do in the morning. And I could use someone with quick eyes and a quick mind to help me."

"Yes, father," I replied as I stood and made for the beds prepared for us.

CHAPTER 5

Over breakfast the next morning, my father asked Vesalius about the smiths. "Do you still have smiths in the area? I remember some of great skill."

"Oh yes, many foundries and a fair number of smiths ... some right here on my estate. I have formed a partnership with the guild. I provide ore, timber, and space on my estate; they provide their skills and labour, and we split the profits. It is, shall we say, an equitable arrangement." He laughed as he patted his considerable bulk.

"Could you spare a smith or two?"

Vesalius' eyes widened almost imperceptibly. "Ah, so we come to it. I wondered why my old friend would travel so far. I had hoped it was to sample my wine and drink in my friendship once more," he feigned offence. "But now I see a more mercenary reason for your visit ..." His voice trailed off as he shook his head slowly in mock sadness.

My father smiled ruefully and asked, "Shall I be honest with you, old friend?" After a slight pause and a nod from Vesalius he continued, "My journey has several goals. In truth I have long wished to see you and the fair fields and orchards of Avallon again - to soak in the healing springs, to drink the wine, and to rest myself in the presence of a true friend. For true friend I call you who took pity on us in our time of need. I also came to see my son installed in the school at Avallon. But two greater needs have brought me to your door again. Firstly, I am commissioned by the lords of all the Britons to seek friendship and alliance with the Burgundians. Second, I have come in search of smiths ... weaponsmiths in fact. We have men but not enough weapons for the dark days we see ahead. These are the reasons I have come." With these last words, my father swept his arms across the table as if scattering his thoughts before them, then folded them across his chest.

Vesalius rubbed his naked chin with his hand as he considered all he had heard. "I hear you, my friend; and I understand your troubles. As you know, the Visigoth lands are less than two days' ride from where we are seated. The Burgundians are strong warriors and good

Christians, but I fear with Euric's death the Franks will only become bolder. As to your desire for an alliance, I fear you may be too late. The Franks have already sent an ambassador. They passed this way a few weeks ago. Of course, you must try to execute your commission, and I wish you well …" He shook his head slowly, breathing deeply before continuing.

"Now as to the smiths, there I may be of service to you. As I mentioned, we have smiths here; but I do not command them. They are free men - and some of the best, I fear, know their worth too well. I will take you to them. You can examine their work and invite whom you choose. They alone will make their choice. I do warn you, though - they know their craft and their value. Do not take offence too easily. Some perhaps esteem themselves too highly … you will be the judge."

As we were getting up to leave the table, Scapilion asked my father for permission to continue alone to Avallon. "As you know, it is but a short ride from here; and I know nothing of smiths and smithies. So, if you would not mind, perhaps I could take my leave of you today, and Illtyd can join me there soon?"

"Yes, of course. Thank you for your service to my household. I will send Illtyd to you soon. We are indebted to you," my father replied.

Turning to me, Scapilion added, "Fear not, Illtyd. Soon you will find better labours for your mind than worrying." And, placing his hand upon my head he blessed me, made the sign of the cross over me, and departed.

As we rode to visit the smiths I was struck again by the beauty of the area. Although it was only mid-summer, the trees were heavy with apples. And despite the impending doom of my abandonment in Avallon, a cheerfulness settled on me.

We heard the smiths before we saw them - the clanking of their hammers and the roar of the fires. Soon, we could smell them. The smell of an active smithy always reminds me of a lightning strike.

"Ah master smith, how are you today?" Our host greeted a bear of a man wearing a thick leather apron standing near a large clay cone. He looked up but a moment and held one finger aloft as he turned his attention back to the cone. Men clustered around … some using bellows, some carrying buckets of ore, others shovelling charcoal, still others using pokers and other implements. I watched as the master smith looked into the orange glow, sniffing, and extending his hand to feel the heat. Those around him watched him closely. At some signal I did not perceive they all leapt into action for a few moments; and then just as rapidly stopped, stepped back, relaxing and smiling at one another while keeping a close watch on their master.

The man turned towards us. Vesalius addressed him, "Guielandus, this is Bicanys, prince of Britons and my old friend." The smith did not seem overly impressed. He looked us up and down. I watched as his eyes drifted over our weapons.

"What do you want with me," he started, but then added, "… or rather, to what do I owe the honour?"

"I see you are a busy man, as am I," my father began. "I will not mince words. We need smiths. Even better if that man were a master weaponsmith who could instruct others. I remember the smiths of Avallon as they mended our weapons and forged new ones for us after our ill-fated battle with the Goths, before this young one was born. I see you have the command and respect of those who serve you, which speaks much for you. Would you consider joining us in Armorica?"

"A man who gets to the point … I like that. I often say there is nothing that is not worth considering. Come down off that horse of yours, Bicanys; we shall have a drink and see where that leads us."

As the man turned to give orders to his men, I saw a look of genuine surprise on Vesalius' face. "Well now, an invitation to drink with Guielandus. That does not happen every day. I will leave you to your cups, my friends, and look in on the mines before I head home. I will see you at the villa this evening." He turned his horse north with a bemused expression still covering his face.

We dismounted and made our way toward the house of the smith. As we did so I marvelled at the hive of activity of all sorts - digging, carrying, chopping, and hammering. The din decreased somewhat as we rounded the corner of the house to find a table beneath the shade of a massive oak. A girl of about my age appeared with jars and cups on a simple wooden platter.

Guielandus shooed her away and poured the ale himself. "Try some of this. I brewed it myself," he said, handing the first cup to my father and waiting to watch him try it.

My father obliged by taking a huge gulp. "Very good indeed," responded my father, looking impressed as he examined the contents of his cup.

"Some for your boy, then," Guielandus said as he offered me a cup. "Now taste it, boy, don't just drink it. What do you taste?"

I took a drink, rolling it over around my tongue and teeth before swallowing it. I tried to practice what Kian had taught me paying attention to everything. "It is smooth and full … oaky," I began. "But there is something beyond the barley and oats - a sweetness that I believe is apple, and perhaps honey, with a spicy afterglow."

Both Guielandus and my father looked surprised. "Well, look at you!? A spicy afterglow is it?!" Guielandus let out a roar of a laugh, "Here … give that back before you out all my secrets." He made a playful lunge across the table as if to snatch the cup from my hand. Laughing and rolling from side to side on his bench. My father reached over and ruffled my hair, smiling at me.

"You've got quite a lad there … quite a lad," added Guielandus, still smiling and shaking his head while pouring some of the dark liquid into his own cup. He turned to my father. "So you are looking for a master smith. Well, you've found one. As you can see, I've built a home for myself here. Everything I need is close to hand. Why would I consider coming with you?"

"Truthfully, I don't know. But you are already considering it. Why else invite us to share your hospitality?"

A smile crept into Guielandus eyes as he replied, "Yes, you have read me aright. I am considering it. You are a Briton, and so were my forefathers. Far back in time, we worked for the legions in Britannia; but we hitched our cart to Constantine III's wagon and ended up here in Gaul. It may look like Roman Gaul, but this is Burgundia now. The king may give lip service to the Emperor when it suits his purpose, but they are not like us. We are children of the empire and they of the wilds. I feel it in my bones; it is only a matter of time before it comes to open warfare between these tribes. When that time comes, I don't like our chances here in the middle of it all." He paused to take a drink, watching my father over the rim of his cup.

Then he added with a gleam in his eye, "Not to mention that I'm a bit bored here. You say you are looking for a weaponsmith, and that is what I am. But here, although my life is easy, I make mostly farm implements; and the weapons I make I would not see in the hands of these barbarians." He eyed my father carefully. "Come," he said, rapidly rising. "Bring your cups with you if you like. Follow me."

CHAPTER 6

We followed Guielandus into his house, through to an inner room. Closing the door behind us, he moved aside the bed and a coarse woven rug and pulled up a floorboard. Reaching down into the hole, he pulled out a sword. The scabbard alone was a work of art, covered with silver and gold in an intricate design of swirls and shapes. He handed it to my father and stepped back, folding his arms across his chest.

Taking just a moment to admire the scabbard work, my father slowly drew the sword. Before he even had it fully drawn, we knew this was no ordinary blade. First we noticed the bright steel on the edges then the swirling shapes, almost like tendrils of smoke that seemed to flow down the centre of the blade. This was no common sword.

My father felt for the balance in his hand and then tested the sharpness on his thumbnail. Nodding his head approvingly, he proceeded to shave some hair off the back of his arm. "This is a marvellous blade. It feels lively in my hand, light. It is very sharp, and I like the shape. It looks almost like a spatha but handles with better balance."

"Yes. Yes! I have tried many methods of forging and tempering to develop a blade that is light but strong, flexible but sharp. And the shape of this particular blade is modelled on the spatha, so it is long enough for use from the horse, but light enough to be used in close combat. I am glad to see you appreciate it." He began carefully rearranging everything in the room. Gesturing for my father to hold the sword, he said, "Follow me."

We followed him outside and around to the back of the house. They had slaughtered a hog earlier, and it was hanging head down to drain the blood into a bowl. After moving the bowl and clearing some space around the carcass, he said, "How about we let the young man have a go?" I reached out my hand toward the sword, but he shook his head. "No - first show me what you can do with your blade."

I drew my sword and approached the carcass. I felt I was being tested. I rehearsed my footwork in my head and chose my attack. I slashed at the carcass just below the hip, my blade cutting deep into the flesh, breaking bone. Proud of my work, I turned toward my judges.

"Not bad," said Guielandus. "Now try with my sword, on the other side this time."

I carefully wiped my blade on the edge of my tunic before returning it to my scabbard. I saw my father nodding approvingly out of the corner of his eye. "It's the little things that make all the difference," Brennus used to say.

As I drew the sword from the scabbard my father still held, I could immediately tell it was lighter than it should have been. It did feel almost alive in my hand. Once again, attentive to my footwork, I approached the carcass - my momentary foe. This time I used a backhanded slash just above the shoulder. I was surprised how easily my blade passed through. Not only did my sword find the mark, but it carried on through the side and out the front of the carcass, passing through several ribs. I smiled as I looked up at the face of my father. I handed the sword back to him. He spun it in his hand.

"Draw your sword. Trust me, and do what I say."

Having been drilled by Brennus to recognise the tone of command, I immediately obeyed. Drawing my sword and stepping back a few paces.

"Defend yourself." Turning to Guielandus, he asked, "May I?"

Guielandus nodded.

My father swung his sword slowly through the air, and I quickly turned it aside with my own. "Again," he said. Swinging his sword in the same arc of attack again, I parried. "Again." I parried, but this time I felt the shock run down my arm. I looked up cautiously at my father. "Again!" this time I turned it away with more effort and my teeth shook from the force of his blow.

My father stepped back, examining his blade. "Not a mark on it!?" he said. "Illtyd, bring me your sword. There were several notches in the blade. I must have looked disheartened at the damage to my blade.

"Never you worry, with a smith like Guielandus around, your blade will be good as new by …" he paused, looking toward the smith.

"Tomorrow. I can have it repaired for you by tomorrow evening," said Guielandus with a laugh.

Just then, a woman came out of the house. "Oh, look what you've done to my pig!" she cried.

"Don't worry my love … just a little early carving saves the job for later," replied Guielandus with a wink. "Now how about another draught of my ale?" he said to us, scooting us around the corner and away from his wife.

We were all chuckling to ourselves as we returned to our ale.

"So, you are pleased with my craftsmanship I assume?" he asked, gesturing to the sword that was now lying on the table among the cups.

"It is like a magic weapon from the old stories!" I gushed.

Both of the men smiled at that. "It is a fine weapon, but we will need more than one fine weapon for the days ahead."

"Oh, don't you worry about that. My men and I can make many serviceable swords, spears, shields, mail, and helmets. But to make blades like this or lorica segmentata takes more time. Of course, quality also depends on materials. Here I have everything I need."

"What you need, I will find," my father replied.

"But in enough quantity and quality?"

"What do you need?" my father rejoined.

"Quality iron ore, wood for charcoal, geese, clay, salt, oil, and wine."

"These we have in abundance."

"There is just one more thing," he paused and looked my father directly in the eyes and held his gaze. "Safety."

"That is something we have at the moment; and with your help, I have real hope we can secure it in the days ahead. We are a united people who have the sea on three sides and every intention of defending our lands. In times like this we cannot promise more. Let me add this - I know you are a freeman here, and your terms of agreement with Vesalius are generous. We would match his terms or even better them" My father folded his arms across his chest.

"If you can meet his terms and add safety to the mix, you will have bested them in my estimation. I saw those longhair Franks ride through the other day. As if the Burgundians were not bad enough, those arrogant Franks are spoiling for a fight. It won't be long. Mark my words."

"I fear you may be right, master smith. I fear you may be right," my father quietly repeated, shaking his head and drawing the cup to his lips once more.

"Then we have ourselves a deal, and that's something we can drink to." And so saying, Guielandus filled our cups again, with a wink and a grin.

We sat in the shade of the old oak, enjoying the sunshine and ale in silence.

After a few minutes, Guielandus started. "Well, I'm cooking a bloom and I better get back to it. Leave your sword with me, young man. You can pick it up tomorrow evening. We can talk about the arrangements then. And don't forget to take your sword with you, Prince Bicanys," he said as he gestured to the exquisite weapon on the table. "Consider it a gift from a friend," he added with a wink.

And so, not a day after our arrival, my father had accomplished half of his mission.

Vesalius was surprised and a bit disappointed to be losing Guielandus. He indeed was a master smith, but there were others nearby. After all, they lived in the middle of things, not on the fringes as we did.

My father retrieved my sword the next day, and made arrangements for Guielandus and his household to join us before the summer was out.

We stayed with Vesalius for a few more days, visiting the springs and enjoying his hospitality, and making preparations for the next stage of our mission.

One morning my father approached me, placed his hands on my shoulders and looked down into my eyes.

"We do not always choose our path. Sometimes the path is set before us and our choice is merely how we will walk it. I set my face toward Lugdunum to meet with Gundobad, the Burgundian king. I do not have high hopes but I will walk this path to serve our people. You will not accompany me."

I made to protest, but my father merely shook his head. I opened my mouth again, but he held up his hand and continued, "You will not accompany me. Our paths diverge here. Yours leads to Avallon and from there to the church. You too will serve our people. Pray for us. Pray for me, my son."

My father pulled me into his strong embrace. He held me there for but a moment; then, grabbing me by both arms he held me out in front of him measuring me with his gaze. He nodded, turning decisively on his heel, and was gone. I never saw him again.

CHAPTER 7

Vesalius accompanied me to Avallon and installed me in the school of Germanus. It had been named after its founder Germanus of Autissiodorum. Upon arrival, I learned that my childhood tutor, Scapilion, had just been made the head of the school. Most of the students were highborn members of the Gallo-Roman aristocracy.

I found my years there a strange mix of joy and sadness.

The joy of learning came fully alive in me in those days of study and debate. Our education was sevenfold: grammar, arithmetic, geometry, law, philosophy, rhetoric, and the Holy Scriptures - both Old and New Testament. Of these, I most enjoyed philosophy and rhetoric.

One unexpected source of joy was a letter I received from my mother. I discovered I had a brother, Sadwrn. It would be several years before I met him, but I rejoiced in the gift the Lord of Life had bestowed on my parents. To know of Sadwrn but to be unable to see him made me sad. I often wondered what he was like and when - or if - our paths would cross.

When fits of melancholy came upon me, I found solace in my studies. Scapilion had us read Aristotle and Plato alongside the Scriptures. There is much truth to be found among these old pagans. They may not have had all the light, but what they had they put forth clearly. I was like Plato's man in a cave; having only seen the shadows I was now beginning to look on the real things. But alas … I was still blinded to the true Light.

For rhetoric, we added Latin masters to the Greeks, Quintilian's twelve volumes, and Cicero. We learned to make our case in plain speech, middle, and grand, and how to choose the right form of address for each situation. We became adept at selecting the proper appeal - to the passions, to ethics, or to logic - and which would best sway the audience to our oratory. The rigorous declamations were among my favourite pursuits in those years.

Our teachers presented a legal or ethical situation and with just moments to prepare, we had to create our position and convince the school. Often we would be set in opposition to each other, one for and one against, only to have the roles reversed. I found myself as invigorated by the cut and thrust of intellectual battle as I had been in the hardscrabble school of Brennus, the warrior.

Occasionally we were invited to weigh in on legal issues in a more practical way. Gundobad was compiling the Lex Burgundionum in those days. Scapilion was widely respected and keen to help in the codification of the Burgundian laws, if for no other reason than to protect the Gallo-Romans. The Burgundians brought tribal traditions but no written law when they came into the empire. They recognised the laws of Rome as applying to relations between Gallo-Romans but did not subject themselves to this law. Gundobad was the first of their rulers to recognise the value of clarifying relations between the various people under his kingship.

We also read Augustine, Jerome, and other fathers of our faith alongside the Scriptures. The study of the Scriptures was a mere academic pursuit for me in those days. I used them as fuel for my rhetorical battles but remained ignorant of their real power … or rather, the power behind and infusing them.

I committed much of what I learned to memory, for Kian's training of attentiveness and memorisation held me in good stead. Creating a labyrinthine repository in my mind, I stocked the rooms and shelves with information that I could later access by wandering the halls. I walk those halls still, pulling out things both new and old according to the need of the moment.

I am deeply indebted to Kian for the early training of my mind. Had it not been for that old druid, I doubt that my journey would have led to my King. Kian gave me the tools to store all I would need; and all I had led me eventually to God.

In the idyllic years of my learning, the threatening storm finally broke in full fury over Gaul. Word reached us just a year after my arrival that Clovis and the Franks had defeated the legions of Soissons - no mean feat. The rapacious Franks spread through the land plundering as they went, eliminating any perceived threat through battle or murder.

No one knew where Clovis - that voracious wolf - would turn his gaze next. In Avallon I feared for my own safety. My mind flew across Gaul to pray for my family and all the Britons in Armorica. Would they be able to hold that precious peninsula against the Franks?

It seemed God smiled upon us in Avallon and Armorica. It took the wolf time to digest his new lands; and then he turned upon his own. The Frankish wars among themselves kept their attention focused elsewhere and left us in relative peace for some years.

But in those years of peace with the Franks, the Saecson predations only increased. The old forts on the Saecson shore of Britannia fell one by one. Those on the coast of Armorica still held against the rising tide of violence. But these Saecson raiders were swift and ruthless. In Britannia they sought conquest; but in Armorica they were content to raid. And when I say raid, I mean pillage, kidnap, rape, and burn. All too often by the time my father or other warriors arrived all that was left of a coastal settlement was smouldering wreckage and occasionally the scars in the sand left by the keels of their swift ships. The sand would smooth with the next tide, but not all wounds are so quickly or easily healed.

I studied in Avallon for five years, growing in wisdom, knowledge, and stature. I hope you will not think me immodest to report that I was not among the lesser students of Scapilion. In my later years there, Scapilion often entrusted the instruction of the younger boys to me. By then the basics of grammar, arithmetic, and geometry held no mystery for me; but in teaching I truly mastered them. It is often the case that we only come to master a subject once we are called upon to instruct others.

I was well on my way to fulfilling the wishes of my parents. While not a Christian of any particular conviction, I did not consider myself an unbeliever. It wasn't that I disbelieved in my Lord; rather, this belief had not moved beyond mental assent. The hearth had been prepared, the tinder and logs heaped up; all that remained was for the spark of true faith to fall on the dry materials. But many more years would pass before that day.

What might my life have been like had Brennus not appeared one morning? Would I have become a churchman or a bishop? Would I have received the tonsure and ordination? I do not know. I assume I would have. But such musings are meaningless, because Brennus did arrive and set my life on a different course.

CHAPTER 8

One morning, as I was drilling the students in arithmetic, Scapilion interrupted my lesson. I could not divine the reason for the interruption. It was unlike Scapilion to let anything interfere with lessons. From his dour expression, I could gain no insight. I followed him into the hall, and he merely gestured toward a grizzled warrior.

As I approached him, I saw something familiar in his form. Could it be? It must be! It was Brennus! As the moment of recognition parted the mists of my mind, my heart leapt to see my old battle master again. But no joy lit his eyes. His brows were knit, and a dark expression soured his countenance.

He watched my approach casually at first; but as I came closer I could see recognition dawn in his eyes, mixed with something else. What I could not tell … but I knew something was wrong.

"Illtyd, it is you, isn't it?" he began.

"Yes, my master. It is I," I responded still smiling but not as wide as before.

"You have changed much since our last parting."

"As have you, my master," I replied, embracing him. I was surprised to find that we were of a similar height. Brennus loomed large in my memory, but he seemed somehow smaller now.

"I come with bad tidings, Illtyd." I stepped back so that I might see his face. "Your father is dead."

I felt the ground unsteady beneath my feet. Brennus reached out a hand to help me, and sobs surged up through me. I shook, though I knew it not. I don't remember how, but we ended up outside on a bench in the courtyard. As I regained control of myself one question demanded an answer.

"What happened?"

"Saecsons. We spotted smoke on the horizon and swiftly moved into action. With 100 men we rode hard to meet them. We did not expect to reach them in time; we rarely do. By the time we arrived, they were usually away in their fiendish boats. But this time - I do not know why - three ships full lay in ambush for us. Your father was felled by a throwing axe before we even knew we were under attack. He never even drew his sword and was dead before he hit the ground. I am sorry, Illtyd. I would gladly have changed places with him for your sake and the sake of all our people. He was a great warrior and a great man."

"Thank you, Brennus," I replied simply. "I am grateful for your service to my father and to me in bringing me this news in person. How is my mother, and how fairs young Sadwrn?" Although I had yet to meet him, I knew he was nearly five years old.

"She is well." He smiled and continued, "And Sadwrn seems to be hewn from the same stone as yourself. He is just as quick and nearly as mischievous." He paused before continuing. "Your mother sent me with a message for you; although I don't know that you will welcome it." He looked at the ground, shuffling his booted feet upon the stone.

"Well?" I inquired.

"She would bid you stay here. She expects you will want to return, but she bids you stay here. She said, 'Tell him his father is avenged, his brother comforts me in my grief, and the people are kept by the war band and myself. The Lord has need of you to build his church.' That is her message."

"Is he? Is he avenged?"

"Yes. Not a Saecson survived that ferocious battle. Seeing your father fall set a fire in the hearts of our men. We slew them all. Even those trying to escape or surrender found no mercy that day. We piled the dead into their boats and let the retreating tide carry their corpses out to sea as a warning to any who might be tempted to follow. There is no one left upon whom to avenge yourself."

"And yet as grief swells my heart, my heart yearns for vengeance!" I cried, dashing the tears from my eyes.

45

"Yes, Illtyd. That is often the way of grief."

"Be careful, my son, not to be hasty," I heard another voice over my shoulder. I turned to find Scapilion standing over me. He lay his hand on my shoulder. "May God grant you to grieve well for your father and for all who fall in these dark days. May his kingdom come, and his will be done on earth as it is in heaven. And may God show you the road marked out for you today and every day for the rest of your life." His blessing washed over me, but brought scant comfort.

Scapilion relieved me of my duties from that moment so that I might devote myself to grief and to prayer. I grieved much but prayed little. Retrieving the memories of my father from the labyrinth in my mind, I pondered. He was not an expressive man, and yet I never doubted his love for me. He was not a tender man, but I had many memories of his care expressed through service and strength to me, to my mother, and to our people.

A week passed, and my heart still ached. I grieved for the times we would never have now, man to man, not just father to child. I wished for one last time to talk with my father … a wish that will never be fulfilled this side of eternity.

I often spoke with Scapilion and Brennus in those days. I knew that a fork in the road stood before me. My mother bid me stay on the path they had chosen for me, but now I must decide. Brennus and Scapilion, good fathers to me both in their own ways, were kind and put forward no answer; both insisted I must choose for myself.

"Such a momentous decision must be made by the one who will walk the road he chooses. I cannot choose for you and would not if I could. You and you alone must make that decision. I offer only this word of advice: Although you alone must make the decision, do not make the decision alone. Seek the counsel of the one who knows the end from the beginning. The Alpha and the Omega knocks on the door, if anyone will hear his voice and open it, he will come in and fellowship with you as our brother and your God." With words like these, Scapilion urged me toward prayer.

Brennus was no less philosophical in his brevity. He tersely responded, "It's up to you."

They waited and they listened. They waited with me for ten days, besting Job's friends by three, until I arrived at my decision.

I stood one morning after breakfast and addressed the gathered school. "My friends, my brothers, my fathers," I began, nodding toward my peers, my students, and my teachers. "As you know, I have sojourned among you for five years. In many ways, these years have been pleasant for me; in others, they have been an exile from my homeland. But like the Israelites in the days of Jeremiah, I have settled here and prayed for the good of the city of my exile. Also, like them, I have waited for the appointed time to return to my land … to my people. I believe that time has come. I ask you to pray for me as I take these next steps in the journey of my life. I do not know where these steps will take me, but I know I will need your prayers as I will pray for you."

Scapilion rose from his place at the head table and led us in unison in the prayer our Lord taught his disciples:

Our Father who art in heaven,

Hallowed be thy name.

Thy kingdom come.

Thy will be done

on earth as it is in heaven.

Give us this day our daily bread,

and forgive us our trespasses,

as we forgive those who trespass against us,

and lead us not into temptation,

but deliver us from evil.

Then, approaching me, he placed his hand on my head and blessed me, "May you truly be delivered from evil, my son." He then kissed me on both cheeks and made the sign of the cross over me.

I did not have much to pack, and there was nothing left to say. Brennus and I rode out together that afternoon. After so many years walking about in a robe it felt strange to be wearing trousers astride a horse. I must have looked uncomfortable because Brennus commented.

"You'll soon remember it, my lad. But my do you look awkward astride a steed." He chuckled as he pulled something from the pack behind his saddle and handed it to me as he said, "You may remember this as well."

I immediately recognised it from the scabbard alone. It was the sword Guielandus had given my father. It showed signs of hard use, with scratches and small dents marring the sheath. As we rode through the countryside not far from where my father had received this gift and where we had said our last goodbye, I drew this sword for the first time as my own. It was magnificent. In contrast to the scabbard there were but the slightest marks and not a single nick on the blade.

I looked to Brennus in surprise. "Yes, it is miraculous," he answered my quizzical gaze. "This sword served your father faithfully in many a battle. 'Brathiadur,' he called it - biting steel. It is yours now. I know he would have wanted you to have it, although your mother would never have wished you to wield it. Have you no second thoughts about this path?"

I felt the heft of my father's blade in my hand and knew there was no turning back.

CHAPTER 9

It had been five years since I had been outside of Avallon. The land we traversed seemed empty and sad. The sun still shone, but people were scarcely seen. Many places still bore the marks of the Frankish invasions - groves and villages destroyed. But the Franks were invaders no more. I reminded myself that this land now belonged to them; it was Clovis' by right of battle. "Justice and legality are not always the same," Scapilion had often reminded us.

As we rode through the shattered land, I asked Brennus more about the state of things since my father's death. I learned about the machinations of my cousins. Three kings of Armorica had sat upon the throne since Budic I - sons, uncles, and cousins all engaged in a fratricidal war to own a crown of dubious worth. Budic II, our new cousin king, two years younger than I, wore the crown then, even as he wears it now. I did not envy him then, nor do I presently. To lead is always a burden, to rule in troubled times even more so.

I have often wondered after the ambitions of men. So often we strive to grasp and possess things that in the end bring us little pleasure and often much pain. Isn't it better to live a quiet life, minding your business and doing some useful work than to scratch and strive for more … always more? The insatiable appetite for more devours from within.

My father had opportunities to enter the dynastic struggles. Brennus admitted to encouraging him to do so. "It wasn't just me. Not a man who knew your father would have resisted him. In truth, many clamoured for him to take the kingship. But your father supported your uncle Erich in his attempts to make peace between the squabbling whelps of Budic. Eventually, Erich himself assumed the crown, bringing some welcome peace before passing it to our present king Budic II. He's not a bad lad, and I think he has the making of a fine king. Time will tell," Brennus concluded.

"And how goes it with my mother?"

"Your mother lives up to her name, Rheinwylydd. A good and modest queen among women is she," he replied with frank admiration. "She serves the people well, and in her own name like the queens of old. She is not a woman to be trifled with," he added with a grin.

"That I remember all too well!" We shared a laugh that passed into a thoughtful silence as we rode on.

It was not difficult to tell when we entered our land. Where there had been destruction, we now saw abundance. We had seen but few men on the road, all frightened and guarded; now we were assailed heartily by all. Those who knew Brennus on sight greeted him warmly; those who did not challenged us boldly, and rightly so in those dangerous days.

It was good to be in the land of my youth. There is something in the very rocks and woods of Armorica that called to me then, even as now. And to be surrounded by Britons and hear the language of my heart tripping off the tongues of all around me … it was music to my ears and a balm to my soul. My sojourn in Avallon was profitable, but it was never really home.

I first caught a glimpse of my mother through the gate to our villa. Grey now fringed her dark tresses, tracing descending paths from the crown of her head, but there was no mistaking her regal bearing. She turned to see who approached, and I caught her dark and beautiful eyes. I had always thought my mother the most beautiful of women. I admired her for a moment as she puzzled over the appearance of the young man before her. The moment of recognition was followed by the flash of many emotions, each flitting across her face in rapid succession: anger, sadness, and love.

By the time I had dismounted, she had composed herself. "My son, you have come home to me after all. I had hoped you would not. But now that I see you with my own eyes, I am glad of it. I have missed you." At this, she threw her arms around me and kissed my cheek.

After filling the welcome cups, we three sat down together in the hall.

50

"Ah, dear Illtyd, it is good to see you again. Let my eyes drink you in, my flower." She paused for a moment. "You are even more like your father than I remember. You have grown from sapling to tree in the years since I have seen you. Show me your hands."

Brennus smiled at this, but I offered my hands for her inspection. There was no point in refusing.

"The hands of a scholar just as I wished it. I hope your head is not as soft as your hands," she added mischievously.

"No mother. I believe my head may be as full as that of Scapilion or even Kian, and as hard as my father's."

Brennus grinned into his cup. "You may have your father's looks, but you have your mother's tongue," he muttered half under his breath.

I caught my mother's eye, and we burst into laughter.

"In all seriousness, Scapilion said he is the finest scholar he has ever seen," Brennus continued. "He said Illtyd's mind is a storehouse that is not yet filled to capacity. He was sorry to see him go."

I blushed on hearing this praise, but my mother swelled. With a nod, she replied, "Well, then what are we to do with you now, my wayward scholar? I can see you've not yet received the tonsure. So, you're not a man of the church."

"I've thought much about this," I began. "I am a Christian, but I am not devoted to the church. I will continue my studies in a different direction. I will train with Brennus and do what I can to support you and our people if you will allow it."

"My first wish was for you to stay away, but my heart is glad that you are here. Yes, Illtyd, I will allow it. I will relish your support and welcome you home with all my heart." She was both princess and mother at that moment; I do not know which I admired more.

As I was savouring this experience of home, I heard a squeal and the patter of small feet. "Give it back, I said!" cried a voice. "You started it," said another. "Wait 'til I get my hands on you!" responded the first.

51

Just then, a curly-headed dark-haired imp of roughly five years of age came sprinting into the hall with something clutched in his hand. Right behind him came a girl a few years older. He feinted right to throw off his pursuer before dodging left, intending to run right past us toward the kitchens.

In a moment he was swept off his feet and thrown into the air by Brennus. But the young face registered no fear and little surprise. He clearly belonged here. He was already laughing as he careened back toward earth, only to be caught in Brennus' strong arms.

Brennus was laughing too as he turned toward me. "And this young scamp is your brother of ill repute, Sadwrn." He settled the boy on his feet and made a flourish with his hand as if introducing royalty.

Sadwrn eyed me quickly, and I must have passed his rushed inspection for he took two quick steps toward me and threw his small arms around me, hugging me fiercely as he said, "At last! At last! My brother is home!" Then, without missing a beat, he turned and flung the object from his hand toward the girl waiting sheepishly near the door. "Here's your stupid doll."

The girl caught it in mid-flight and ducked out the door as quick as a flash.

"What have I told you about torturing the girls?!" My mother demanded.

"I know mother, but it's just so fun!" Sadwrn feigned repentance, but everyone knew his heart wasn't in it.

We spent the rest of the evening swapping stories and getting to know each other. Sadwrn reminded me of the young students at the college. We played merellus together, and I caught my first glimpse of his mind. I taught him how to play calculi that evening, and by the end of the night he was already a challenging opponent. Brennus was right; Sadwrn was very bright indeed.

As I lay on my bed listening as the house grew quiet, my mind was flooded with memories of the past and questions about the future. I left my home a child and came home a man, only to find a child taking up space I once inhabited. I knew that it was now my task to take up the space vacated by my father. I had come home to be a warrior, and my training would start afresh in the morning.

Brennus made it his goal to make up for lost time. "Five years in a school have made not only your hands soft. You're soft all over, my boy. Let's see if we can harden you up!"

In the days that followed, Brennus renewed my training. He introduced me to my old nemesis the forest stone again. Although I was the taller now and thought I would find it easier; much to my disappointment, it was not. I resumed my daily strain of muscle and bone against that torturous rock.

Brennus taught me many feats including to juggle - first rocks, then sticks, then knives. "This is not just to impress the ladies," he reassured me. "This develops your coordination and quickness. It also teaches you to quickly master the feel and balance of a blade in your hand. If you master this, maybe I'll teach you how to juggle swords," he added with a wink.

Not long after my arrival, I paid a visit to Guielandus. As I approached his holding I could tell he was doing well. On land granted by my father not far from our villa, Guielandus had built a villa in miniature. A large house at the rear, it had two protruding wings flanking a courtyard of not inconsiderable size. He had also built a wall on what would have been the open side of the court, were we living in more stable times.

"Ho there, master smith!" I cried out as I rode up to the gate.

"Who calls for me now?! Can a man have no quiet to do the work God has given him?" came the flustered reply.

"It is Illtyd ap Bicanys. I bring you greetings and thanks," I replied, taking no offence at his brusque manner.

"So it is you!" Guielandus looked the same to me, if perhaps somewhat rounder in the middle. "I had heard of your return. How are things in Avallon?"

53

"Remarkably peaceful, even in these troubled times. I hope you do not regret your decision to leave such a fair place for our wild lands?" I inquired.

"No, not at all. The iron from your mines is of the highest quality. We have a sturdy home and full bellies. My family is happy. I have work to keep me busy and apprentices aplenty to do the heavy lifting," he added with a wink. I could hear the banging and clanking from all around us, even as we spoke.

"I came to thank you for your service to my family, and to share my admiration for this blade," I laid my hand on the hilt and scabbard as I spoke.

"Yes, I saw it on your hip. I am sorry about your father. I pray the blade will serve you as well as it served him."

"I trust it will. But, if I may be so bold, do you think you could equal the work?"

"Could I? I already have!" He took me into his shop and showed me three naked blades similar to the one I held, although each with its own pattern and some slight differences in shape - one slightly longer, one weighted toward the tip like the old falcata from Hispania, and one identical to my own in all but the pattern in the fuller.

I had hardly taken in the riches before me, calculating the various advantages of each blade when he interrupted me, "And look here!" He gestured to a row of spears with broad leaf-blades and the tell-tale tendril pattern down the centre.

"And here!" He opened the doors on a cupboard within which was a tightly-woven mail shirt and a helmet. "These are made from a special alloy I have devised to be strong but not brittle. Look here, I have added a cross of reinforced ridges over the crown, and one across the brow. See how the central ridge carries down over the brow and covers the nose as well without compromising your field of vision."

As he continued to describe his design choices, I marvelled at his inventiveness as well as his craftsmanship. "These are amazing pieces! Fit for a king, my friend, fit for a king!"

"Thank you; but I did not make them for a king. I made them for your father. But alas - he never saw them. You look to be his size, and as you are his son, they are yours." As he said this, he swept his arm over the lot of them.

I hardly knew what to say to such a princely gift. "Truly, you surprise me!" was all I could muster in response.

"Do I indeed, lad!?" chortled Guielandus.

After his laughter had subsided, I got to the point of my visit. "Times are hard, master smith, and I am afraid they will get worse before they get better. The Franks menace our border to the East and the Saecsons by sea. We will need more weapons and armour in the days ahead. More than you can make, I am afraid. Can you produce enough for the army we will need to defend ourselves?"

"I will do what I can. Weapons such as I have given you are difficult and time-consuming to make; but I can make many a serviceable weapon in the time it would take me to make one of these," Guielandus said, gesturing again to the bench covered with his craftsmanship. And raising his chin in challenge he added, "I believe your father was content with the weapons of my workshop and the speed with which they have been produced."

"Yes, of course, master smith. I meant no offence. I only came to ask if you would be willing to lead the smiths round about and work together to produce even more. I am afraid not all of them share your knack for making weapons."

His face took on a distant expression as he pondered the question. Finally he continued, "I see. I am afraid I must agree with you that the skills required for making a plough do not always translate to the forging of weapons that will not fail you in the heat of battle." He paused, scratching at his beard and studying the sky. "How about this? If you will send me twenty young men of middling intellect and good strength, and if you will provide for their upkeep, I will train them myself. If you will see that I am provided with all I need, I will produce all you need. Yes, that should do it!" He added with a decisive nod of his considerable head.

"I will consult with my mother, but I am sure we can find you what you need."

"Good, then we are agreed! Now come, share an ale with me," he grabbed me by the shoulder, pushing me through the door.

I never was a man to turn down Guielandus' gifts, be they arms, armour, or ale.

CHAPTER 10

Guielandus' unexpected bounty tied to my mount, I returned home with a warm belly and undreamt riches. Weapons like these had never been made in our lands. Guielandus was a wizard of metallurgy and design. Any realm would consider him a treasure, and an expert brewer to boot! I marvelled at our good fortune as I returned to our holding.

As I rode in, Brennus observed my arrival with some interest. "What have you there, young man?" he queried, looking over the spears and sacks tied to my horse.

"Guielandus has bestowed his greatest gifts on me - one who is unworthy to wield them as yet. Come, help me." Together we unloaded the horse and took the weapons to the armoury.

Brennus and I carefully inspected and tested each blade and spear. Away from the watchful eye of the smith, we could be more critical. In truth, we found nothing to criticise; only our personal preferences differed. Neither of us cared for the heavier falcata nor the long sword, preferring the length and agility of the original sword Guielandus had gifted to my father.

"Here, this one is yours. It is the twin of my father's sword, and I know he would have wanted you to have it - you who shared so many things in life and battle. Take this sword and may you be blessed as you use it righteously."

Brennus made to protest, but he thought the better of it as he looked into my earnest eyes and received both my gift and my blessing with a nod.

We each chose a spear as well; there was little enough variation among them. Then I showed Brennus the helm and mail. He let out a low whistle as he considered them, fingering the links and feeling the weight of the coat. "This is some of his finest work yet. I knew he could make a blade, but this should serve you as well or better than any blade. Lord willing you'll never test it," he added with a grim smile.

"But come, let me test you instead, young princeling! There are things you can learn that will defend you better than armour or helm."

And with that we resumed my training in earnest. I had thought the exercise with Myrddin and Arthwyr difficult, but this new season took on a grim determination hitherto unknown to me. My hands so long used for scholarly pursuits were soon blistered and sore from wood and blade and stone. Although it was rough, in truth I relished it.

I was young, and my mind swirled with emotions and thoughts; but when left to itself it always returned to vengeance. I didn't like the colour of these dark thoughts, and my daily exertions left little time for contemplation. Each day spent in hard training was another day I could dodge the darkness of my own soul.

Brennus required me to start each day with an assault on my old adversary - the stone in the forest. Brennus taught me different ways of assaulting the rock - pushing, pulling, and lifting. Each one exhausting and ineffective in shifting my nemesis from his perch, but very useful for building up my strength.

Added to my daily exertion against my stony enemy were tasks to develop quickness and speed. I was amazed at the agility of Brennus. We raced many times across flat and broken ground, and that old man bested me … at least at the beginning.

Eventually, my body began to respond to the regimen designed by the old warrior. I remember the first time I bested him, or nearly so. We were racing up the hill into the forest; I was running hard and just about to reach the summit ahead of him for the first time, when I suddenly found my feet tangled and myself crashing to the ground just short of victory.

Reaching the summit a few yards further, face still red with exertion, Brennus turned toward me panting and grinning.

"You tripped me!" I accused.

He just nodded, his panting interrupted by his laughter. When he finally caught his breath, he added, "Remember this, my lad, old age and treachery will always overcome youth and enthusiasm." He burst into laughter again while I rubbed my smarting knees, dusted myself off and joined him on the summit.

In addition to my physical training, Brennus trained me in the art of killing. "Battle is not about fighting. It is about incapacitating your enemy. The quickest way to do that is to kill him. At the end of the day, you want to protect those you love and come home to them each evening. Make no mistake - your enemy aims to kill you. You must kill him first. That is the grim reality of war."

Brennus' words were not inspiring. He was never an eloquent orator. Nevertheless, he was a great tutor in the school of war.

Our bodies are amazing things - so strong, resilient ... and so fragile. Brennus showed me the vulnerable places - the easiest bones to crush, where to strike your enemy to take away his breath, how to cause the most pain with the least effort. I learned how to open the windows of the soul and end a man's earthbound life. There is an art to killing, a terrible deadly art to doing it well. And doing it well is the best way to preserve your own life in battle. May you never know such things, my children.

Some of these lessons Brennus taught me with words, but many I learned as we grappled or fought with blunted weapons. Brennus firmly believed in the power of demonstration. Many a day I returned bruised or bloodied, but those lessons made an impression on my mind as well as my body.

Brennus pushed me farther than I thought I could go. Many times I cursed him under my breath as he rapped me again with the flat of his sword or caught me under the ribs with the butt of his spear. His response never varied. He watched me for a moment, resumed his stance and said, "Again."

Not content to merely train my body for combat, Brennus began to drill me in tactics as well. He asked me to plan attacks and ambushes, raids against our home and settlements.

When I protested, he responded, "You have to think like your enemy to beat him. It's no good thinking about what you would do; you have to think like a raider - like a Saecson or Scoti. Not all enemies are the same. You have to think like a Frank to beat a Frank. Understanding the motive and methods of your enemy is an essential skill for a leader." He paused, fixing me with his gaze before continuing, "For a leader you will be, like your father before you. You are a young man now ... but you will not always be so," he added quietly, almost to himself. A mist fell over his countenance as he considered something beyond our conversation.

"Be careful, Illtyd. Be careful that you do not become so like them that you lose yourself. You must be fierce and unrelenting in battle. You must outfox the fox, out wolf the wolf pack ... but never become a predator yourself. I have seen too many go that way. Sometimes the skill for killing is followed by the thirst for it. The power of a warrior is to be used for the good of the people, never against them. Become a boar of battle, Illtyd. A boar fights and kills but doesn't live by his killing. Yes, my lad, you will be a boar of battle." He nodded to himself as he looked me over, once again the distance returning to his gaze.

Brennus suddenly looked old to me. His once-dark beard now grizzled, he still retained tremendous strength; but I knew his sun was setting. I think he knew it too.

As my body hardened under the training and my weapon skill increased, Brennus began to train me with others in our war band. We had many men who would fight when called upon, but fewer were truly trained as warriors. In the days since the demise of the legions, warfare had returned to smaller affairs, mostly raiding and skirmishes. We could call upon more than a hundred at a moment's notice, but only a handful were indeed warriors.

These men had already ridden to battle with Brennus and my father. An odd assembly of men, unmatched in look or temperament, they became one in adversity. As I got to know them I was attentive to their strengths and weaknesses, all of which could prove crucial in battle.

Morgan was quick in all his ways - his movements and his wit; and just as quick to take offence. Cai was a wiry, tough man with thinning hair and was taciturn by nature. Llew was a huge man - a head taller than Brennus with arms like oaken limbs, but ponderous in his ways. I did not relish wrestling him. Rhodri was short - almost round - but with a sturdy build and not easily moved, whether on a field of combat or in an argument. Each of these men had earned their place in the war band of my family by their deeds.

They were happy to take turns raining blows upon my shield. I knew I would not truly be one of them until I had been tried in the heat of battle. I enjoyed the rough camaraderie of men who daily tested themselves against one another. It wasn't long until I could hold my own in wrestling and weapons. Slowly, I earned some grudging respect from these veterans.

As members of the war band we also had the privilege and responsibility of hunting. Our quarry was mostly deer, but occasionally wild pigs. We grew to trust each other and rely on one another during those hunting expeditions.

We often would ride to a more deserted part of the land, make camp, and spend several days hunting in different directions. These excursions were good practice for stalking, and they were also good fun. They provided a welcome break from the rigours of physical conditioning, tactics, and weapons training.

One day in late summer we found ourselves creeping through the forest, attentive to every sound and smell. We had chosen this part of the forest because of a family of pigs we had spotted. In addition to the sow and piglets we had sighted an enormous boar on our previous visits. He was a wily adversary, and no one had been able to get near enough for a bow shot, let alone a spear thrust. The previous evening we had joked and wagered on who would be the one to take him. We fanned out across the forest floor within sight of one another, if only just. We had seen several large sows with their young, none too happy to see us on their patch of turf. But they just skittered away into the undergrowth. We knew a boar would not be so easily frightened.

Boars are unpredictable as well. Sometimes they will bolt away, but they are just as likely to come charging directly out of some thicket. Our guard was up, spears in hand as we made our way through the dense foliage straining every sense toward danger and possible victory. I caught a whiff of something on the wind. Smoke.

Looking over toward Llew, I saw he shared my concern.

CHAPTER 11

Our silent hunt was suddenly ended as Brennus called out. "To me now!"

In scant moments we closed around him.

"There is but one settlement near enough for the smoke to reach us this deep in the forest. We must be quick; we may be too late already. Illtyd, you run back to camp and ride for the holding. Muster as many men as you can and meet us at Lehon, on the river. Go!"

I did not protest; although I wanted to run toward the crisis, Brennus was our leader, and we followed his orders without question. I crashed through the undergrowth at breakneck speed, not knowing what awaited my friends nor what was happening in the village by the river. Lehon was a small settlement - hardly even a hamlet - where the forest met the river on the eastern fringes of our land.

It wasn't long until I was back in camp. I leapt on the back of my horse, not even bothering to saddle him. I flew down the paths out of the forest and onto the road toward our villa, the centre of life for our people. As I met people along the way, I raised the alarm. I reached the villa in little more than an hour. Throwing myself down from my heaving mount, shouting the warning, I raced toward the armoury. The stable boys and stewards jumped to my aid. In a few minutes, everyone was mobilised. The men armed themselves while the stable boys prepared mounts for us.

My mother was there in the mix, giving orders and preparing aid for whatever we would find at Lehon. Carts were loaded with supplies while everyone hoped for the best and prepared for the worst. I managed to arm and armour myself and was back in the saddle on a fresh mount, spear in hand, sword at my side quicker than I knew. In those few minutes, our peaceful settlement had been transformed into an armed camp. Fifty men rode with me as we made our way toward Lehon.

We rode hard, skirting the forest to make better time. The column of smoke rising in the distance filled us with dread. As we approached the river we became more cautious but slowed only slightly, balancing our desire to save with the knowledge that death by ambush would save no one. Thankfully, there was no ambush. At least we could be grateful for that. There was nothing else worthy of gratitude that day.

Llew met us on the road before we reached the town, slowly waving his hand over his head in a sad token of resignation. "There is work to be done here, but none that must be done in a hurry," he reported flatly.

It is one thing to train for battle. It is quite another to see the aftermath of a slaughter. I found Brennus down by the river, studying the marks on the bank. "There were two ships. Do you see?" He gestured to the deep gashes in the bank where keels of the swift boats had driven aground. The ground all around the boats was churned by feet and hoofs, and slick with blood. Broken bodies of men and a few women lay scattered near where the landing had taken place. There had been little resistance. What could a few farmers and fisherfolk - no more than ten families together - have done against sixty savage Saecson?

These brazen raiders had not even bothered to sneak into the town by stealth. They knew their advantage lay in speed. Rowing directly into the heart of the settlement, they loaded up their boats with anything they could find of value: cattle, pigs, grain, coin, women, and children. In their haste, they had not ranged around the settlement. I witnessed the grief of those who had been in the fields or forest when the attack occurred. I was too shocked to grieve for the dead, but I shuddered as I thought of the future in store for those who had been taken.

"Illtyd! Pay attention!" cried Brennus, calling me out of my reverie.

"Take the host and ride hard downriver. I know it is unlikely, but you may yet spy them before they reach the sea, or even see which way they travel. Perhaps we may catch them yet. It is too late for many, but not yet for all."

I needed no further instruction. Rallying the men to me, we were back on our horses moments later, in an almost undoubtedly fruitless pursuit. How could men and horses keep pace with boats heading downstream? These raiders had come far inland on their search for plunder. I wondered if we would find other villages sacked along our way to the sea. The day was already half gone, and I knew if we did not spot them by nightfall we would have no chance of finding them.

I also knew that if we didn't find them in the first five miles of our search it would likely be too late. I knew this land well - we all did. The river at Lehon is but a bowshot wide, but the nearer to the sea the wider it becomes. If we did not overtake them before long, we would be powerless to stop them.

We shared a sense of violation that these craven men would come into our land, kill our people and then merely row away. Our powerlessness fed our rage as we lashed our steeds on. Our horses were tired, after only a brief respite from our hard ride to Lehon. Our compassion for the captives outweighing our concern for our mounts, we pressed on.

The road took us some distance from the river at points. Scouts peeled off at intervals to make sure we did not pass them when the river was out of sight. It was a slight chance, but not one worth risking. The only thing worse than a Saecson raiding party in front of you is one sneaking up behind you.

But our scouts repeatedly returned with nothing to report. No movement on the river. We rode on in desperation and a desire for vengeance or justice. It isn't always clear which is which. We wanted to free our people from a life of abuse and slavery. We wanted to avenge the dead. We wanted to kill these raiders to prevent them from wreaking havoc on anyone else. I knew if they were successful they would be likely to come again.

I pondered as I rode, trying to understand my adversary. They had come fifteen miles inland and sacked a small settlement. Why? Why hadn't they struck somewhere closer to the sea? How did they avoid detection as they travelled so far upriver?

"Look! There!" I was startled out of my musings by a sharp-eyed scout.

The light was fading, but it seemed there were two ships far out in the middle of the river and still some distance ahead of us. We rode on, spurring our exhausted horses, whispering encouragement into their equine ears and hoping that some opportunity would present itself.

Pushing ourselves and our animals ever more, we were making small gains. But with each passing moment the river grew wider. Although we were closing the distance, our hope was dwindling. They were far out in the widening channel now, and we were close enough to see them preparing to hoist their sails to catch the offshore winds coming up as the darkness was falling.

As we rode on, we heard a shout go up from the river. The Saecsons had seen us, but they showed no fear. They taunted us from the safety of the river. At that moment, I was silently happy to be ignorant of their language. They began to sing as they readied their sails and continued rowing. With the combined power of oar and sail they gained speed. It was then I realised that even the tides were in opposition to our quest and the retreating estuary was drawing them out to sea. It was as if everything conspired against us. All we could do was watch as our enemy sailed away.

I called our troop to a halt. There was no need to waste the horses. We stopped by the side of the river in hopelessness, silently witnessing the enslavement of our kin. The gaps in the Saecson war song filled with the wailing of women and children.

No longer in pursuit, we trailed them down to the sea to watch them sail away north and east. We watched them disappear from sight. And I cursed them. I called on the God of heaven to avenge himself on those pagan brigands, to smite them with his justice. But nothing happened.

CHAPTER 12

We spent a restless night at the coastal hill fort of Dinard. They too had seen the ships departing but could provide no explanation as to how they had slipped past them to gain access to the heart of our land.

"This is your job -the whole reason you are here!" I raged at them.

They bore my rebuke like men and hung their heads in shame. They knew it was true ... though my censure was uncalled for and my rage misplaced.

I would like to tell you I apologised for my outburst. I would like to say I asked their forgiveness because I recognised that my shame and impotent rage could not find their real target. But I did not. I was young then and did not know myself then as I do now.

The next morning we rode back to Lehon to deliver news of our failure to Brennus and do what we could to help. I found him near the charred ruins of a barn.

"It's okay, lad," Brennus laid a comforting hand on my shoulder. "This is the first raid you have witnessed. I'm afraid it will not be the last. We have endured many a predation from these Saecson devils, although never this far inland. They usually content themselves with targeting the coastal settlements. We have moved most of those to high ground and built sturdy palisades to dissuade them. That is usually enough to encourage small parties to find easier pickings elsewhere. They wouldn't hold out against a force of size nor determination. No, I'm afraid we have learned to live with these raids."

"Live with them?! What about the dead?! What about the captured?! What will they live with?!"

Brennus grabbed me by the collar, shoving me up against the wall. "Who are you to speak to me thus!? You have seen wars only in books. You watch your tone with me, whelp!" Brennus struggled to contain himself. Taking a deep breath he continued, "You are angry. We all are. But you will not pour your anger out on me or the men. These men have fought these long years while you were living the easy life of a scholar, safe behind the shields of others. All your great learning has not prepared you for the realities of life. Look around you boy! This is the real world. These are your people. They don't need your condemnation. They need your help. They need your leadership. Pull yourself together, man!"

With that, he turned and stalked away.

Even then, in the midst of my youthful anger, I knew he was right. I felt the sting of his words as well as the truth of them.

It was some time before I mastered myself enough to join the others in the efforts of clearing and cleansing the town.

There was blood. I had never seen so much blood. The bodies had already been buried, and the cleansing had begun. Some buildings would have to be torn down; they were beyond repair. These raiders were not content to merely steal; they left destruction in their wake. I learned more about their tactics and ways that day as I witnessed their handiwork. They didn't just kill, they mutilated. They didn't just steal, they destroyed. Their goal was more than plunder, it was terror. By the time they torched the settlement they were already loading their boats. There was no tactical advantage to the fire, it was wanton destruction. They sought to terrorise and demoralise their victims to strike fear into the hearts of all around.

I thought them monsters then. But now I know they were merely men. It is easier to kill someone when they are less than us, or even just something other than us. We do not grieve for the loss of life when we eat a pig … even less so when we eat a fish.

To the Saecson raiders we were no more than sheep to be sheared or slaughtered … or at best, animals to be hunted. Their religion also supports them in their war-making. Their gods are deceivers and always at war. Their best hope of the afterlife is to die in battle. For a Saecson to live is war and to die in battle is gain.

I knew little of this and cared even less as I put my back into the work of rebuilding Lehon. We improved the settlement with a strong palisade.

During this time of rebuilding my admiration for my mother deepened. She served and comforted while bearing the immense grief and responsibility of a leader. She did it all with incredible grace and quiet strength. While I observed her, I often caught a fleeting glance of her watching me. We talked little during that week at Lehon.

Brennus, too, was quiet. I looked for opportunities to help him, to work alongside him. I wanted him to see my apology in action, my leadership in deed. My rage had cooled into deep, hard anger, like iron in my gut. It was still there, just not on the surface. I channelled my energies into the work and sought to put our disagreement behind us.

We never spoke of it, but I never again talked to him in the way I had. My passionate outburst and his heated reply exposed the gulf between us. I had lived a life of privilege, although I knew it not. It is a very odd fish who knows he swims in water. We tend to take our environment for granted. While my hands and my body were no longer the soft stuff of the scholar, hardened as they had been by my training under Brennus' watchful eye, I honestly had been insulated from the harshness of our world in my scholarly world of Avallon.

I do not regret my years of scholarship; they shaped me. But that first raid and futile pursuit opened my eyes to a world beyond intellectual training and struggle. The world needs scholars and priests, but the world also needs warriors - men who will stand on the walls and see off the predators among us. Sometimes those predators come from afar in ships; sometimes they are more challenging to spot.

The night after we returned to our villa, my mother invited Brennus and me to sit with her by the hearth. Summer was passing, and the nights were growing cool. We wrapped ourselves in furs and shared a jug of mead while we studied the flames as she clutched a letter in her hand.

"So, the sea wolves have come again," she began. "This attack demonstrates their craftiness as well as their boldness. Never before have they come so far inland. As you know, our strategy has been a defensive one. We have done what we can to make it more difficult for them to find easy prey in the hope they would look elsewhere. But I grow tired of burying our dead and comforting the grieving. What is your counsel?"

"Could not my cousin the king raise a fleet to seek out the wolves' lair? I know we do not have the strength nor the ships for such a task, but with the combined power of the Britons we may end this scourge once and for all," I suggested.

"No, Illtyd," She sadly shook her head. "That will not happen. King Budic seems more concerned with reclaiming the throne of Dumnonia than defending his kingdom in Armorica."

Brennus added, "While I applaud your youthful enthusiasm, I fear you do not yet understand the situation thoroughly. Defence in depth has been our practice. We cannot take the initiative and so we are left only with responsive tactics. I too would seize the initiative from our foes, but we cannot. We are but a small boat on a large sea. Events beyond our ken are at play."

My mother nodded slowly before continuing, "I agree with your heart, my son; but I agree with Brennus' head. We lack the resources and information we would need to launch an attack on the Saecson homeland. Budic has pressing matters with the Franks as well as his ambitions." She paused, looking at us both closely in the firelight.

"Although we cannot take the fight to the Saecson lands, we can take the battle to the Saecsons. Our situation is dire, but that in Britannia is far worse. I have just learned that the last of the British forts on the Saecson shore has fallen. These pagans know no decency, nor should that surprise us after what we have seen. They gained access to the fort under the guise of negotiation with your uncle Meurig, Arthwyr's father. They poisoned his drink as they drank to his health. Then they slaughtered every man woman and child in Anderida - not just the fort but the town as well. They nailed some of them to trees as homage to Wotan, their so-called god.

"Arthwyr has been appointed Dux Bellorum - war leader - of Britannia as was his father before him. He calls for all Britons to rally to him and drive the Saecsons back into the sea. Perhaps their arrogance to claim British land will be their undoing. Here they slink away; but there they can be faced, fought, and killed."

"These are bitter times." Brennus shook his grizzled head as he sipped his mead, rolling it around his mouth.

"I will go," I responded quietly.

My mother studied my face, nodding slowly to herself, "I knew you would, my son. There is much of your father in you," she added, reaching over to cup my cheek in her hand. "He did not love war as some do, but neither would he stand by when there was a battle that needed fighting. There is a time for everything under heaven, and this is a time for war. I prayed we could make a peaceful life here, but it seems that is not to be."

Turning to Brennus, she asked, "Is he ready?"

"Oh, aye, he's ready!" Brennus responded with a wry smile. "He's far more ready than I was when my spear first found its mark. He has fire in his soul and steel in his arm. I dare say he is as ready as any man can be. His mettle can only be tested now in battle, and I pray he passes the test."

My mother stood while declaring, "So be it. Tomorrow, I will spread the word that any who would go to fight the Saecson on the shores of our once island home have my blessing. Let preparations begin and may the wars fought there bring peace to us here!"

CHAPTER 13

It didn't take long for the word to spread. As the harvest was gathered, the news travelled from market to market across our lands and beyond. As weeks passed and autumn gave way to the first real chills of winter, I found myself growing impatient. One morning, as I complained in the armoury, Brennus chided me.

"Patience! A man weakened by hunger will not fight well. We needed provisions. Preparations take time. We've just received word that Budic himself has blessed our cause and pledged his support. His men and ships will be a welcome addition and should speed you on your way in the spring."

"'You'?" I took Brennus by the arm. "Don't you mean 'us'? Surely you are coming!" I exclaimed.

"No. This is your campaign. I will remain here and see what can be done to shore up our defences and keep the raiders at bay. Do not forget the Franks are knocking at our door. They are busy with the Goths and likely the Burgundians after that, but I fear it will not be long before they turn their attention to us. No, I will look to our defences while you take the fight to our foes."

I nodded as he finished speaking. He was a brave man and a great warrior. I knew he would not shy from a fight. He never had. His wisdom was shown sooner than anyone anticipated.

"Smoke!" a voice cried out.

After the previous raid, Brennus had overseen the creation of signal fires along the coast and up the rivers. At the first sight of raiders, the flames were to be lit. A column of smoke was rising in the east. Soon followed by another, then another. These additional fires leading to the interior.

"To arms!" Brennus cried out.

In a moment, our languid preparations for some future battle took on new urgency. We grabbed our weapons, saddled our horses and 150 rode out armoured and with dire purpose.

Only one coastal fire had signalled, that of Dinard at the mouth of the River Renk. It seemed that our adversary, having found easy prey once, had returned to their newly-favoured hunting ground. We did not make directly for Dinard; assuming the Saecson had passed the point, we made to intercept them at Taden, where the river narrows. Brennus also made care to send swift scouts all along the coast to Dinard itself, and settlements on the coast and along the river. These were to report to us at Taden with all speed.

We arrived at Taden to find everything quiet. Having seen the signal fires, the people had drawn inside the palisade and armed themselves as they could. Relieved faces greeted our arrival. They had noticed no activity on the river nor in the forest.

Pleased but puzzled, we dismounted, rubbing down our weary mounts. Brennus sent Morgan and me to scout the bank along the river toward Dinard. We had been carefully making our way downriver for some time when we first spotted the ships. They were still mid-channel, but just out of bowshot. Their number concerned us more than their nearness. Six Saecson ships sliced the waters of our placid river!

We carefully retreated from the riverbank before running back to Brennus in haste. Brennus immediately dispatched scouts to track their progress and keep us informed. Pondering our news for a few moments, digesting it and turning it over in his mind, he quickly formulated a plan.

"I wonder what drives these wolves from their den so late in the season," he mused aloud. "No matter." He scratched at his chin as he considered our options. "They will no doubt be on their guard, having seen the signal fires themselves. We will not catch them entirely unaware. The fact that they did not turn back shows their bravery or foolhardiness; let us hope it is more of the latter than the former, shall we?" He shared a hard smile with us before continuing.

"They are continuing upriver, so they must have some target in mind. Let us choose their target for them. We will provoke them to attack us here, at Taden. Let us divide our forces for maximum effect. I will lead a group in a shield wall to meet them on the beach." He gestured to the landing before the settlement. "Fifty men will stand with me." Some in our group gasped at this.

Someone muttered, "What chance have 50 men? They'll have three times as many in those boats."

Brennus scowled at us, holding up his hand. "They will be upon us before long. Listen and obey!" He gave quick and clear instructions, dividing us into bowmen, slingers, cavalry, and spearmen and assigning us our place and tasks.

As he concluded, one of the elders of Taden spoke up, "And what of us? Are we to do nothing?"

"My friend, if all goes well there will be little for you to do," Brennus declared with a broad grin. "But if it does not, you will be busy enough and will need no orders from me. Stay within the palisade and defend yourselves if you must," he added grimly.

He paused to look around him. "Now, only one thing remains. Illtyd, as we have no proper priest, you will pray for us. Put your piety to work before your spear."

Surprised by this invitation, I could not tell if there was mockery in his words; but there was no humour in his eyes. And so I prayed.

"God of heaven. Fix your eye on us this day. Avenge the blood of your people upon the heads of these pagans. Put your courage in our hearts. Put your strength in our bodies. Use us as your avenging wrath to rid the world of these evildoers. You know their purpose. You know the justice of our cause. Slay them, Lord, by your hand or by ours. Lay them waste. Let not one of them live another day to do evil on your earth." Straining my voice and pouring all my pent-up anger into that prayer, I called upon the Lord.

When I finished, I saw a quizzical expression flit across Brennus' face before he turned away to see to the final disposition of the men. This done, he turned back to me.

"That was quite a prayer," he said, smiling.

"What did you expect?"

"I don't know. But that was …" Brennus paused, searching for words. "Thank you." He ended as he clapped his hand on my mailed shoulder. "Today, we will be battle brothers. You will fight on my right-hand today. May God hear your prayers!"

We formed a double rank on the beach, perhaps half a bowshot from the waterline, the smoothly flowing river oblivious to approaching violence.

CHAPTER 14

We did not have long to wait. The first boat rounded the bend in the river and immediately sighted us. They paused their rowing and allowed the other ships to draw near. Soon all six were near, and we heard voices in their strange tongue drifting to us from across the water.

A great shout went up from the boats, and they fairly sprang forward in the water toward us as their oars bit the water. They seemed to be racing each other toward the shore. They were singing as they came - perhaps some hymn to their gods - as they quickly closed the distance between us.

Brennus, holding his spear aloft, stepped forward from the shield wall, shouting his defiance.

"Come! Come to your death! Come to your doom, sea wolves. We wait to measure our swords on your necks, our spears in your chest. Come to us and die!" He pounded his shield with his spear.

Brennus stepped back into line as their first ship ploughed an unholy furrow in the bank, followed quickly by five more. They leapt from their boats, not even bothering to form a shield wall. They raced towards us bellowing like bulls.

Our archers sprang to action, and many invaders fell in that first volley.

As they poured from their ships, I feared we would be overwhelmed before Brennus' plan could be fully realised. They came at us with a speed and fury I had not anticipated. I felt fear creeping up like bile in my throat.

Racing towards us they let fly their throwing axes; one buried itself in my shield, unbalancing me for a moment. I saw a mountain of a man howling and rushing straight at me.

Hardly knowing what I was doing, I thrust my spear through his throat. I still remember the startled look on his face as he grasped weakly at the shaft of my spear. I withdrew it deftly and found myself stepping back with my brothers-in-arms.

An instant later, another foe appeared before me. Knocking my spear-thrust aside with his sword, he grabbed the handle of the axe still stuck in my shield, trying to tear it free while throwing his full force into me. Were it not for the second row of men at my back, I am sure I would have gone down.

But I was not alone. As I fought to push this brute back, a spear thrust from my left skewered his leg. As he bellowed in rage, my spear found his armpit, and he too lay bleeding on the beach.

We continued our fighting retreat. What had been planned as a feigned retreat became a battered reality as we were pressed back by their numbers and ferocity. Concentrating on only what was directly in front of me, I did not realise we had fallen back across the road until I heard the cries of our horsemen and watched as the hunters became the hunted.

Our stealthy slingers sprang up and picked their shots well as some of their number tried to fall back to the boats. Between the archers and the slingers, they had no chance.

But these men! Such a foe! Surrounded on all sides, being ridden down by horse and rider, peppered by arrows and slings, they did not lose heart. They formed themselves into a circular shield wall and began to make their way back toward the boats.

More than half their number lay dead or dying, but still they fought on. Harried by the archers and slingers, their ranks steadily thinned. Our horsemen formed a wedge and charged again.

Breaking through, they mowed down all in their wake with spear and sword while trying to keep from being dragged from their saddles by the enraged mob. We rushed upon the broken foe, the erstwhile slingers joining our attack now with sword and shield.

Still they fought on. Not one surrendered nor sought mercy. The battle that started with a rush and a roar ended with little more than whimpers. They asked for no mercy and received none. We killed them all. Brennus' plan worked perfectly; not one made it back to their boats.

Although we lost but few, there were cuts and bruises aplenty and a few broken bones. Only twelve of our men died that day. I did not know them well but grieved them deeply.

Men had been gathering at our holding in preparation for our voyage to Britannia. Nearly all of them had accompanied us to repel this raid. The people helped us wash the bodies of our dead and load them on a wagon to be transported back to our villa. There the priest would say prayers for them, and they would be honoured and remembered before their bodies were buried.

I opened the doors for the souls of eight men that day … eight men whose earthly lives were ended by my hand. I hardly remember the decision to kill or choosing where to strike. My training made the choices for me. My hands found work to do and did it well. These men had come to do evil, and God blessed us our work to cut them down before they could do so.

The battle ended well before evening but our work was far from over. The grateful people of Taden emerged from their palisade to help in the aftermath. We laid aside our weapons and waded into the river to wash the gore of battle from our bodies. We rested briefly before joining the villagers in their grim labour. What had been our battlefield had to be returned to a beach.

We stripped the raiders' bodies of anything valuable. Aside from their weapons and armour, there was precious little. They came expecting to fill their bellies and their boats in our rich land.

What spoils we found we set aside to deal with later. We loaded a wagon to be brought back to my mother, our princess; to her belonged the right to distribute the spoils.

As we gathered their bodies and carried them to the pit the villagers had dug in the forest, I found myself hauling the body of a huge brute with Cai.

I asked him, "Why did they leave their homes and families to come to our land? What beliefs drove them to their deaths?"

He just shrugged.

"Are they nothing more than thieves and murderers? What about their families? Who have they left behind?" I shook my head in wonder, adding, "This man must be someone's son, someone's brother or father." I motioned to Cai and stopped for a rest.

Cai stopped with me, looking from the battered face of the body between us to mine. "He came to kill and now he's dead. Does it matter why he came?" He shrugged again motioning to me, and we resumed our filthy work.

Returning to the shore to find the rest of the bodies gone, we rowed the six sturdy Saecson ships upstream beyond Lehon. We stored them in the wood, some small way from the shore. They were remarkably light for their size. We knew the day would soon come when we would use these very boats on our own expedition.

By the time we returned to Taden, the grateful people had prepared a feast for us. The beach was cleared … only the furrows ploughed by the prows of the ships remained; that, and the blood still soaking into the ground. We would trust God to wash away the blood with his rain and renew the beach once more.

As I entered the palisade, I was surprised to find my mother there. Of course she would have come to care for her people, whatever the outcome. She did not see me arrive, as she was deep in conversation with Brennus and the elders. As I approached, she stepped away from them and looked me up and down with eyes full of emotion. Apparently, I passed inspection. She embraced me, kissing me on both cheeks.

"Thank God you are safe, my son! I know you are a man and a warrior. But still, a mother worries after her son. Brennus tells me you did well today … both in your fighting and in your prayers," She added with a smile. She drew me away from the crowd preparing for the feast.

"Tell me, now that you have seen battle, do you regret leaving your life in Avallon? It's not too late. You could still be a man of the church."

Until my mother asked, it had not even occurred to me. I told her frankly, "No, mother. Although I was afraid today, I do not long for Avallon. I do not wish to turn back from the road I have chosen. I am a man of faith but also a man of war."

"There is no shame in fear. Only a great fool feels no fear. There can be no bravery without it. Today you faced yours and stood in the line of men forming a protective wall around your people, like your father before you." Her dark face betrayed a proud smile as she continued.

"I wanted a different life for you, but I respect your decision. You are not the boy I sent away. You are a man. A man makes his way in the world. Brennus and I are in agreement. You will lead our warriors to Britannia; I will announce it tonight. They witnessed you in the thick of battle today, and you are my, a true son of your father. Do not be afraid, my son; they will follow you as they followed him."

There, in the growing gloom, away from the fire and the others, I confessed, "Mother, I am not sure I am ready to lead. There are others better known, more experienced than I. What if I should fail them?"

A kindly smile lit my mother's eyes. Nodding, she said, "Good. Good. You feel the weight of leadership as you should. Those who wear it too lightly or grasp it too greedily will fail in the end. You will make mistakes; but if you do justly, love mercy, and walk humbly with your God, you will not fail. A wise leader will consult those with experience and wisdom. Seeking counsel is not a sign of weakness. But, having taken counsel and made a decision, do not fear to step boldly to the work God puts before you. Come now, they will be missing us."

CHAPTER 15

As we made our way back into the centre of Taden we were hailed and greeted by our warriors and the people. Piled near the fire were the spoils from our battle. I did not know then, but they had been impatiently waiting for my mother. A good sword or armour, battered and used though it might be, holds more worth than most poor farmers would see in their entire lives.

My mother raised her arms to the acclaim of the people. As they quieted, she gestured to the warriors around her. "These men have stood between us and death today. What are these things of metal compared with the flesh of our kindred?" She paused to let her words find their mark. "They have risked their lives for us, and their bodies bear the marks of it. Each one did their part today with honour, and so tonight we honour you. Tonight we will feast, and were there a bard here I would have your deeds sung as well." There were nods around the fire. "But before we feast and celebrate your victory, I would see you rewarded in some small way for your labour this day."

I was not prepared for what she said next.

"Illtyd, my son, come here." Heads swivelled in my direction as I approached my mother, unsure as to her purpose. "Today, my son became your sword brother. Together you bathed your feet in the blood of our enemies. May all who come against us have the same fate." Cries of "Here, here!" and "Always!" rang out.

"As you know, we did not seek this battle; but we go seeking one in the days ahead. Any who wish to carry the fight across the sea to the Saecson have the blessing of Budic, your king, and myself. A great effort will be made to rid Britannia of the Saecson scourge which has troubled our people these many years. My son, Illtyd, will lead you as you go." A murmur rippled through those gathered. I knew I was not the only one surprised by this news.

"Brennus, who has led you for so long, will stay by my side to defend our lands from Saecson and Frank while you take the battle beyond our shores. Illtyd will lead you with my blessing." She scanned the crowd, willing them to accept her decision, daring them to gainsay her.

"His first act as your war chief will be to distribute this as he sees fit." She gestured to the pile of goods collected from the Saecsons.

I stepped forward, hardly knowing what was happening, but knowing I must lead. My mother's words still echoing in my ears, I spoke thus, "My sword brothers and my people, I know it is scarcely a year since my return from Avallon. Today is but my first battle; I make no claims for myself, but I plan to earn your trust in the days ahead. Many of you served my father; all of you know my mother." I looked into her face as she stood beside me, but she gave me no encouragement. She looked the very form of stoic authority as she watched her people closely.

"These are but trinkets compared to the blood of our brothers. One-tenth of this shall be given to the families of those who fell today. One-tenth shall be given to survivors of Lehon, so recently bereft. The rest will be shared out equally among all who fought this day. I will take no share, as my share has already been given to me … to lead you from this day onward. I claim that as my gift and my share in today's victory. Come, enough talk. Let us eat and be glad to be alive this night!"

With that, my first act of leadership was concluded. Brennus rose, clapped me on the shoulder and wrapped me in a manly embrace. "Well done, lad. Well-spoken and well-done!" he whispered in my ear. I turned toward my mother. She merely nodded, but I saw the affirmation in her eyes and knew she was pleased.

As we feasted that night the men made their way to me, slapping me on the back and acclaiming my leadership.

As the rigours of the day took their toll and we found places in the settlement to sleep, Morgan, Cai, Rhodri, and Llew approached me. "Come, we would speak with you," Cai said. I followed them out of the gate.

"Your father spoke very highly of you," Rhodri began. "As a child, you did not know us, but we have watched you grow from acorn to sapling to oak. We loved your father - a love born in the fires of battle. Your mother has made you our leader, and we will do as she bids. But more, we would pledge ourselves to you as we did to your father before you. We will fight, and if need be, we will die for you. May we serve the son even better than we did the father."

There in the darkness, these men knelt before me. Each one kneeled, offering their empty hands, palms pressed together and raised to me. I recognised this ancient pledge of fealty. They were binding themselves to me and I to them. They would follow me in absolute loyalty; I accepted their allegiance and bound myself to ever consider their wellbeing and to lead with a heart devoted to them.

"You served my father well. You have been the wall around our people for many years. Your labour in fields I know not of has made the prosperity of our people possible. I am humbled by your offer, and I gratefully accept your fealty. May I grow worthy of it in the days to come."

Truly awed and humbled by their gesture, I placed my hands over each of them in turn, marvelling that these men - these warriors - would honour me in this way. I had done little to earn their loyalty, but in exchanging this vow I knew I must become the man they believed me to be.

Having completed the ancient rite, Morgan spoke first, "Right! Now that's done, let's have another drink!" With one arm around me and the other around Cai, he fairly pushed us back through the gate while he broke out in a song that doesn't bear repeating. Something about a woman he met at a fair … I'll just leave it at that.

The next day our bodies ached from the previous day's exertions and our heads from the night's drinks. But our hearts were light as the joy of living dawned again. This was subdued by the grim reality of the deaths of our sword brothers. We made our way back to the villa to bury our comrades.

In the following weeks we resumed preparations for the expedition with fierce determination. Having defeated our foes on our land, we moved with renewed purpose and confidence to take the battle to them in Britannia.

Brennus disappeared for days at a time, riding out to see to the defences and strengthen the network of forts and signal fires. He added to this the placement of horses at each settlement to be cared for by the people and designated a rider from each village to raise the alarm. With many men away, they would need to be able to respond quickly to bring what force they had to bear with all speed.

I know he also did this to allow me room to grow in the estimation of the men. They would naturally look to him were he there. In his absence they would look for leadership, and I provided it. I relied on the experience of those who had campaigned before, especially Rhodri and Morgan. They were quick with a word of wisdom or encouragement and seemed happy to serve.

In just a few weeks our preparations were nearly complete, and many men swelled our ranks. In Brennus' travels he also served to keep us abreast of other developments. Budic's ships would meet us at Dinard in a few weeks. We would make the crossing on a spring tide and pray for a smooth sea and strong winds.

I was filled with anticipation, sailing to a land I had never known. For some it was going home; but the land of my forefathers was not yet my own. I was also looking forward to a reunion with Arthwyr and Myrddin. My childhood compatriots were now seasoned warriors, and Arthwyr a great leader. Although still young, Arthwyr's renown had already spread far and wide. I longed to see my friends, to feel the soil of Britannia beneath my feet, and to take the battle to our enemies.

Beneath this anticipation lay a hidden level of apprehensions. First among them - although it amuses me now to tell it - the sea. Up to that time I had always lived near the sea, never upon it. Also, we would be traversing this unfamiliar terrain in unfamiliar boats. Our band of men would make the crossing in the Saecson ships. While we had been making our preparations our fisherfolk and shipbuilders had been learning the ways of these boats. They were impressed with their design and versatility, but it was all new to me.

I also continued to wonder about leading this expedition. Some of the men muttered. Some called me "princeling" - their own fears expressed towards me. I had no concern that I would falter in battle, only that some decision I would make might cost the lives of my men … or perhaps even worse, that my failures might reflect poorly on the honour of my family.

The hopes and expectations and the combined military might of Armorica weighed heavily on my young shoulders.

CHAPTER 16

Budic's forces arrived on schedule and our combined fleet of 50 ships carried 1,000 men, 600 horses, and supplies for all. We hoped to be enough to tip the scales in the long-running war against the invaders.

I need not have worried about the crossing. It was as uneventful as I had been assured. That first crossing awakened in me a love for the sea. I found the wind and waves invigorating. While several in our number were frequently and violently ill, I adapted quickly to the pitch and roll of our ships on the water.

We landed in Dumnonia to a less than enthusiastic welcome. This was my first introduction to the politics of Britannia. Although King Geraint of Dumnonia had been expecting us, he did not meet us at the port. Instead, we were greeted by his war chief. I was invited to attend him at his fortress, a full day's ride inland, while my men were billeted in port. Surprised by his lack of hospitality, but with little choice, I agreed to these terms. I left Rhodri and Llew to see to arrangements in port. With just Morgan and Cai as my companions, we rode into the heart of Dumnonia not knowing what awaited us.

Geraint's fortress was immense and indeed imposing. Rising high above the surrounding countryside, it looked impregnable to my young eyes. Geraint received me in his great hall with stiff formality rather than the open-hearted welcome we had hoped. He knew I was kin to Budic, who had designs upon his throne, and that I came with 1000 men. I could not entirely blame him for being suspicious and did all I could to allay his concerns.

That first night, I presented one of Guielandus' spears as a gift. I asked not about his kingdom nor the disposition of his forces, only about Saecsons and the wars. I also took pains to emphasise our urgent desire to move quickly to join up with Arthwyr and engage the enemy. Much to my surprise and joy, I did not have long to wait.

Before our meal was complete, the door to the hall opened to reveal Arthwyr and several of the kings of Britannia. Geraint rose quickly to welcome his new guests. I recognised true friendship in his greeting of

Arthwyr, if some stiffness in his demeanour towards others. These kings, although allied at the moment, battled each other nearly as often as they fought the Saecson. Some had taken Saecson brides or given their daughters to Saecson kings. The lines of loyalty were blurry at best. I was introduced to Pawl of Penychen, Meirch of Cerniw, a nephew of our host, and several others. If only these kings had been more full of faith than ambition. Oh, the greed and fickleness of men!

Although younger than the kings, they showed Arthwyr honour and deference. Geraint made room at his table to honour our new guests. As they approached the high table, Arthwyr's gaze swept the room as if looking for something or someone. Suddenly he recognised me and greeted me warmly, calling my name and sweeping me into a bear hug. I do believe his warm greeting of me did much to raise my estimation in the eyes of all present.

Respect is a fickle thing. Do not put your trust in reputation. Reputation is something you have but never own. It is but the opinion of men, and that can change in a moment and for many reasons. Respect can be earned by truly noble deeds but lost so easily. The smooth tongue of a slanderer finds fertile grounds in the hearts of ambitious men.

That first night in Britannia, reunited with Arthwyr and surrounded by the nobility of the land, my confidence swelled. Surely we would be victorious. How could the Saecsons hold their ground before the combined might of the Britons?!

The next morning, I found Arthwyr at breakfast early. He bid me walk with him.

"It is a boon to see you and to hear of the host you have brought. We will put you all to good use in the days ahead; and may God bless us and grant us victory, for our enemy is cunning. The Saecson reckons not honour as we do. They gain honour through deceit. Their gods are deceivers, so why should they not emulate them? You may have heard that my own father was poisoned when he accepted a cup offered in peace from Aelle, that worthless dog."

"I am sorry for your loss," I responded. "I have heard of the slaughter that day at Anderida, and we hope to avenge your father and all those who have been betrayed and murdered by the Saecson hordes."

"If you would avenge all those who have been murdered, you will have to take more than just the Saecson into view." He paused, looking off into the distance. "Forgive me," he continued. "I am sometimes taken by melancholy thoughts. These kings have their own ambitions; they care more about themselves than their people, their thrones than their kingdoms. If we could but stand together as one, I am sure we could drive the invader from our shores. But ..." He grunted in frustration. "Forgive me. It is good to see you and to have someone I know I can trust by my side. Especially now that Myrddin is gone."

"Myrddin! Gone! What has happened?"

"We do not know. Myrddin too was at Anderida when it fell. No one has seen him since. Some say he perished in the massacre. Other say ... say ... other things."

"What? What do they say?"

"Oh, what does it matter what they say? They will say anything if it suits their ambitions. Some even question the virtue of my mother and say I am a bastard. They mean to keep me from any claim to kingship ... as if that mattered to me. I tell you, Illtyd - watch yourself. These kings of Britannia are not to be trusted. I fight their battles, and they spread rumours behind my back even as they feast me in their halls."

"I am sorry. Are there none of honour among them?"

"Oh yes, there are some I would trust enough, at least in battle. Our host, Geraint ap Erbin, has been bold and faithful in battle. And yet I wonder, once the Saecsons are defeated ... how will his relations with his neighbours be then?"

"And Myrddin? What else can you tell me?" I returned to our previous topic.

"Some say he lives still in the forest of Anderida, stalking the Saecsons and besting them in their game of terror. The stories grow darker and more outrageous as time passes, and it hasn't yet been a year! They say he practices human sacrifice. They say he has returned to the old ways and that the gods of our ancestors walk the land with him."

"Strange tales indeed, my friend. What say you?"

"I say people love strange tales in dark times. I say people believe what they want to believe! I say my friend is dead and they won't let his memory live in peace!" Arthwyr's face contorted fiercely as he growled out these words about our lost cousin.

"I am truly sorry. You have suffered much. I had hoped to see Myrddin again. I brought gifts for both of you. Come, at least I can give you yours."

We returned to the corner of the hall where we had slept to find Cai keeping watch. "Rest easy, Cai; we are among friends here," I greeted him, laying a reassuring hand on his shoulder.

He returned my greeting with a scowl. "Are we?" was all he said before nodding at Arthwyr in a sign of recognition and respect before wandering away toward the hearth and breakfast.

I turned my eyes toward Arthwyr, but he was looking in another direction. My eyes followed his, and soon my attention was captured as well. Near the hearth, two young women were talking … one dark and dusky with hair of raven black and one with fair skin and hair like golden corn … both of surpassing beauty.

"Who is that?" I whispered hoarsely.

"That is Gwenhwyfar, the daughter of our host, and the woman I hope to marry. She is talking with Trynihid, the niece of Pawl of Penychen."

I traced his line of sight more closely now, to try to figure out who was who. Despairing, and not wanting to find myself at cross purposes with my cousin, I asked, "Which is Gwenhwyfar?"

Arthwyr looked surprised and annoyed as he gestured, "The raven-haired beauty is my desire" … as if it was obvious, and I was thick to not immediately recognise his choice.

Beauty is a puzzlement. Of course, I recognised the beauty of Gwenhwyfar. She reminded me of the beauty of my mother. Dark hair, dark eyes, only her dusky skin differed from the fair skin of my mother. She was a beautiful woman, indeed. But I only ever had eyes for Trynihid. Her golden hair and fair skin seemed to catch all the dim light in the hall and reflect it like a beacon. I felt my heart like a moth drawn toward the flame. We must have been staring like two dumb oxen because the next I knew the girls were giggling and twittering to themselves. They fairly flew out of the room with just a glance over their shoulders in our direction.

"Your Gwenhwyfar is a beauty, my friend … if it is not too soon to call her yours?" I gingerly enquired.

"There is no arrangement, but Geraint knows of my hopes. He is perhaps concerned that in marrying her, I mean to stake a claim to his throne after him. He is zealous to protect his son Cadwy's throne. I cannot blame him. There are always schemers about. But I would never do anything to harm Cadwy, nor do I covet his throne. You will meet Cadwy soon enough; I'm surprised he is not here already. Your arrival has set things in motion. A war council is gathering here." He glanced over his shoulder to where he had last see Gwenhwyfar as he ruefully pronounced, "Now is not the time for love."

"Here my friend is my gift for you. A gift you may find fitting to the times," I added as I presented him with the long sword from Guielandus.

Arthwyr's eyes shone as he drew the sword from its scabbard. "It looks like it would cut steel, so bright is the edge." He tested the edge with his thumb approvingly. "And wonderfully light for the length, I expected it to be heavier!" He checked the balance and weight as he swung it to feel it play in his hand. "But oh, it is well balanced! Light enough for close combat, long enough to be effective while mounted. Oh, I will cleave some heads with this! Thank you, my friend. This is a gift of great worth; I am hungry to test it in battle!"

CHAPTER 17

Over the next few days, more men gathered from kingdoms across Britannia. They came from every corner - even beyond the already ancient wall of Hadrian. Llaennog of Elmet, Cynfelyn of Cynwidion, and Gawain of Gododdin were among them. They came together, but not truly in unity. Wary of one another, they were pleased to consider the expulsion of the Saecsons, if only to have a freer hand to advance their individual agendas.

Although a member of the council, as the commander of the forces of Armorica I held back, thinking it better to observe than to press into the thick of things. I began to see why these ambitious men were pleased to let Arthwyr lead their combined forces. Of course they recognised his tactical genius, and no man doubted his courage or prowess in battle. But they were pleased to have Arthwyr command because he had no land, no base from which to stake a claim to dominion. No man would allow another king to make a name for himself at the expense of others. They continually needled one another while feigning friendship. It was a dangerous game they played.

In the end, Arthwyr was confirmed as Dux Bellorum. As the war leader, he would continue to command the war effort. A general strategy was agreed. The Saecsons, having established themselves solidly in the southeast, steadily pushed north toward Elmet and Linnius. They also pushed west into the heart of the island. Their constant pressure and settlement in the valleys had almost completely encircled Cynwidion already. The northern kingdoms advocated further defence of the north while the western and southern kingdoms demanded the halt of eastward expansion. In the end, the decision was agreed to blunt the eastward advance first.

This did not please everyone. The kings of the far north affirmed the will of the council but declined to send men or material help of any kind, insisting they needed to look to their own defences. The remaining kings and princes at the council agreed to marshal their forces and meet at Caer Guintguic. We decided to gather there in a fortnight or sooner. I sent Morgan back to the coast to move our men east by sea and then march them north to meet us. I travelled with Arthwyr, who sent scouts immediately to the east of Caer Guintguic to learn what we might about the strength and movements of the enemy.

All went well. By the time Morgan rejoined us, we found ourselves with a force of nearly 3000 men wanting only a target to strike. While we waited for the return of the scouts, Arthwyr drilled us in tactics he had found useful against the Saecsons. Arthwyr was a creative and stern war chief. He pressed us in our training and integrated our ranks. We got to know men from across Britannia as we traded blows and shared grim smiles on long marches.

We did not have long to wait. As the scouts returned, they brought word that Aelle was moving west and north with a large army, at least 1000 men, from his new base at Anderida. It seemed he was intent in joining with the Saecsons in the Tamesis valley. Arthwyr would have preferred to choose to take the fight to them, but this unexpected development might provide a chance to smash Aelle's main force and exact vengeance for the slaughter at Anderida.

Arthwyr gave orders for us to march into the river valley of the Bassa, wary of ambush and betrayal. We moved in full armour, mounted scouts screening our flanks and probing ahead of us. We met no Saecson on our approach to the ford over the river Bassa.

Arthwyr was determined to prevent Aelle from joining forces with the Saecson forces in the Tamesis valley. "If we can crush Aelle here we can turn our attention to driving the invaders from the heart of our island and back across the sea."

Our scouts kept a wary eye out for our enemy as we prepared for the day of battle.

Our training had forged bonds that in turn boosted our courage. Having traded blows with a man is a rough sort of friendship. Having tasted the strength of his blows and given a few of your own can weld disparate men into a single weapon. Arthwyr had been carefully preparing us for battle, honing our skills and boosting our courage. Now, he made preparations of another kind.

Deception - I shudder to give voice to these words - deception is as much a part of war as is courage. In the years since I had last seen Arthwyr, he had proven not only a skilled and courageous warrior but also a brilliant tactician. Some may practice tactics or learn them from books. No doubt Arthwyr had been trained by Brennus and his father, but Arthwyr lived and uncannily breathed war tactics as if it was his very nature. Deception became a sharp tool in his capable hands.

Hear me when I say - do not walk in the ways of the deceiver. When Satan lies, he speaks his native language. May you never learn to walk in his ways. Once you start down that road it is hard to return; Lord knows few do so. But in a time of deceit and brutality, the weapon of trickery was readily wielded by the hand of Arthwyr.

As war leader, Arthwyr was always careful to screen the movements of his troops. We marched and camped so as to move stealthily through our own lands, lest word of our strength or numbers reach our enemy. Only Arthwyr would choose the time and place of battle, all the while revealing as little as possible to the enemy.

And so, there at the ford of Bassa Arthwyr called a council, laid his trap, and baited it with me.

"Our scouts have been shadowing Aelle's movements for days. He is but three miles from here at present. But there are still many ways he could move, and I know not what he will choose if left to himself. So we will not leave it to him. You will be the bait to lure the wolf into the noose we will use to hang him. Choose twenty men to draw blood from our foe. In doing so, he may charge heedlessly across the ford and onto the waiting spears of our men."

The council of princes watched me closely, but I hesitated not at all. I knew this was an honour as well as a challenge. "I will lead this attack, and may God grant us success," I said. I found many men eager to join me on this mission. I chose mostly young men who looked like they could move quickly. We would have to strike hard and move swiftly to escape back across the ford ahead of the Saecson host.

Twenty men to challenge 1000 may seem foolhardy, but one uses a small worm to bait a hook for a large fish. I chose Cai and Morgan from among my companions, leaving Llew and Rhodri to lead the rest of our contingent. We were dressed as a hunting party. Lightly armed and with no helmets or armour, we rode out to prick our foe. Several of the scouts rode with us, as I was unfamiliar with the terrain.

And so, having only been on the island a few weeks, I found myself boldly riding out. Costumed as a nobleman on a hunt, I hoped to find my quarry. It did not take long.

We had not ridden far when the scouts called us up short. This was their corner of the world, and they knew it like I knew my patch in Armorica. We had expected to have to ride further, but it seemed we were not the only hunting party in the forest that day. The scout pointed out a man some yards distant creeping through the woods. Staying in character, I called out a bold challenge.

"You there! What are you doing?!"

The startled man stood up straight, staring in our direction. He glanced over his shoulder. I made straight toward him, quickly covering the ground between us, all the while watching him carefully and assuming a haughty expression. The remainder of our party fanned out behind me. I could tell by his weapons and clothing he was a Saecson. He carried a bow, with an arrow notched on the string. His saex, the traditional Saecson knife, hung from his belt which also secured an axe to his side.

Berating him as I rode, "You, what are you doing in my forest? Who are you?! Answer me, poacher, or you'll pay for your silence with your head."

As I approached, he seemed wary but not terribly concerned. Eying our party as if making some calculations of his own, he stood almost casually, shifting his weight slowly from foot to foot.

"I am not a poacher, but I am hunting. Are these your lands then?" He addressed me in my own language but with a strange accent.

"Yes, they are. Be gone with you! I have come to hunt, not to argue with a Saecson interloper! You have no permission to hunt in my forest, nor would I grant it."

A small smile crept across his face as he replied, "You did not grant my permission, and yet I have it. My lord has tasked me to bring meat to his fire."

"And who is your lord who dares to give permission to hunt in my forest?"

"Who really owns the trees and the land? They were here before us and will be here after we're dead. After all, all men die - some sooner than later. Perhaps it will not be your forest forever."

As he spoke this last word, he raised his bow so quickly and fluidly that he nearly caught me. I confess I was thinking more about how to respond to his somewhat philosophical observation than I was about defending myself. His arrow nearly felled me, but God was gracious and I heard it whistle by my head. Two inches to the right and it would have buried itself in my eye.

I dug my heels into my horse and planted my spear in his chest. He had just managed to pull his saex from its sheath and his axe from his belt. But he would never use them again.

Arrows flew at us from the forest beyond where he lay. We made quick work of the remaining hunting party. We found eight of them had stealthily approached while I had questioned the interloper. We knew there were no Saecson settlements nearby. These men belonged to Aelle.

We left their bodies where they lay and pressed on. I shall not bore you with the tedium of our search - how our scouts found and followed their trail, knowing we would find Aelle at the end of it and our real task would commence. War is like that you know … hours of tense boredom punctuated with seconds of sheer terror.

We rode the trails as if hunting for game, unable to be sure we went unobserved, while the scouts probed forward and watched our flanks lest we stumble upon another hunting party.

CHAPTER 18

We did not have long to ride that day. We soon found ourselves not far from the Saecson camp. It appeared they had not moved. We observed them spread across a trampled meadow from deep within the safety of the forest.

Morgan spoke first, "Look at them … as if they don't have a care in the world … tramping through Britannia as if they belong here … as if it is their land … like a bear sprawled out on the ground after eating too much honey. They've barely even posted a guard at all."

"Well, now that we've found the bear, I say we rouse him from his honey stupor and lead him in a merry chase," I responded. Cai nodded his agreement.

We quietly retreated deeper into the forest to remount our horses. Although armed with only spears and swords, we would have speed and surprise on our side.

Moments later, all twenty of us came thundering out of the forest. We rode down the sentries and were well into the camp before the alarm was raised. As they rushed for their arms, we thrust and slashed, causing as much damage as we could. Just a few minutes later, we rushed back out of the camp, retracing our bloody path to the edge of the forest before they could encircle us.

Having reached the relative safety of the forest edge, I turned to taunt our foes. I found Cai at my side. He was holding a Saecson banner, red with a black raven upon it. With a sly smile, he offered it to me.

Brandishing their banner above my head, I bellowed my challenge: "You Saecson wolves! You come to steal, kill, and destroy! How is the destroyer so easily ridden down in his camp?! Easily we have snatched away your lives, your banner, and your honour! I will remember this hunting day. I left home this morning to find boar; but instead I slaughtered Saecson dogs. My spear drips with your blood and thirsts for more!"

We had done our work well. Their first ranks flew across the field toward us. We turned our horses and rode hard back toward the ford. We rode recklessly to make sure we left an easy trail to follow. We heard their reckless pursuit. We passed the bodies of their one-time hunting party in the forest. A few moments later, we listened to their howls of rage as they came upon their dead bodies.

The rest of our hunting party were halfway across the river when Cai and I reached the ford. I hesitated but a moment before crossing. The cries and curses of a thousand Saecsons at my back, I hurried across the river. Having gained the far shore, we turned to see what we had wrought.

The Saecson host assembling on the far bank most closely resembled a storm-tossed sea, a heaving mass of men and arms only loosely under control. I brandished their banner at them once more before turning and ascending the embankment some small distance from the shore. There, I planted the raven flag and turned to face the foe whose fore ranks were now waist-deep in the middle of the ford.

As I waited for the impending storm to break, I marvelled at the power of their rage. These thousand warriors had chased us miles through the forest and still they came on. We dismounted, took up our shields, and arrayed ourselves along the top of the embankment, spears at the ready. Hundreds of Saecsons were now on our side of the river, not even bothering to form their ranks in their eagerness to kill us. Hundreds more were swarming into the river while still more emerged from the forest beyond.

In their blind rage, they came on. Little did they know nor even imagine what Arthwyr had in store for them.

We watched them from the top of the embankment, while behind us, just out of sight stood 1000 men rested and waiting. Arthwyr appeared at my side, plucked the flag from the ground and cast it down before him. As he drew his sword, the slaughter commenced.

The men behind us rushed to the top of the embankment forming a solid wall of shields and spears before the onrushing Saecsons. They faltered at this sudden change, but having come this far there was no turning back. With terrible cries, they rushed up the embankment as fast as their exhausted legs could carry them, only to be mowed down like so much grass by the waiting spears of our shield wall.

Only once they were fully engaged on our side of the river did our horsemen appear from their flanks on the far side. Their forces, already divided by the river, were further divided and crushed by the repeated charges of the armoured cavalry. Those in the river faced the unenviable choice of moving forward to death before the shield wall or back to meet the rampant warriors upon their charging steeds.

Behind the safety of our shield wall, our hunting party properly armoured ourselves in full to join the battle in earnest. By the time we were armoured and ready the fight was all but over. I mounted my horse and watched as Arthwyr's trap consumed the stalwart foe, turning their desire for vengeance into the means for their own destruction.

The Bassa ran red with blood that day. Hundreds of Saecsons lay dead before the sun had reached its zenith. It descended from battle to butchery as Arthwyr's plan worked all too well. Not all were slain, however; Aelle and many of his men retreated into the forest, beating a rapid path toward their coastal domain. Those cut off from retreat fought in isolated pockets on either shore and in the river. Most preferred death, but some hundred or so were captured.

The captured were stripped, bound, and marched before us. We returned to our camp in high spirits that night, with spoils as well as captives. Even as we rejoiced at our victory, we were careful to post a watchful guard, lest our foe fall on us unaware.

The victory was overwhelming, and we were filled with hope for Britannia. The fierce Saecson war host lay slaughtered before us.

A council was called. Some called for the heads of the captives and some for slower and more painful deaths. None called for mercy.

Arthwyr, as battle chief, Dux Bellorum, had the right to divide the spoils and decide the fate of the captured. He called for silence and bid the captives brought before him. They came, still bound, into our midst, with blows and spittle launched at them as they came. And yet, they came with heads held high.

After quieting the assembly, Arthwyr called the kings and princes of Britannia to join him. The captives stood before us, surrounded by the war host of Britannia fairly baying for their blood. None doubted that these men deserved to die for their predations on our land. Arthwyr asked what we would have him do.

I knew justice would be served if they were killed, but I dared to speak. "Cousin, might we give them a choice?" All eyes turned to me.

"Yes - a choice of drowning or hanging. A sword, axe, or spear is too good for the likes of them," called someone from the assembly.

"We have all suffered at the hands of the Saecson. Death is a just sentence. But what if we give them a choice of death or banishment. Might not some accept the offer?" I ventured.

"For what purpose?" Arthwyr queried. He seemed none too pleased I had taken this tack. "Why should we let our enemy live? Especially, sly and conniving enemies like these?" I noticed those nearest us nodding as he spoke.

Still, I went on. "I have as much against the Saecson as any man, and I do not know why this idea has seized me now. But didn't the apostle Paul suggest that kindness can lead to repentance? Might not a demonstration of kindness in the face of their savagery be a shock to their system? Do we want vengeance more than peace?"

"Yes, vengeance is what we want!" someone called out. The men of the council shook their heads and shuffled on their feet, casting fierce looks in the direction of the waiting captives. More cries for vengeance rang from the British war host.

King Pawl of Penychen spoke up, "Young Illtyd has earned our respect in battle today. Let us not doubt his mettle or cast his ideas aside too hastily. But neither would I trust the word of a Saecson. If we offer them life or death, I do not doubt they would choose life. Then they would use our kindness against us, slitting our throats at the first opportunity. They are oath-breakers, the lot of them. They pride themselves on that point." Heads bobbed in agreement.

Pawl continued, "But we need not trust them to allow them Illtyd's choice." This was met with some confusion. "I say we mark them."

He paused to let his idea settle for a moment before continuing, "Many among us bear the indelible marks of tattoos. The Romans branded their slaves, and often their legions. I say we offer them the choice of a quick death now, or the chance to live as marked men far from our shores. If a marked man is found again on British lands, he will surely die and not quickly. How does that sound to you, Arthwyr?"

Arthwyr pondered this new option for a few minutes, eying the assemblage of warriors, lords, and captives in turn. There was a discontented and angry murmuring as he silently deliberated. At last he stood, "Here is my decision: We will offer them a choice." A wail of rage rose from the crowd. "Hear me now!" bellowed Arthwyr. The assembly quieted, and he continued, "They can choose to surrender one eye and one cheek to a hot brand and life beyond our lands, never to return upon pain of death. Or they can choose death by hanging now."

This was hardly the choice I had in mind; but under the law of an eye for an eye, all of their lives should have been forfeited. There was a limited sort of mercy in Arthwyr's offer. They could keep one eye and their lives if they chose. But a hot brand in the eye is tough to accept under any circumstance.

I could tell the assembly was weighing Arthwyr's decision and seemed divided. Not that they had any say in the matter. Arthwyr's decision was final. The murmuring had started among the captives as well. Clearly, some among them had learned our language, and they were discussing the situation among themselves and began to grow agitated.

Arthwyr demanded silence from the prisoners. His decree was swiftly enforced with cries, blows, and kicks.

CHAPTER 19

Arthwyr called the assembly to order. Addressing himself to the captives, he asked who would speak for them. For a few moments, no one moved. Finally, a huge man stood in their midst. He looked to be nearly as tall as Arthwyr, though several years older. His body bore the marks of many a past battle; his face, although spattered with mud and gore from the day's action, bore a proud expression some might call noble.

Arthwyr asked him if he understood our speech and the man replied he did. Arthwyr gestured for the man to approach. As he did, Arthwyr asked him his name and how he came by his knowledge of our language.

"I am Hild, son of Bada who came over on the first ship with Hengest and Horsa. I was born and raised here in Britannia. I have ever lived here. Why would I not know my mother's language as well as my father's?" He concluded in a surly yet straightforward manner.

"Your mother is a Briton and you have lived your whole life on our islands, yet you and your people have repeatedly broken our laws and every treaty which bound you. Do you deny it?" Arthwyr challenged.

"I do not know treaties or laws. I am a warrior like my father before me. I am loyal to my kindred and my king. I fight when and where I am told, and farm when I'm left to myself. I am no better or worse than any man here." This was met with angry jeers from the crowd.

Arthwyr looked him hard in the eye, for they were but a few feet apart now. "I will not be drawn into a debate with you. You and your people this day are waging war against the Kings of Britannia. As the Dux Bellorum of the Britons and the commander of the army who has defeated you this day, I will give you a choice. You can die today, hung from the trees in yon forest, or you can submit yourselves to an oath to leave British lands forever. The price of your oath is your right eye and a brand upon your cheek. This will show your submission and be your punishment for your crimes against us. If you choose life, you will be taken from this place to the shore. You will be given a boat and supplies to last one week. Should you ever be found in British lands again, we will not be so merciful. I give you leave to discuss your choice."

I did not envy Hild as he turned to address his countrymen and sword brothers. He laid the choice before them as we watched. I found myself praying for them to choose life, while many hoped for another outcome. I noticed some of the men of Cynwidion and Rhegin made a show of gathering ropes and making nooses, throwing these down in a pile near the captives. Others heated pokers in naked flames, silently taunting them.

While the prisoners debated their options, King Pawl laid his hand on my shoulder. "Only a very brave or very foolish man will argue for mercy after a day like today. Which one are you, Illtyd ap Bicanys?" he asked with a wary look.

"I don't quite know myself," I answered. "I know the Saecson depredations. My own father was killed from ambush by Saecson raiders, my people slaughtered. And yet, I wonder if the Apostle may be right. Could kindness lead them to repentance? I confess I don't know. But is this offer even a kindness?" I asked.

"These men would not have hesitated to kill us today. Even now, if the situation were reversed and you were their captive, they would not hesitate to kill you. You must know this," Pawl insisted.

"I do not doubt it. I have killed in battle and will do so again. But is there not something in the words of Hild? Is he worse than other men? Are they not like us?"

"He may not be worse, but these heathen pillaging Saecsons are not like us. We have not invaded their lands. We have not pillaged or burned their villages. We have not raped and enslaved their women and children. They worship pagan gods and delight in blood and war. They are men, but not like us. Their gods are not like Christ. They delight in deceit like the devil himself. No, young Illtyd," he concluded finally, "they are not like us."

We eyed each other thoughtfully but had no more chance to continue our conversation at that time, for the prisoners had concluded their debate and Hild was approaching Arthwyr.

Motioning for quiet, Arthwyr asked, "Have you made your choice?"

Hild nodded sombrely, "To return to our people disfigured and blinded would be an even greater dishonour than to be hung like a dog from a tree. We do not ask for mercy; we only ask that you kill us like men. We have fought with honour; let us die with honour."

"So, you reject our offered mercy and make demands instead." Arthwyr retorted. "You say you fought with honour. Maybe you did today. Today when you found yourself faced with British warriors; you did not shrink back. But many other days you and yours have behaved treacherously and without honour! You stalk our children in the night and dishonour every gesture of hospitality shown to you. You ask for no mercy, and you will receive none," he declared.

"Do you think we are the only ones to practice treachery?" Hild shouted. "Do not your own people stalk us in the woods of Anderida? Many mornings we have awoken to find our animals gone and the headless bodies of kinsmen upon our thresholds. Many have gone into the night only to be found bloodless and headless hanging from the crossroads or on the trees along the road. Do you think only the Saecson hunts at night?" Hild stood defiantly to the last.

"I'll not bandy words with you," Arthwyr said quietly. Then, turning to the Britons, he cried, "Let justice be done upon them. String them up!"

The men needed little encouragement. Leaping into action like falcons freed for flight, they were on the prisoners in a moment, dragging them from the camp to the forest. They made short work of them and left their bodies to swing in the wind.

I didn't watch. I was pondering Hild's words about the terror stalking them from the depths of the forest of Anderida. Headless and bloodless bodies struck an old chord and a dark one; I recalled tales from my childhood of Bran the Blessed and the warriors of old. I knew that the old ways were still alive in our lands. Kian was not the only apostle of druidism in those days, but these stories and rituals went beyond mere superstitions about mistletoe or herbal potions to cure or curse.

I remembered Kian's stories of power residing in the head, of heads speaking beyond death, of oaken chests full of oiled heads. I knew of ancient druidic practices that called for libations of blood and the heads of our enemies. In the days before the Romans, our people had practised the old rites for the old gods.

Although it had been generations since these dark arts had held full sway among the Britons, I was not foolish enough to believe that all of my countrymen had been converted. But until that day I had not considered that the old ways could come again. Surely not, I thought to myself.

Arthwyr stood before the spoils with the kings and leaders, distributing the weapons and valuables among them. I received a significant share and left it to be shared out among our men by Llew and Cai who had led our men this day.

As Arthwyr turned to go, I kept pace alongside him.

He looked at me. "Why did you do that?" he whispered. "Why did you ask for mercy for these men who killed your father and mine? You made it much more complicated than it needed to be!"

"I know. I am sorry. It suddenly came upon me that they could be led to repentance."

"The only way to end these wars is to kill them and drive them from the land … our land. They may claim it, but we know it is ours! They understand only power." Arthwyr was already planning his next move. "Having defeated Aelle today, our southern flank should be secure. We will head north and drive them out of the Tamesis valley and east beyond Londinium, and back into the sea." He gestured as he spoke as if he could push them into the sea with his hands.

"You know my troops are yours to command. We will follow you, but may I ask for a boon?" I asked.

He eyed me warily. "What now?"

"I would take the same twenty men I had today and explore the forest of Anderida before joining you at Londinium."

"What do you hope to find there?"

"I hope to find a remnant of my father's people. I also hope - and fear - I will find Myrddin. Hild's words give me hope he is still alive, but fear of what he is becoming."

Arthwyr nodded. "The stories ring true. Go with my blessing. But be careful. You will not be the only party endeavouring to solve this mystery."

CHAPTER 20

The next morning I assembled the men. We gathered our supplies and prepared our mounts. While we made to move south and west, the rest of the army was preparing to move north. I knew Llew and Rhodri would have no trouble leading the men in my absence.

I was grateful to have Morgan and Cai with me. I wanted familiar men I could trust as well as men who knew the land and would serve as guides and scouts.

We rode in full armour, as we did not know what we would face. Riding single file and picking our way carefully, we tried to make our way stealthily into the heart of the lands of Rhegin. We camped each night in hollows and glades away from trails and with no fire … always with a rotating watch, constantly on guard.

As we travelled, I wondered if these lands would have been familiar to my father. If ever he spoke of Rhegin, it was in glowing but vague terms. As we rode through the forest of Anderida, I was impressed by its sheer size. After two days of careful riding, I was informed by the scouts that we were still only on the edge of the forest. It would be denser further in, they assured me. I could only shake my head in wonder.

Another day in, and they brought grimmer news. They guided us warily to their find. We smelled it before we saw the pile of rotting heads, stacked in a pyramid beside the track where two tracks converged. No doubt a warning to anyone passing this way.

We doubled the watch that night and pressed on even more slowly and warily the next day, our Rhegin scouts leading the way. That day we found more signs and warnings, strange signs and symbols painted on rocks and trees in blood, headless bodies hanging over our track.

As we passed beyond that place, we were startled by a booming voice.

"Who are you? Who foolishly treads my forest heedless of signs and portents!?"

The voice seemed to come from nowhere and everywhere. With weapons drawn, we drew nearer to one another. Instinctively forming a defensive perimeter, we scanned the forest for danger and the source of the challenge.

Seeing no alternative, I answered the challenge, "I am Illtyd ap Bicanys, a prince among Britons. I come in search of a friend."

After a few moments the booming voice rang out again, "What friend do you seek?"

"I seek Myrddin ap Cynwal and the remnant of Rhegin," I answered simply. Then, issuing a challenge of my own, "And who are you who lays claim to the ancient forest of Anderida?!"

I believe I heard a chuckle in response. "A fair question Illtyd ap Bicanys. I do not own the forest, but I am its keeper. You might say the forest owns me."

As I was puzzling over this. A hooded figure swathed in green, covered in leaves and branches suddenly emerged from the forest as if by magic … and spoke with a more familiar voice. "Perhaps you may find two friends instead of one." The figure drew back his hood, and there before me stood Kian, my old master. "At least, I would claim as much. Would you?" he said, stepping closer.

"Of course, my master," I said. Sheathing my sword and leaping from my horse, I crossed the distance between us and embraced him. As I did so, I found a large brass horn slung across his back.

"Ah, this is the source of your godlike voice, is it?" I declared.

"Well, you can't blame a man for trying," He chuckled. "In troubled times like these, we must use whatever power we have. With the right kindling and a spark, the fears of men can be stoked and fanned into a flame that burns only them. Their fear makes them easy targets for those who might hunt them."

With that, he waved his hand and ten men appeared above us in the surrounding trees, bows in hand. The enormity of our peril was suddenly apparent, as our heads swivelled this way and that.

"We could have taken you easily enough, but we hunt only Saecsons and traitors. We know you are not Saecson …" His voice trailed off, leaving the question hanging in the air.

"No, my master, we are neither Saecson nor traitors. We have come not a week hence from a great slaughter of Saecsons that would undoubtedly have pleased you."

Kian studied my face for a moment. "Yes, I think you'll do. Come along then." With that, he turned and started making his way deeper into the forest. His men, following his lead, descended from their perches in the trees and followed.

I gestured for my nervous comrades to put away their weapons; returning to my horse, we followed. It wasn't long before the paths they took forced us to dismount and lead our horses by hand. The tracks were narrow and low, but just passable for man and horse.

The trails felt more like tunnels and crisscrossed many others as we continued following. Then suddenly, we were out in a large clearing. It took a moment for our eyes to adjust to the bright light of day after so long in the gloom of the forest. As they did, we saw what looked to be a substantial settlement of simple but sturdy-looking structures around the edges of a vast clearing. Next, our noses took in the smell of roasting meat, and we saw several pigs turning on spits over open fires.

Then, Myrddin was before me. My long-lost brother approached across the field clad all in black, looking every bit a lord. Although we had not seen each other in years, we embraced like old friends.

"I thought you were dead …" I began.

"Come, there will be enough time for talking. Let us eat and drink." Then, looking beyond me to my men, he gestured, "Come, my new friends - you are welcome here!"

After weeks of hard rations, cold camping, and constant danger, it was good to eat hot meat and relax in the safety of this forest fastness.

As we ate, Myrddin explained their situation. "We are the last remnants of Rhegin. After the fall of Anderida, we could not hold our coastal lands. They have the coast, but we still command the forest. We provide haven here for any Briton who needs it and sure death to any Saecson who is foolish enough to hunt us. We have over 500 men, and scouts spread out in the forest in every direction. We have been watching you for two days."

I shook my head at how easily we had been taken in. "I thought we were so careful!"

Myrddin laughed, "Careful enough to catch a Saecson unawares no doubt, but we have forest craft they do not. The ancient ways have many secrets unknown to them."

"I see you play upon their fears and use their fears against them. They do fear the forest. Men we captured told us stories, and we have seen for ourselves your bloody handiwork on our journey here," I said. "I understand the tactic, but surely the ancient ways have dangers as well as powers. There are reasons we have abandoned them."

An awkward silence followed.

"You have not seen what I have seen." Myrddin said, breaking the silence. "I was there when they poisoned Meurig's cup. We showed them hospitality, and I barely escaped the slaughter that followed. Your god may be good enough in times of peace, but we need gods who will fight for us, not just die for us. I watched from the forest as they nailed my people to trees, powerless to stop them. I need power, and the old ways offer me that. I will have my revenge, whatever it takes."

These words were spoken with such certainty and fierceness that I feared for my friend. I knew all too well the feelings of rage and vengeance. But even then, in the early days of my own tentative faith, I could feel this was wrong. Words failed me. I placed my hand on his shoulder, and we sat together in silence as darkness fell over the clearing. I silently prayed the Lord would give me words.

"I have not seen what you have seen. I do not know what you know," I began. "I have my own pain and reasons for hatred. But this I know, my redeemer lives. Christ will reign upon the earth. I would be found on his side on that day."

"Maybe on that day he will reign. But who will help us in the meantime? I remember, 'Vengeance is mine saith the Lord, I will repay.' But his vengeance, if it ever comes, will come too late. No, I will use whatever power suits my purpose. I will see Britannia free from these Saecson dogs and our dead avenged not someday, but this day!" Myrddin growled.

"Let us not quarrel. Yesterday you were dead, and now you are alive. I did not seek you only to fall out with you. I have brought you a gift … a gift and an invitation. Come."

I stood motioning for him to follow me to where our things had been stored.

As we walked I continued, "All is not lost. I did not come to Britannia alone. A thousand men and 600 horses came with me. We ride with Arthwyr, and the combined host of Britannia rides with us. At Bassa, we had over 3000 and smashed Aelle's forces. I bring an invitation from Arthwyr. Join us. Together we can drive the Saecsons from our shores." I could tell he was turning my proposal over in his mind.

"Why leave the fastness of our forest?" he asked. "We can avenge ourselves from here."

"Yes, you can seek vengeance; but can you win the war with 500 men? Join the remaining forces of Rhegin to Arthwyr's, and we can win battle after battle until the war is won." By this time we had reached our assigned lodgings.

Drawing aside the door covering, I invited my host inside. "I come with an invitation from Arthwyr and a gift from myself." I retrieved from my belongings the remaining sword of Guielandus and handled it to Myrddin. "This is for you."

As he drew it, he took his time to examine the blade and test it in his hand. "The blade is exquisite, but the balance is different. It feels something between an axe and a sword, but lighter than either." After testing the edge, he added, "I accept. I accept this gift with thanksgiving and hope before long to test it upon my enemies. As to Arthwyr's invitation, I will discuss it with Kian and my men. I want both vengeance and victory. Perhaps Arthwyr can deliver both."

We parted then for the evening, and I slept well within the safety of the ancient forest. But my sleep was disturbed by dark dreams.

CHAPTER 21

I awoke the next morning with a strange heaviness in my chest. I was glad to be reunited with Myrddin; yet there were disturbing elements to our conversation … a situation made no better by Morgan's arrival while I was dressing for the day.

"Come with me, there is something you should see."

He led me across to the far side of the clearing. There I found an entrance to an oak grove, flanked by two ancient-looking stones covered with swirls and symbols - some known to me, and others I did not recognise. This was an ancient place, fairly pulsing with power.

As we entered between these blood-stained pillars, the heaviness in my chest increased and I found myself temporarily unable to see and struggling to breathe. As our eyes adjusted to the darkness, I discovered we were standing in a circle within a ring of standing stones about the height of a man, each covered with different symbols and topped with a human head. These were surrounded by an outer ring of oaks, their branches forming an almost solid ceiling above us. In the trunk of each ancient tree was carved a niche, and in each slot a human skull. In the centre of the circle stood a stone table over what looked like a stone trough.

Morgan stood beside me as I took in the macabre tableau before me.

My thoughts were interrupted by a greeting, "Welcome Illtyd ap Bicanys. I wondered when I might have a chance to speak with you again." It was Kian. I had not seen him enter. Perhaps he had been here before us.

"I am here, my old master. I did not come to speak with you, but I would be glad of the chance."

"Would you now?" He smiled. "Would you? Even now that you have entered this holy place?"

"Oh! Do not call this place holy!"

"And why not? Do you not call your churches holy where you pour out the blood of your god week by week as you remember his crucifixion? Shall I not call holy the place where we pour out libations of blood to our gods? Our gods were ancient before your Jesus was born. Arawn, Beli Mawr, Gwydion, Mabon, Gofannon, Cerridwen, Lleu, and a host of others have watched over our people for ages. You bow before some foreign god if you like. But here on the island of the mighty, I apologise to no man for worshipping our gods as they require."

I bowed my head, made the sign of the cross, and prayed.

I wish I could tell you that I refuted him. I wish I had found the words. I was just so profoundly grieved. Finally, I found my voice, "And Myrddin, does he worship at your altars?"

"Aye, he does. He brings me heads and prays for power to avenge his people. He brings me captives and watches as the gods drink their fill of the blood of our enemies. Did you think they were just stories? Did you think that my faith was weaker than that of Scapilion? My religion is older, and my faith is stronger than you can imagine. The struggle is real and our gods, the gods who have served us well from time beyond time, will help us to expel these invaders with their strange ways from our shores. They will expel all foreigners and foreign gods even as they ever have, even as they rid us of the Romans. The old ways are full of power, young Illtyd. You will see."

Morgan stepped around me toward Kian. I grabbed his arm. "No, Morgan. Come, let us leave this cursed place."

Kian laughed as he called after us, "Go on then. Your prayers are not welcome here. You call it cursed; I call it blessed. The blood of our enemies waters the soil and plants the seeds of our victory. Call it what you will, but from places such as this, worship has long arisen. Worship like this is the protection of our people - the power of our people. You will see."

Professing to be wise, they became fools! Even now, I am grateful for the training I received at the feet of Kian. My childhood memories are not all gone - the lore of nature, the vast store of wisdom at his disposal. His knowledge was so impressive. If only … if only Kian would have turned his heart and bowed his knee to the High King of Heaven. Not content with his own wickedness, he recruited others to follow his dark path. I had such high respect for Kian; but in that moment I knew he was lost to me. I still held hope for Myrddin.

I found Myrddin a few minutes later, talking with his men. As he dismissed them, I noticed he was wearing the sword I had gifted to him the previous evening. Noting the direction of our approach, he asked, "Have you been talking with Kian then?"

"Yes, we have. This is no tactic to frighten the enemy, to distract them and make them easier to kill. This is something much darker," I warned him.

"It may be dark, but it is potent. Surely you felt it! This is the ancient and tried way of our people. It is the way of power. These long years since we parted have been difficult. I returned to find my father dead, our people in constant danger, and in need of guidance. Kian, the greatest of the druids, has served us well these several years. He has consoled the grieving, and it was his counsel to come here and strike back at our enemies from our new forest home. He is the reason there is a remnant of Rhegin at all. I will not abandon him. I will not abandon our people. I will not abandon our ways," he pronounced with finality.

"I will, however, accept Arthwyr's invitation," he continued. "It may surprise you to know that Kian himself counselled for it. We will leave a small contingent to care for our forest home, the crops, and animals. Kian, I, and a full 500 men will ride with you to find Arthwyr and see what may be done to drive the Saecson from our shore. That is if you will have us?" he queried.

"Yes, brother! By all means, yes. Let us leave this place! Come with us. Arthwyr would rally all Britons to his side. You answer his invitation, not mine. But for me, I say yes!"

Myrddin smiled at this. "Preparations have already begun. We will be ready in just a few days. Until then, take your leave and rest yourself here in safety."

CHAPTER 22

Myrddin's forest home was a peaceful and prosperous one. Though darkness hung about it, they had made a home for themselves. Apparently Kian had known of this place for many years; but it had never held a settlement before the fall of Anderida.

They had converted a portion of the substantial clearing to crops - mainly barley - while grazing pigs, horses, and cattle in this clearing and in others nearby. The forest also yielded many useful things for their lives.

While it was peaceful and safe, it was not happy. A shadow covered the place. I was not sure then how to understand this. Was it the result of so much grief in the hearts of people so deeply wounded by treachery or war? Having lost so much, did they fear it happening again … and so they could not give themselves to the small joys available to them? Was it the spiritual oppression they welcomed in their midst because they hoped it would provide them with power? I suspect it was some combination of these.

Whatever the source, my men were uneasy and eager to be gone. As usual, Morgan gave voice to their concerns. "Something is not right about this place. There is too much death and not enough life. They have food and safety and roofs over their head. They have swords at their side and are protected by the walls of the forest better than any palisade, and yet they have no life in them. I'll be glad to be gone. Can't we just go and let them follow at their leisure?"

"I feel it too, my friend; but we will not leave without them. Besides, I'm not sure we could find our way out."

"Too true," Morgan replied. "It was a right maze getting in here! But still, the men - even the men of Rhegin who came with us - are feeling jittery. I think we should be going sooner rather than later. It's just not right, I tell you."

I felt the same. The settlement bustled with the gathering of supplies and the preparations for war. I had presided over similar activities just weeks before in my home in Armorica. And yet, this felt different. I found myself wondering about Brennus and my mother and how things were there.

Within just a few days everything was settled, and we made our way back out of the forest by use of another path. This one took us north toward Londinium and our rendezvous with Arthwyr.

We reached Londinium just three days later and received a bit of a rough welcome when we did. I don't suppose the people of the city were keen to find 500 mounted warriors riding up to the southern end of the bridge. By the time we reached the bridge, the gates were shut; spears and archers lined the wall.

We halted perhaps two bow-lengths from the wall. We decided that Myrddin, Kian, and I would approach alone.

"Ho there, who are you? And what brings you here?" shouted a voice from the gate tower.

"We come in peace. We are here to meet with Arthwyr, Dux Bellorum of Britannia. We left him nearly a fortnight ago at the fords of Bassa."

"I heard about that. You were there, were you?" the guard tersely asked.

"Yes, I was. Has Arthwyr arrived?" It was my turn to be terse.

"No. I heard of him though. They say he's off to the west of here. Good luck to you then."

With that, the man disappeared, and our interview appeared to be over. The people of Londinium have always had peculiar ways about them.

So without further ado, we returned to our men and headed west. We followed the Tamesis along the south shore.

We were eyed warily in each settlement we approached. These people had seen troubles of their own, no doubt.

As we rode, Myrddin and I spent time reminiscing about our childhood in Armorica. Our lives had taken such different paths since then; we found it easier to discuss our shared connections.

"So you say Brennus is still there, looking to the defences of the eastern march?"

"Yes, although the Saecson has been more trouble than the Franks as of yet," I offered.

"Ah yes, the Franks and their axes … I remember Brennus' lessons in the weapons of our enemies. 'Know your enemy, understand his weapons, and you will have the advantage when the battle is joined.'" Myrddin's mimicry of Brennus voice and manner had us both laughing as we road along. "And Scapilion … what of my old teacher? You went with him to Avallon, did you not?"

"Yes; and he lives there still, as far as I know. He trains many young minds, but as always his goal is to draw men to Christ."

"I envy him, in some ways, Illtyd. He has the luxury of meditating on the cross while others bear the brunt of keeping the storm-tossed waves of the world at bay. We must live in a harsher world - a world where love, grace, mercy, and charity are weaknesses. So I leave Scapilion with all goodwill in his tower of learning, isolated from the real world." Myrddin looked almost wistful as he spoke.

"I hear you, my friend. It is true … my hands and my body grew soft in Avallon. But my mind was sharpened and expanded. Perhaps it was a fair trade. I cannot say," I added grinning at him. "I can say this: The battles we fight against the Saecson or the Frank are not the only battles that matter. Violence is a part of this life; but what of the sources of violence? If we can restore balance by doing justly, loving mercy, and walking humbly with God, then violence may yet fade away. The final answer is not in the sword or the spear, but in the heart of men," I concluded.

A long, thoughtful silence followed as we rode on together.

"I like your vision," Myrddin admitted, "but until balance is restored I will trust in the sword and shield, the spear and the bow, and in anything else that will grant us the victory over our cursed foe."

I would have said more, but we spied one of our scouts cantering back toward us and spurred our mounts to meet him.

They had spotted Arthwyr's troops. We would soon be reunited.

CHAPTER 23

As we rode into camp, we felt the spirits of the men around us lift. As you might imagine, the infusion of 500 mounted warriors to our army was an unexpected boon. But their enthusiasm was tempered by the measuring of their new comrades.

I rode straight to Arthwyr's tent and left Myrddin to see to settling his men in the camp. I heard calls ring out as men recognised each other and reacquainted.

"I found him!" I cried out as I pushed aside the entrance to Arthwyr's tent, only to find many sets of eyes fixed on me none too kindly. The tent was full of the lords of Britannia. I had stumbled into a council. I motioned my apologies and made to leave, but Arthwyr bid me back.

"Illtyd, come; it is good to see you again, my cousin. I heard horses and men; tell us what you have found," Arthwyr asked.

"Forgive my intrusion, my lords. The sound you heard is the remnant of Rhegin. Myrddin ap Cynwal is alive and leads 500 mounted warriors to support our cause!"

Smiles and nods greeted my news as the lords looked around at each other approvingly.

"Good. I am glad to hear of it. Now, stay with us as we return to the matter at hand." Arthwyr motioned for me to join him in the circle as he turned to address the lords, "This army is under my command. There are Saecson strongholds to take. I say we move on."

A cup was placed in my hands and I turned to thank the bearer … but the words never came. I found myself looking into the face of my love. Of course she wasn't mine then; but oh, was she beautiful! I had only seen Trynihid once before, and then from afar; but in that moment it seemed that time slowed down as I mutely took in the features of her exquisite face and the dazzling blue of her luminous eyes. Then, with just the hint of a smile flitting across her face, she was gone. It took me a moment to gather my wits. When I did, I found the lords were debating about what to do with the Saecsons in the valley of the Tamesis.

"The valley fairly swarms with these Saecson barbarians! They boldly roam about with impunity. They are settling there as they once did on the eastern shores. Londinium is but a shadow of itself! It's amazing that the bridge still stands. Calleva, my own city, will be next. They say they seek only land and a place to farm, but their numbers swarm as their boats slice up the Tamesis. We've seen this before. If you let them get a foothold, more are sure to follow. And what do you think these farmers would have become had Aelle's forces not been stopped? Their hands would have flown to their weapons, and suddenly peaceful farmers are warriors again. No, they must go - and we must drive them out!" concluded Emrys, King of the Atrebates.

Cynfelyn of Cynwidion spoke up as well. "We must clear the valley to secure my lands." Many others cried their agreement.

"This isn't really a question for the Dux Bellorum, is it?" came a familiar voice from behind me.

Kian stepped into the centre of our circle. "The bards of Britannia have long been invited to councils. I assert my right as one of the leaders of our people, although I possess no kingdom and no kingdom possesses me. I carry the lore and laws of our people within myself. It seems to me that the question you ask is one of law and statecraft, not war. Are these people arrayed before you in battle?" He paused and scanned the room, daring anyone to challenge him.

"Arthwyr is the war leader you have chosen, and I say you have chosen wisely." He continued, "He was born to lead and fight as I was born to be a bard, a priest, and a judge. But there is no battle here to be fought. This is a legal question. These people have settled on land that does not belong to them, have they not?"

"Aye, they have!" came affirmations from around the circle.

"They are foreigners and as such, have no legal standing among our people. Is this not so? Unless one among you has offered them hospitality and would stand with them, that is?" He smirked as each man violently shook his head. "What then is the penalty for a foreigner who steals? He must forfeit his ill-gotten goods and be hung! It seems, my lords, you know what justice demands. The only question that remains is who shall execute justice upon these lawbreakers."

Heads nodded all around.

I did not like the way this was headed. "Under the laws of the Romans, might they not make restitution?" I offered. "They could be made to pay back four times what they have taken."

"A fair point, Illtyd," Kian rejoined. "if thou would live as a Roman rather than the laws of our people, that is. I know little of Roman laws and little like even what I do know. I speak only of laws that are older and deeper than the laws of Rome. Our laws are written in the stars and the soil, handed down from Cerridwen by Awen, not voted on by some feeble foreigners in a far-off senate. So, Illtyd - are you British or Roman?"

"Kian, you are wise and eloquent. I mean no disrespect to you. I simply reject your premise. Is it not so that a single element may possess more than one attribute or form? Does not the ice become water and water become steam? Many here are both Roman and British. I am a proud son of a prince of Rhegin and a princess of the Silures … British to my marrow. I am also heir to the wisdom and technology of Rome. It has long been the way of our people to look for wisdom wherever it may be found, has it not? The question before us is not who is more British, but where justice lies for the Saecson villages over the hill. Does not the deeper meaning of our law concern itself with the restoration of balance? How will hanging these people restore balance? But if they make restitution might not restoration result?"

Kian smiled and nodded when I was finished. Stroking his voluminous beard, he continued, "Your problem, young Illtyd, is not that you have learned too much but that you still skim along the surface of things like a stone from a sling across a pool. You must sink into the depths of the pool of knowledge before you can arrive at true understanding. Do not your Scriptures say that without the shedding of blood there can be no restoration? Do not your Scriptures record sacrifices for purifying the land? Our ways are not as different as they might seem. Did not your God command his people to drive out the evildoers from their land? Would you deny our people that same right? He commanded them to lay them waste and leave no survivors. I humbly suggest we do the same. Do not forget that these men bring their own gods, and they pollute the land by their very presence. Do not all the laws of Christendom and Britannia require that we cleanse the land? But come, my lords, what say you?"

Arthwyr stood, "I agree with Kian. This is not my decision. Where there are battles that need fighting, I am your servant and your leader. You lords must decide this among yourselves. Come, Illtyd; let us leave them to their deliberations." Arthwyr bid me rise, and I followed him from the tent.

"Why did you do that? You can't really agree with Kian! Don't you see what he is doing?! He asserts his authority and would twist these men to his bloody ends."

"I hear you, cousin; but you must hear me. Kian has authority. It is his right as a bard of our people. I may not agree with his ends, but I know those men. You are still new here. You have made a favourable impression, but you cannot compete with a druid in their estimation. Many a man would call himself a Christian, but far fewer think like one. Kian will carry this day, mark my words. These men want vengeance. They are scared. Frightened men hunger for power to protect them. They are eager to lash out. Your words may sink in over time, but today they want simple solutions. Kian knows this and is telling them what they want to hear. Your responsibility here is to the men of Armorica. Command your men … and follow your commander." he added, "You came to help me drive the Saecson from this land, denying them a haven to build their forces from which they attack your land. You may find that Kian is accomplishing your purpose, even if not by your method. Come, let us find Myrddin and be reunited once more."

As we turned to start our search, Myrddin came striding up to us. Arthwyr greeted him warmly while also taking stock of his old friend. "It has been too long, my friend. I feared you dead."

"It seemed so to me at times; by the gods I often wished it. I would have gladly exchanged my life for that of your father. He was a great man who deserved a better death than that offered him. I am truly sorry." Myrddin embraced Arthwyr.

"You will be wanted in there," Arthwyr gestured. "You are the leader of the remnant of Rhegin are you not?" Arthwyr answered Myrddin's quizzical expression. "The lords of Britannia are deciding a legal matter; your voice should be heard as you are a prince of the land, if not a very king." Arthwyr propelled him toward the tent. "Come and find me with the men of Armorica when your council is concluded." With that, our brief circle dissolved once more and Arthwyr and I retired to my camp.

Llew and Rhodri, as seasoned leaders, laid our camp out well. I noticed they had wisely chosen a high dry patch of ground. They called for cups to be brought and we drank to my health and our safe return. Morgan and Cai had a head start on us. They were only too happy to have another round, drinking the health of everyone. I was glad to be back among my men and delighted to find they had done well in my absence.

We did not have long to wait. Myrddin found us sitting around the fire that evening.

"Well, what has been decided?" I asked.

Myrddin coolly summarised, "They will be given a choice. They can hang for their thievery, or they can leave with just their lives and a week of provisions. Either way, all of their belongings are to be paid as galanas - reparations to the Atrebates. Should they choose to leave, they will be branded on their right hand as thieves. If they return, their lives will be forfeit."

"And who will deliver this news and carry out these actions?" Arthwyr asked.

"As these lands rightly belong to the Atrebates, Emrys, their king, will lead us. The remnant of Rhegin will ride with them. All are welcome to join us." Myrddin eyed us carefully, gauging our reaction.

Arthwyr shook his head, "My men will not ride with you. We will save ourselves for battle. God knows there will be enough of those in the days ahead."

I chose to follow Arthwyr's lead and keep the men of Armorica fresh for the days ahead. I have often wondered what would have happened had we chosen differently.

CHAPTER 24

Early the next morning we heard the camp stirring. It discomfited many of our men not to be riding with their sword brothers of late. Camp life is not exciting, and even a little activity is better than none.

Arthwyr and I decided to make good use of the day by setting our men to training. Formations, like letters, take practice before they can be formed fluidly, naturally. And so we drilled the men in formations and tactics; and as the day grew longer, we integrated cavalry into the drills.

But the real fun of the day happened when Llew, growing tired of the lax attitude of one of the young men, grabbed him by the collar and hurled him to the ground. "If that is how you will move on the day of battle you will die, and take your sword brothers with you!"

The young man, one of Budic's men, mumbled something under his breath as he dusted himself off. "What's that, cur?! Do you have something to say to me?" Llew bellowed.

Showing a severe lack of sense, the young man responded, "I have been tested in battle. You took me unawares on a practice field. You would not throw me so easily a second time."

"Challenge accepted!" Llew answered decisively. The young man's eyes grew wide as he watched Llew laying aside his weapons and armour. He sought to score a point with his words, not to issue a challenge.

Howls of laughter and catcalls rang out as the men saw his hesitance. A broad circle gathered around Llew and his unwitting challenger, who had now laid aside his weapons as well.

"Shall we say three falls?" I interjected. "I shall judge it all be fair."

"If it pleases your lordship, as Llew is your man perchance I could request another judge the contest," one of Budic's men requested.

Seeing Arthwyr riding toward us, I agreed. "Very well. What say you, Arthwyr? Will you judge a wrestling match between Llew and this young man?" Turning to the young man in question, I asked, "What is your name?"

"I am Madog ap Owain."

"Very well, Madog. I will gladly judge between you and yon giant. May God bless you and the task you have set for yourself this day!" Arthwyr laughed as he responded. "The first to fairly throw his opponent to the ground thrice is the victor. Begin!"

With surprising speed, Llew fairly flew at Madog, driving his shoulder into the centre of his chest. Madog was on his back before he knew what hit him.

"Fairly done!" rang out Arthwyr's judgement.

Madog, more angry than hurt, slowly rose from the ground.

"Again!"

Llew came at him quickly again, but Madog, not caught unawares this time, stepped aside trailing his leg behind him. Llew tripped over his leg and nearly fell before regaining his footing, much to the disappointment of the crowd that was now beginning to warm to the fight. Llew's supporters offered wagers, but there were no takers.

Having arrested his fall, Llew spun around just in time. Madog, seeing Llew off balance, had flung himself headlong at Llew's back to topple him. Catching his movement out of the corner of his eye, Llew whipped his arm around, the back of his hand catching Madog across his temple. Madog went down for the second time.

By this time, the whole of the men of Armorica as well as Arthwyr's men had gathered for the sport.

"Fairly done!" Arthwyr's judgement rang out. There were a few grumbles as Madog stumbled to his feet. "Again!"

Llew approached Madog once more, and seeing him somewhat dazed, put his heavy hand in the centre of Madog's chest to almost gently push him over backwards. But as Madog fell, he suddenly snatched Llew's wrist, jerking him forward while throwing his weight back. He moved the mountain that was Llew and proceeded to trip him. No one was more surprised than Llew to find himself on his back.

The crowd exploded into shouts and laughter. Arthwyr's call of "Fairly done!" was greeted with more laughter and cries from the crowd.

Madog allowed himself a cheeky grin and a wave to the crowd as Llew picked himself up after Madog's sly trick. The angry scowl on Llew's face did not bode well. He circled his young opponent carefully now, deciding how to finish the match and perhaps the man.

Llew feinted in and Madog jumped back, throwing his hands out before him to keep his balance. An almost imperceptible smile drew across Llew's face. He kicked his leg out, but Madog jumped over the attempted trip and kept his distance. Llew circled him again, then changed his rotation. Feinting again toward his midsection, Madog jumped back, as before; but this time Llew grabbed his trailing wrist and pulled him into an embrace. Pinning his arms to his side, he squeezed until I feared Madog's ribs would crack; then he threw him to the ground like a child would throw a doll. Madog lay there gasping for breath but unhurt. The crowd cheered the champion!

Arthwyr strode into the middle of the circle "All fairly done! Well won Llew ap Gruffydd!" he said as he removed one of his armbands and held it up for all to see. "A prize for our champion, with my blessing!" He made to place the armband on Llew. It took some doing to pry it open wide enough to fit on his massive arm, much to the delight of the crowd.

This gave me an idea. Snatching one of Guielandus' spears from my horse, I made my way to stand beside Llew. A few whispered words in his ear, a nod of his massive head, and I put my plan into action.

"Who is next?!" My challenge rang out. "Who will fight the champion?" Silence fell over the assembly. "Arthwyr's generosity shames me. I now offer this spear as spoil to anyone who can defeat my champion." I held the fine smoky spear aloft. Guielandus' weapons were already gaining a reputation. I suspected that the chance to own one might induce some to try their luck. I had several remaining and men needed the sport. Still, none stepped forward.

"Surely, there is someone?! Have you not seen Madog fell the tree already once today?"

Before long, there was a veritable queue of men vying for the opportunity to wrestle Llew. And Llew fought them all, one after another. Some matches were closer than others, but none could fell the tree again.

As evening came on and the fires were lit, Arthwyr and I agreed to draw the contest to a close. "As not one among you has felled the mighty oak, Llew himself will claim the spoils," Arthwyr announced, handing the spear to an exhausted but grateful Llew.

"Not bad pay for a day's labour!" he exclaimed. I clapped him on the back and bid him drink the victory cup with us, but that was not to be.

CHAPTER 25

Just then, we heard riders approaching and knew the men of Rhegin were returning from their own day's labour.

It wasn't long before disturbing rumours rippled through the men. Words like sacrifice and massacre whispered through the crowd.

Arthwyr and I made our way toward his tent at the centre of the camp.

There we found Kian riding toward us, with heads tied to his saddle like some grisly phantom out of the old stories. He rode with his head held high, wearing a look of supreme satisfaction. Myrddin rode beside him with a fierce and terrible look upon his face, his stare alone daring any and every man to confront him.

We let them pass in peace, only learning from the reports of others about the activities of the day. They had ridden to the nearest Saecson settlement and delivered their judgement. As you may imagine the appearance of an armed host did not do much to allay their fears. When their leaders objected to the proceedings, Kian announced they had made their choice. In truth, Kian made the choice for them. He got what he wanted. The men moved in, the farmers resisted, and a great slaughter ensued. They left not even the children alive.

Myrddin and Kian then split their considerable force, and each led a contingent, one up and one down the valley. They slaughtered all.

But even this was not enough. Kian ritually sacrificed three men to Don the Queen of Rivers to purify and reclaim the Tamesis for our people. I will spare you the details of his heathen sacrifice. They then hung corpses along the river as a sign to any wandering Saecson.

Emrys of the Atrebates got what he wanted as well, and had already distributed the settlements to his people. It was over.

I have sometimes wondered if my presence might have averted the slaughter. Yet another massacre of the innocents. So often in history, the mighty trample and violate the weak to get what they want. The kingdom of our God is a different kind of dominion, an upside-down kingdom where the weak are strong. But on that day darkness reigned.

It was clear to me from that day that Kian was fighting a larger battle. He had been biding his time, waiting until the people were prepared. He wanted more than to push the Saecsons into the sea ... or better yet, into the otherworld. His goal was to restore the old ways, to turn the hearts of the people to their former religion.

The next morning, Arthwyr called a council.

"The Tamesis valley has been cleared of Saecsons. What now? If you are done with your proceedings, can we get back to the war?" Arthwyr asked.

Emrys stood. "My part in this war is concluded. We scored a great victory and sent Aelle's men scattering. They must be halfway across the sea by now ... what's left of them. Then yesterday we cleared the Tamesis as far as Londinium. We have our lands recovered. My men have other work to do. By your leave, I withdraw."

"Surely not!!" I cried out. "We have come from far and wide to win the war against the Saecson, not to slaughter children. I call that no great victory. They still hold the Saecson shore! Have you forgotten Anderida? They have been bested but not defeated, not pushed into the sea."

Emrys eyed me coolly. "I have not forgotten. But my responsibility is to my people and my people alone. I do not answer to you." With that, he turned on his heel and left.

Geraint of Dumnonia stood. "Emrys has made his choice," he said. "What of the rest of you? My lands lay safe in the west. No Saecson marauds my borders. And yet, here I am with my men because I know these wolves will not go away. They must be driven from our shores. Having tasted the sweetness of our land, they mean to have it all. They will not be satisfied with a bite or two. They have been on our land for fifty years, gobbling it up piece by piece. Emrys 'victory' yesterday was against farmers and their families. There is no honour in this victory. Perhaps it had to be done. We will leave that for now." He shook his head as if trying to clear the images from his memories.

He continued, "Yes, his land is empty of Saecsons now … but for how long? How long until their cursed boats come up the river again? They will keep coming until we retake the shore … until we hold the shores and the river mouths against them. Unless we build a bulwark to thwart them, they will simply return like the tide surging up the Tamesis. Let us take the land and bolster our defences. Then let them come and crash against the shore and wreck themselves if they choose; but first we must drive them from the land utterly, or surely they will drive us. We know these wolves have no mercy. As for my people and me, we are with you Arthwyr, until the end!" His eyes swept the room, fairly willing the men to choose his path as well.

"The men of Armorica stand with you as well!" I cried.

"And Rhegin!" Myrddin stood.

It felt good to be united with Myrddin at least in this.

Kian spoke from behind me, "Hear me now, Lords of Britannia!" He intoned in a solemn voice. "Emrys is gone. His vision is too short. But I have a vision for you! There was a time when the Kings of Britons ruled these islands unopposed. If you would have it so again, harken unto me!" As he spoke, he walked around the outside carving a circle in the turf with his staff. "Inside this circle are the lords of Briton bound together in common cause. But our cause will falter if the ties that bind us are weak." He continued marking the circle as he strode around us.

"We must drive them into the sea or send them to the otherworld. They have upset the balance of our land. They have brought foreign gods into our midst, and this must be avenged. Do you think you and your people are the only offended ones?! The gods' honour is affronted! This has been their realm longer than you can imagine. They have watched over our people, and our people have given them worship … as they ought. But you have been unfaithful to them, and they have abandoned you to the sea wolves - a people without mercy, without beauty, without honour. They are like their gods. Let us become like ours! Your gods stand ready to help you! They would give aid if only you would ask and ask properly."

"Kian! Enough of this!" I was on my feet again. "You would have us return to the darkness of our pagan ancestors!" I turned my gaze to the assembled lords. "I stand here in the circle with you, committed to the safety and security of our people. Although I have known Kian since my childhood and I respect his wisdom in many things, I cannot stand aside while he weaves his words to trap us in darkness. God, in his mercy and wisdom, allowed men to walk in darkness for a time; but now the light of Christ has come! Let us follow Christ in all things and Arthwyr in war. We defeated Aelle with no help from the old gods. Let us do so again and again. Let the hammer of God's justice fall upon them. We do not want or need the old gods to drive them into the sea! Let us do so ourselves with the Lord of heaven and earth on our side!" I paused, looking for words to press home my point.

I spoke softly then. "My first battle master, Brennus, taught me to know the ways of the wolf, but never to become one. He trained me to be like a boar in battle. A boar will kill to defend but does not delight in the killing. The bard Kian would turn us into wolves, would have us drench ourselves and our land in blood to placate and appease brutal, merciless, and capricious gods who are not even gods. My brothers, there is a better way. Let us follow the Lord of light and forsake the darkness." I sat down.

Kian nodded as if considering my words. "Well-spoken young one. In time, your eloquence may convince some. But let us not forget what brought you to Britannia. You desired vengeance - vengeance for your father, vengeance for your people. Isn't that what we all want? Yes, we desire safety and security, but if you look deeper and answer honestly, you know the truth. Beneath your calls for justice burns hatred and vengeance. Our gods also thirst for vengeance. Your god offers love, mercy, and forgiveness, a god too tame for times like this. Morrigan, the great warrior queen of the gods, and Arawn of the underworld love battle - they live for vengeance. They are the gods we must entreat. But great magic requires great sacrifice. Who would carry our message to the gods? Who would exchange his life for the lives of our people?"

A voice cried out, "I will!"

We all swivelled our heads around to find Myrddin standing, arms folded across his chest, wearing a resolute visage.

CHAPTER 26

Chaos enveloped the gathered lords of Britannia as voices clamoured, asking what could be meant by this.

Kian cried out over the tumult, "Lords of Briton! Let not your hearts be troubled. Arthwyr is our champion on the fields of battle. Myrddin will be our champion in the otherworld. We have not hesitated to lay our lives down in battle and men of courage will ever do so. But does not even the Christ of Illtyd say, 'Greater love has no man than to lay down his life for his friends'? Myrddin knows he will lay aside this body and rise anew in the otherworld to implore our gods, our former guardians, to fight for us once more as they have from time immemorial. A life freely given is a sacrifice worthy of demanding their attention. Myrddin's sacrifice will show our devotion. He will intercede on our behalf, and they will rise up and help us drive the wolves from our shores."

I sat in stunned silence as Kian twisted the words of our Lord to suit his purposes. I still remember the look of determination on Myrddin's face. Myrddin, my cousin-brother was slipping from my grasp.

The encircled lords of Britannia mumbled among themselves, scratching their grizzled chins and pulling at their moustaches, murmuring among themselves about this unexpected turn.

Kian watched silently and beckoned Myrddin to his side. I watched as Myrddin made his way through the circle toward Kian. As he passed near me, I stood and embraced him. He returned my embrace warmly for a moment, and then thrust me from him, gripping my wrists. "It must be this way." He continued his journey across the circle and toward the doom that awaited him at the hands of our mentor and tutor.

I could not let this happen without a fight. "This is madness!" I cried. "Lords of Britannia, would you stand by and watch as one of your own spends his life so cheaply? Has not Myrddin, prince of the Rhegin, shown himself to be a valiant warrior among us? We risk our lives in defence of our lands and people, but we do not waste our lives for no reason. We do not sacrifice our lives in the hope that gods long abandoned - for good reason no less - would save us. The druids have great wisdom, but they also enslaved us to fear and darkness. We stand now united against darkness encroaching on our lands from the seas, let us hold the line against darkness in all forms. We must not pour out libations of blood to these dark forces. We must stand in the light of Christ and strive against the darkness, wherever it is found."

Myrddin now stood with Kian looking on from the edge of our circle. Kian rested his left hand on Myrddin's shoulder and raised his right hand, palm outward with the back of his hand pressed to his forehead. "This council has no authority over me. I am Kian, Druid of Druids, Bard of Briton, Keeper of the Ancient Ways of our people. I accept this man's sacrifice, freely given. This is a matter for the gods now, not for men or councils." With that, he spun Myrddin about, and they stepped into the night together.

I pressed through the assembly, but by the time I reached the entrance to the tent they were nowhere to be found.

That was the last time I saw Myrddin. I pray still that our paths may cross again in the next world. That night my hope for his earthly life was lost, but my hope for his soul lives on. Who knows but that the grace of Christ may cover his sins? He willingly stepped into the darkness, but perhaps even then his soul was tethered to the rock that is higher than all.

In the years since his disappearance, strange stories have grown up around him. People have made him into some sort of wizard. Some hope that he will yet return and bring some boon from beyond the mists of time and death. Kian wandered the lands for many years, seducing any who would listen; but we will leave him for now. I do not wonder what befell Myrddin. He placed his trust in Kian, and I have no doubt that Kian inflicted upon him the threefold death. Kian ritually sacrificed my friend in a vain attempt to sway the gods who are not gods.

Standing at the entrance looking into the darkness, I felt a hand on my shoulder. I turned to find myself staring into the weathered face of Pawl of Penychen.

"Take heart, young Illtyd. All is not lost."

"Perhaps not all … but a great deal," I replied, shaking my head.

"Myrddin was his own man. He and Kian will answer to a judge much higher than our council one day. May God have mercy on their souls."

"I have known them both from my childhood. I never thought it would come to this. These are dark times, but we need not embrace the darkness."

We stood there on the edge of the circle staring silently into the night.

"Kian was right you know," I said quietly, shaking my head.

Pawl looked at me with mild surprise. "Was he now?"

"I did not come to this land for justice or for Christ. I came for vengeance. Who among us has not lost someone in these treacherous times? I have faced death and felt the heat of rage during battle. I have struck down foemen before me. But the fire of anger and hate remains. I feel it here!" I pounded my chest. "I also feel the pull of the old ways, the allure of a power we can wield against our enemies. But that is the cunning lie … these death demons masquerading as guardian gods are not on our side. They only mean to enslave us and drag us backwards."

"And the Christ, is he on our side?" Pawl looked closely at me.

"I would not be so bold as to say that he is. I am reminded of Joshua before the battle of Jericho. He met a warrior in the wilds near the city and made bold to challenge him. 'Are you for us or for our enemy?' The warrior responded, 'Neither, but as the commander of the armies of the Lord, I have now come.' We mistake ourselves to think that we are at the centre of all things. God is not on our side. We must make every effort to be on his side. There is a battle between light and darkness. Jesus is the Light of the World and darkness has been defeated. But darkness is dangerous still even in the throes of death. Darkness has been defeated and the devil thrown down; but oh, he thrashes about on earth. And so we pray that Our Father's will be done on earth as it is in heaven."

Catching my breath, I added quietly, "I know that God is opposed to the deceit and death-dealing of the Saecson. He is not on their side. I know he promises to work all things together for good; and yet his ways are not our ways, and his thoughts are not our thoughts. As high as the heavens are above the earth, so are his ways higher than our ways and his thoughts higher than ours. I do not pretend to know the plans of God in any specifics, but I know his is the side of justice as well as mercy. We can strike down our foes in justice; but when we give ourselves over to vengeance and hate, that is something else. That God cannot bless, nor can he ignore."

King Pawl watched me for a moment, seeming to weigh me or my words - or maybe both. "Come, I hear voices in the council. Let us return."

"... north it is then. North to Linnius and if all goes well to Gododdin beyond," Arthwyr was saying as we entered.

The next morning we discovered the men of Rhegin were gone. They had apparently left with Kian and Myrddin. This seemed to confirm my suspicions that they were headed back to the Forest of Anderida and the fetid ancient grove of blood I had seen there. I hate to imagine the gruesome end of my friend. Myrddin willingly rode to his death under the persuasive power of Kian.

We spent the next days provisioning the army and preparing for a long march north to areas of Britannia unknown not only to me but to many. Arthwyr sent riders out to the kings of the north, hoping they would join us as we now aimed our forces at Saecson threats closer to themselves.

As we moved through the heart of the island, riders returned with news of new allies joining our cause, marshalling their forces and providing provisions as well as men. I will not bore you with the details. Suffice it to say we were well provisioned as our numbers swelled and we looked to meet the foe on the northeast coast of the isle of the mighty.

As we moved we met no real opposition. I prevailed upon Arthwyr and the council to offer mercy to Saecson villages. I could not undo the massacre at the Tamesis, but I hoped to prevent more injustice even in war. They were given the option to demonstrate allegiance by providing provisions or to become our prisoners and be expelled forever once we reached the eastern shore.

I know that a village of farmers is not likely to take to this situation kindly. I expect they viewed our act of mercy much more like extortion or theft. If only they knew how even that mercy was hard-won. They were no threat to our massed war host. I considered it a small victory to have simply left them alive as we rode on or to see them travel before us under the watchful eyes of our scouts.

CHAPTER 27

As we travelled, I found myself spending more time in company with King Pawl. He was a thoughtful man and devout, if not particularly learned. He was not the taciturn warrior my father had been, and we shared many a conversation as we rode. Often our discussions were around the times in which we lived and the mysterious purposes of God.

Much to my surprise and delight, Trynihid rode up quietly beside us one day, her golden hair swept back and cleverly knotted. There were not a few women travelling with the army. Most of them were attached to the households of the various lords, and Trynihid deftly ran Pawl's house for him. Pawl smiled and nodded toward her to acknowledge her arrival before continuing.

"So, what is your understanding of the will of God in this war then?" Pawl asked me, continuing our conversation.

"That I cannot say with any degree of certainty. I cannot believe that God would approve of the actions nor the beliefs of the Saecsons. He is the God of justice. But then, our people have been guilty as well; and we both know that Kian's gods, although called by different names, are as capricious and vindictive as the gods of the Saecson."

Trynihid spoke up then, "So, are you saying that we are no better than the Saecson?"

I looked at Pawl before responding. The faint glimmer of a smile crossed his otherwise solemn countenance.

"In some sense, perhaps no better and no worse. As the Apostle Paul tells us, 'All have sinned and fallen short of the glory of God.'" Her face darkened, and Pawl's smile broadened as he cast a sideward glance at his niece.

"These dogs come from over the sea to raid and murder and steal, and you say we are the same?!" Her blazing blue eyes and angry tone showed me something new about Trynihid. Beneath that beautiful exterior lay a deep well of fire.

"I do not mean to say that we are the same. I have suffered their depredations as have you. I have come to fight them, as have we all. I believe they must be defeated in battle to protect our people. I share your anger, believe me. I see their evil actions for what they are."

"But you would have us offer mercy and forgiveness, I suppose?" she retorted. Her back stiffened and she held herself erect, looking as imposing as any queen.

"I would," I responded. "But I do not think it would accomplish our ends. Men determined to be wicked must be opposed. Steel must be met with steel. God has given us the sword to oppose the sword. God, the God of forgiveness and mercy, is also the God of justice and righteousness. The sword and authority to use it is given so that we might oppose evil and defend the good. But I cannot call the slaughter of innocents good no matter who does it."

"But didn't God command his people to slaughter the peoples of Canaan utterly?" Trynihid rejoined, tilting her head as if it were a humble question rather than a deft attempt to turn my God against me.

Taken aback by her knowledge of Scripture, I asked, "How do you know so much about the history of Israel?"

"Why shouldn't I know the Scriptures? I have read them since my childhood." Her chin jutted out defiantly.

"Have you now?" I asked, looking to Pawl for confirmation. He nodded.

"I have given my niece every opportunity to better herself. I know her father would have wished it, God rest his soul," Pawl added. "If perhaps her tongue is too sharp, I apologise. That is an avenue of betterment she has not yet fully explored." He frowned in her direction.

If Trynihid was cowed by his gentle rebuke she showed no signs of it. "So, what do you make of God's command to leave no Canaanite alive? Perhaps that is God's will for the Saecson as well. What say you?"

"I allow that it may be God's will only inasmuch as I do not know and cannot ultimately know his will. But in the Law of Moses, God instructs his people to offer hospitality to the alien and stranger in their land. Might not those injunctions also be God's will for the Saecsons that would live in peace among us?" I asked.

"I might allow for that if we could trust the Saecson to abide by their word and by our laws. How many times have they preyed upon our trust?" she rejoined again.

"A fair point," I granted. "You cannot blindly trust. It is difficult to know whom to trust in these days of darkness and confusion, even among our own people. But neither can you blindly slaughter."

We eyed each other over the pommel of Pawl's saddle, taking the measure of each other. I must tell you, I liked what I saw. I had known she was beautiful … but now her intellect, strength, and passion were revealed to me.

I was enjoying this conversation on many levels and did not want it to end. "Any who would take up arms against us, we must fight; and if they do not submit, we must kill. Any criminals must be punished for justice' sake and for the sake of those who might otherwise be tempted to learn the wrong lesson from leniency. Agreed?" Both Pawl and Trynihid nodded. "So the question is … what do we do with the others - men, women, and children in our lands who have committed no crime and who do not oppose us?"

As Pawl stroked his beard, Trynihid responded, "Is it true they have committed no crime? They are here in our land without invitation, and they live upon lands seized from those who have been murdered, even if they did not do the killing."

"I see your point," I admitted. "But in times of chaos and disruption are not many being displaced? My family is from Britannia, and yet we have settled in Armorica. The Franks, the Goths, the Vandals, and other nations have overrun the empire. The Romans themselves came as conquerors to our shores. I do not say that this is justice, only that this is the way of the world. In Avallon, we worked with the Burgundians to find a way to live together peacefully."

"But the Saecson don't want to live with us peacefully!" she protested.

"Some of them might," I countered. "I do not know. I know that we must arm ourselves for battle and fight them, but I do not know when this will end. How many more of them lay across the sea? Even as we fight the Saecson in the east, the Scoti attack us from the west and the Picti from the north."

"These are hard times," Pawl interjected. "But God in his providence has placed us in this time for his own good purposes. It seems to me that the question is not so much about what God is doing, but rather what he would have us do with the time he has given us in the place he has put us."

I nodded and looked across at Trynihid.

"Yes, uncle. That is the question. What should we do with the lives we've been given?" Trynihid was looking right back at me.

I have often wondered about the way of love. I believe it was this conversation that moved me beyond merely fancying Trynihid. I had admired her beauty, but now she dazzled me on many levels! How is it that in one moment we know someone and in another we love them? What changes in our soul when we move from curiosity to desire?

I am sure I have not yet plumbed the depths of this mystery to my satisfaction; but this I can say - something changed in me that day.

My desires led me to seek Trynihid whenever I could. I often rode beside her as we moved camp, continuing to sound the depths of her mind and heart. Pawl often invited me to dine with them. I think he enjoyed the debate and banter between us nearly as much as we did.

Subtly at first, but with greater clarity day by day, something beyond just vengeance or justice grew within my heart. The cut and thrust of mental and physical battle had honed and hardened my body and soul for battle, but now, a softening of sorts was creeping into my depths. I was not altogether sure I liked it.

With softness comes vulnerability, and vulnerability was to be hidden at the very least … and better yet, avoided altogether. To be vulnerable was to be weak. Weakness leads to victimisation and ultimately to death.

But therein lies the mystery. What if death is not something to be feared or avoided? What if death is a tool in the hand of God? What if death is a doorway to another world - a better one? What if weakness and vulnerability are part and parcel of the Kingdom of God?

The Lord Jesus Christ embraced death, willingly laying aside all things, and was resurrected and seated at the right hand of God. He trusted God enough to make himself vulnerable.

As we rode through the country with the war host of Briton, I pondered these questions while puzzling over the love growing in my heart toward Trynihid.

CHAPTER 28

I rode with Arthwyr and the Britons through that summer and into autumn.

As we rode north and east, we encountered sparse resistance. As we pressed further north, the kings of the north came to our aid. We were nearly continually resupplied with men and provisions. We mostly drove the Saecson before us. As word spread we found more settlements deserted upon our approach … the choice to leave, supply provisions, or die being made even before our arrival. The diligence of our scouts and the blessing of God averted several ambushes. As the weather grew colder, we knew our campaign was drawing to a close.

We fought the Saecsons when we found a settlement they deemed worthy of defending with their lives, or when they massed to attack us. Arthwyr desired to finish what we had begun and pushed us hard toward Linnuis. We fought a series of battles against the Saecsons as they fell back toward their island fastness at Lindsay. We defeated them six times but could not drive them from the island before the weather turned.

One chilly morning Arthwyr called the lords to gather in his tent. As we gathered, stamping our feet against the cold and drawing near to the smoking braziers, talk turned to the harvest and the men yearning for the warm hearth of home.

Arthwyr sat apart on his camp chair, chewing his moustache and scowling. I could feel the frustration of my old friend but did not approach him; allowing him to choose his own time to reveal his thoughts.

Finally he rose. "My lords, my friends," he called out, gesturing to the seats arranged in a wide circle. Striding to the centre of the ring, he waited for us to settle. "I call you friends. More than that, I call you brothers. We are Britons all and have forged our brotherhood in the heat of battle. We are brothers in blood and toil. We have shared the victories and have borne the cost of many clashes. I count it a great privilege to have led you. You chose me as your Dux Bellorum, and I believe I have borne the weight of command as well as any man can."

He paused, looking around the circle and found only nods of agreement before continuing. "The Saecson have tasted our metal and been pressed hard. They cannot doubt that we are no longer the easy prey they may have thought. We have the upper hand, and I would have had us crush them utterly." He shook his head sadly and went on, "But it was not to be. Not this year, anyway. The weather has turned … the snows are coming. It is time for us to end our campaign. Not forever mind you, but for now. So, as I have commanded you in war, I now release you to find what peace you can this winter. But before we go our separate ways, I have a proposal. I propose we gather a council of war in mid-winter to plan for renewing the campaign in the spring. We will drive them from our shores yet!"

There were nods and murmurs of approval around the circle as Arthwyr strode back to his seat.

Geraint of Dumnonia rose and addressed Arthwyr, "You have served your people well, Arthwyr, Dux Bellorum! I am proud to be your sword brother. You have made us a proud people again and your father, God rest his soul, I'm sure is proud of you as well. No doubt he looks on from heaven with more peace having been justly avenged by his son. This spring, these many months past, we gathered in my home before launching our campaign. I propose we meet there in mid-winter for the council you have called. After all, the chill winds of winter afflict us less in fair Dumnonia." He smiled grandly around the circle, but the Kings of the north did not smile back.

His subtle joke having fallen flat, he pressed on. "Come to me for a mid-winter feast. Let us celebrate together the birth of our Lord Jesus Christ and ask his blessing on our endeavour to drive the pagan Saecsons from our fair lands."

This proposal was met with more cheer, as it is not hard to get a Briton to agree to a feast - particularly one when someone else is providing the provender.

Gawain of Gododdin rose next, "My lords, I speak only for myself, but I am happy to accept the invitation of my sword brother Geraint. I will travel far indeed to taste his hospitality again. I have but one request - that we decide today to retain Arthwyr as Dux Bellorum. I can think of no one better to command our forces. Have we not tasted sweet victory under his banner?! Let us rest well this winter and return to plough the backs of our Saecson foe in the spring with Arthwyr the dragon pulling the plough of rough justice!"

Cries of affirmation rose from the circle now as men leapt to their feet, crowding around Arthwyr.

The results of the council speedily spread through the camp. By the time we left the tent, the mood was high. Despite the chill weather, men strode happily about the field greeting their comrades, rejoicing in their shared victories. Food and drink were shared liberally that night, as there was no longer a need to ration our provisions for the campaign. We would soon be heading home.

I found Rhodri, Llew, Cai, and Morgan amid our portion of the camp. They were drinking around the fire with our men. I had no need to share the news of the council, as they were already sharing a version of Arthwyr's speech as I approached. I settled in to enjoy Morgan's best impression of Arthwyr, followed by a not too complementary impression of Geraint as well. The men roared as Morgan added witty asides and commentary to his performance. Morgan was no bard, creating history from story; but he had a sharp wit and readily mined comedy from observation. This night needed not the solemnity of the bard, but the merriment of a fool. Laughter really is a balm for the soul.

I watched the faces of the men and marvelled, not for the last time, at the way we Britons can find joy so readily even on a cold night on campaign. I marked each face as I looked around at these men at peace; memories of their faces in the heat of battle forced their way across the borders of my mind. We had faced death together. We had endured hardship and pain. We lost some of our company over the months of our campaign. While returning home, some would carry a remembrance back to waiting family whose loved one would not be returning with the host.

My heart was heavy that night. To lead men to war is a heavy thing. To lose men heavier still. I rose and gave Morgan a hearty slap on the back as I made my way out of the circle. Wandering through the camp with my own dark thoughts for company, I skirted the edges of fires and found a similar scene playing at most of them. From some came laughter and from some music rose; but at each one, thoughts of home lifted the hearts of the men to a world beyond war. But I could not shake the melancholy that wrapped its clammy arms around me.

I started as I felt a hand on my shoulder. Looking around quickly, I found Pawl beside me. How long he had been walking with me I did not know.

"Your thoughts plague you tonight, young prince."

"Yes, my lord," I responded. "I find myself reflecting on those whose laughter is not lilting among the fires this evening."

"I see," he responded. We walked along in silence together for so long that I nearly forgot he was there again. "This is your first campaign," he observed. "It is right that you feel the burden of command and ponder the loss of life, even on a successful campaign like this one." He paused again. "I have seen many battles in my time. The weight of command never lifts, but becomes easier with familiarity. The grief is still there, but now I can welcome him as an old friend. He will sit at my fire and tell me sad stories for a time; and then, when I'm not looking, he will slip out and I will find space for joy again around the fire. Some find it too hard to welcome him and would rather pretend he didn't exist; but I say it is better to let him come in than to leave him outside to bang on the gates. Grief will not be denied. He will come in. Better to welcome him and have the conversation than to be tortured and annoyed by the banging in your head."

I looked at Pawl and wondered at his offering of himself to me. I had teachers in Brennus, Scapilion, and even Kian; but Pawl was fast becoming a father to me. Until that moment, I had not realised the place he now held in my heart. Suddenly, grief rushed in and would not be denied. I found tears running down my face as the sadness hit me like a club. There, in the darkness between the fires, I dropped to my knees and cried. I cried for my men. I cried for my father. I cried for myself. At first it was quiet tears; but once the gates were open, I wept and wept. I had no words, only pain long pent up and now released through tears and groans too deep for words.

I do not know how long I knelt there, but I know Pawl stayed with me. Sometime later I rose from soggy knees into his rough embrace.

"I'm sorry," I murmured, wiping my face with my cloak.

"For what?!" he responded. "There is no shame in feeling what you feel. Every good leader, every good man, feels grief. Only a great fool ignores it. It is hard sometimes to find the right way, the right place to express it; but it is there and must be released. Didn't King David express his grief when his son died? Didn't Jeremiah write a book of lamentations? Didn't our Lord Jesus Christ weep? Then why shouldn't you?" He paused, grasping my shoulders and looking me square in the face. "Come. You have laughed. You have wept. Now come have a drink and hear what I would say to you." He turned me what direction he would, and I found myself walking with him toward his tent.

CHAPTER 29

As we walked in comfortable silence toward his tent, I found myself reflecting again on my father and Pawl. I think Pawl and Bicanys would have been friends … different men from the same generation, both warriors and leaders in their own right.

Pawl drew back the curtain and motioned me inside. As I entered, warmth and light enveloped me as did the sweet smell of roasting meat. The remnants of a banquet lay scattered on a table. Pawl had spent the evening with his men before finding me wandering the camp. I had not realised my hunger until that moment. I eyed the food with a scarcely hidden desire.

"Help yourself, young Illtyd … don't be bashful now!" Pawl said with a laugh. I didn't need much encouragement as I took a seat, gathering meat and bread to myself.

As we sat, Trynihid appeared and poured us cups of mead before pouring one for herself and joining us at the table. Her golden hair shone in the soft light of the candles.

As I devoured a joint of venison, washing it down with sweet and warming mead, Pawl watched me thoughtfully across the table. Rubbing his beard, he began, "So, our campaign draws to a close. Tonight we celebrate and remember. Tomorrow preparations will begin in earnest as everyone returns to their home for the winter and spring planting." He paused, eying me carefully. From the corner of my eye I noticed Trynihid watching us interestedly as well.

"I would like you to come back with me … with us …" he added, looking toward Trynihid. "Come and winter with us at Penychen! Come and see the land of your fathers and enjoy the ancient hospitality of the Silures. You will not be disappointed."

I looked from Pawl to Trynihid and back to Pawl. There, in the warmth and the glow, I could imagine nothing better than spending the winter with them.

"I wish I could, but I must return to Armorica - our little Britannia across the sea - with my men."

"Why?" Trynihid interjected … and she did not look happy. "Why can't you send your men back to Armorica for the winter while you winter here … with us?" She emphasised these last words with a pleading look in her cerulean eyes.

My young heart leapt at that look. Despite our many conversations, I had not dared to think she might return my love. Could it be that this invitation to winter in the land of my mother's people could be a prelude to love?

From the first moment I saw her I was caught, ensnared. These months on the campaign had only heightened my feelings. The more I got to know her, the more I wanted to know. The first glimpse showed but her outward beauty; now her character and her mind unfurled before me. I found myself wanting to spend more and more time unravelling the mystery of this woman. And now she was looking down the table at me and if I was not deceived was imploring me to spend time with her away from the worries and hardships of war.

I do not know that this was the wisest decision of my life, but I found myself saying, "Yes … yes, I will come with you!"

I said this watching her face. My head was spinning as I watched a dazzling smile break across her face, followed by a shy glance down and then at her uncle. She looked somewhat flustered as she quickly rose and began to clear the table. Pawl looked mildly surprised but very pleased.

As she left the tent she looked back over her shoulder and flashed another of her beautiful smiles. I have always loved that smile. At that moment I knew for certain the purpose behind her questions. She was not probing and fencing with my decision. She wanted me in her life, and I knew I wanted her in mine.

Pawl broke into my revelry, "Well now that that's settled we will have many things to plan and prepare."

"Yes," I replied, shaking my head slightly to bring myself back to the present moment. I had been miles away. "I will tell the men tomorrow, and I must write a letter to my mother. They will be expecting me. I will put Rhodri in charge of the men and Llew in charge of the boats. I'm sure everyone will get along well as they are heading home." My words poured out in a torrent.

"Yes, yes," Pawl laughed. "You will have many things to do on the morrow. But can I ask you what changed your mind?" There was a twinkle in his eye.

I was just plucking up the courage to answer when the tent opened, and Trynihid fairly skipped into the room with a jug of thick brown ale sloshing inside. "Here!" she said happily. I have brought ale to fortify us for the journey!" She poured out three cups and plopped down on the bench near me.

Pawl sat across from us, not doing his utmost to allay his mirth as he watched the two of us.

There is something magical about the blossoming of young love ... enchanting and wonderful and terrifying all at once. A man of battle and strategy who spends years studying and sharpening his intellect and implementing tactics on the battlefield can be entirely undone by love. I had started the evening with plans to return home, and reflecting on the vagaries of chance and the griefs of life; only to have my plans unravelled by the eyes and smile of a woman.

Don't misunderstand me. This was no tragedy befalling me. I was not bewitched, but I was beguiled. I was captured by the dream of love with this vision of loveliness. We had known each other a few short months but in that time I had scarcely let myself dream of her. My mind and body were occupied with so many things. Love had not been foremost in my mind.

But it had been there all along - that dormant thought, that bulb of a feeling just beneath the surface. Then, as if suddenly, it blossomed from bulb to flower in a moment ... the long desired but unexamined moment when love reveals itself, surprising even the heart where it blooms. One moment it is all bare soil with nothing there, then suddenly it is teeming with life, like daffodils springing up after a long cold winter where you least expect them. Oh, my children, love is a mystery and a gift!

All love is a gift from the all-wise God: The love of brothers. The love of parents. The love of children. But the greatest and perhaps the rarest gift is the love between a man and a woman. This love is a gift all the more precious because God so rarely bestows it. Just as salvation is a gift of God - not a result of works so that no man can boast - so romantic love is a gift from God. And when the gift is given it must be tended and nurtured like a precious flower. But do not confuse the tending of the garden with the life of the garden. There is only one who is the source of all life and all love. To God alone be the glory.

I sat there sipping my ale and grinning like a madman, pondering this sudden turn of events. If I was reading the signs correctly, love had arrived in my life. What would this winter hold for me? Not to mention who might I hold that winter?

As my thoughts and dreams rattled around in my head, a none too gentle push on my shoulder nearly unseated me. "Hey, where have you been?!" Trynihid's mock confronted me.

I laughed, "I have been to paradise and back in the space of these few moments. But now that I'm back, I have something I would like to say to you and your uncle ..." I paused and took another swig of ale.

"Just a few short months ago we were strangers to each other. I still remember the days of our first acquaintance at Dumnonia. God alone knew all that would befall us from that day to this one. Over these months, we have grown to know each other in travel and conversation. You know me. You know my men, my thoughts, my character, my deeds, my leadership, and my faith. And I believe that I know you." Pawl nodded sagely and Trynihid, impatiently. I continued, "You have invited me to come with you for the winter. I propose something more. I ..." turning to Trynihid, "I would pledge myself to you, body and soul, if you will have me."

Tears formed in my beloved's eyes as she took my hands in hers. "I will have you. I will love you now and forever."

"Hold on now you two!" Pawl bellowed, slapping his hand down on the table hard enough to make us jump and nearly upset the cups. For a moment I thought he was angry; and he let us believe so. But a moment later a smile split his face and he said, "I would bless and solemnise this union, but not before me as your only witness. The camp is still alive tonight. Now that you two lovebirds have finally arranged things, let's give them something to celebrate. Get thee gone, young Illtyd. You make your preparations and we will make ours. You will be married in the morning."

I rose from the bench when suddenly I remembered, "You must have this!" I removed the clasp from my cloak and pinned it to hers. In doing so I made bold to snatch a kiss from my betrothed and strode out of the tent a newly-minted groom.

CHAPTER 30

In my excitement I nearly bowled over the first few people I met as I ran back to our portion of the camp.

Breathlessly I made my way to the centre of the fire. My rushed entrance hushing the assembled revellers.

"Congratulate me! I am to be married in the morning!" A great cry arose from the men and I was soon surrounded in a maelstrom of back-slapping and toasts to my health and that of my bride. Not a few ribald jokes were made about what awaited me on the morrow, but I let them pass.

"It took you long enough! I wondered what was taking so long!" Morgan cried. Llew wrapped me up into a huge embrace and then threw me into the air where much to my surprise I landed on a shield carried on the shoulders of my men. I scrambled to my feet and declared my love for Trynihid with wild abandon as I was paraded aloft through the camp. Soon the field was in an uproar as the new cause for celebration gave renewed vigour to the revels.

As we made our way toward the centre of the encampment I noticed we were nearing Arthwyr's tent. In high spirits I called out, "Arthwyr ap Meurig! Great bear and dragon of the Britons! Come out and celebrate with me, for I am to be married!" Arthwyr strode from his tent looking none too pleased, and I wondered what I had interrupted. Several of the kings of Britannia followed him out to witness the commotion.

Arthwyr took in the sight of the gathered crowd and me. For a moment I feared he would rebuke us. But then he called out, "Who is this I see, standing in the sky like heroes of old?! Is this young Illtyd ap Bicanys? We know he is brave in battle against the foe, but is he armed and prepared to battle a wife?!" He broke into a huge grin. A great roar of laughter and catcalls rang out from the crowd. Arthwyr continued, "Illtyd, come back to the earth and let this mere mortal embrace you with all joy!"

I leapt from the shield and landed before my cousin-brother. He swept me into an embrace as fierce and powerful as Llew's. "I wish you all joy! It is of course Trynihid, is it not?"

"Yes, it has to be. But it seems I am the last to know!" I laughed, shaking my head again at it all.

"You have chosen well! You have chosen well. She will match you and together you will do great things." With that he turned me forcibly back toward the crowd, announcing, "I give you Illtyd Farchog, lord of battle - a prince among Britons! Feast him well tonight, for tomorrow new adventures await him." Another great shout and laughter erupted from the gathered host.

I was propelled back into the tumult with congratulations and approbations hurled from all sides. The kings of Britannia wished me well before returning to their consultations in Arthwyr's tent. I wondered about that … but not too much. I had celebrating on my mind!

The rest of the evening was a blur of music and drink and friendship. The camp was primed to celebrate, and our impending union gave yet another reason to cut loose after so many months of tension and hardship.

I woke the next morning in my tent, with only the vaguest recollection of how I got there. My head was swimming as I attempted to sit up, only to fall back on the rushes. I tried again a few minutes later and managed to make it to standing. I stepped outside looking a dog's breakfast no doubt, only to be greeted by the cries and cheers of my men once more.

Rhodri and Cai quickly shooed the men away and took charge. Rhodri handed me a cup of cold water and oats, with the terse admonition, "Drink it!" I did. The two of them helped me clean up and get ready for the most important day.

One does not bring wedding clothes on a military campaign, but somewhere they had procured finery I did not recognise and some that I did. We made quick time of it, and soon I was looking and feeling as good as possible given the circumstances.

Arthwyr arrived and presented me with a golden torc and armbands. "These are for you. May you enter your marriage looking every bit the prince that you are and may you ever be the prince that she deserves."

Taken back by the enormity of the gift as well as the solemnity of the blessing, I embraced Arthwyr. "Thank you! I hope that you too will share my joy sometime soon. Are you not returning to Dumnonia for the winter? Perhaps Gwenhwyfar waits for you?"

"Perhaps she does indeed," he answered with a slight smile. "But today is your day, not mine. Shall we go?"

"I would have you stand with me. Would you honour me in this?"

"Of course I would. Why do you think I came to you this morning?!" He shook me by the shoulder, pushing me toward the entrance to my tent.

As we stepped out, I found my men dressed and armed for battle, ready to accompany me to Pawl's encampment. "There will be no bride-stealing today my friends, but let us go armed should the necessity befall us, for I will not be denied!" I cried.

Arthwyr and I strode side by side through the camp flanked by Rhodri and Cai on our left and Morgan and Llew on our right with the host of Armorica making way for us through the surrounding crowd. Shouts rose on every side as we made our way across the camp.

Suddenly an opening appeared, and there the host of Penychen was arrayed before us. Pawl was at their head, resplendent and armed for battle, lacking only his shield. As we approached he stepped toward us. "Who comes to take my kinswoman from my side?!" He bellowed his challenge.

I stepped forward, my men ranged about me. "I do claim her as my own! Who would gainsay me?!" I bawled back at him.

Pawl eyed me across the few paces still between us, seeming to weigh me in his estimation. "Bring me the cup!" Pawl pronounced as he handed his spear to one of his men.

A beautiful silver drinking cup with a golden rim was brought to him, filled with wine. "I offer you this cup full of all my blessings and invite you to drink to our peace and union." He offered it to me with both hands. I received it with both of my own and drank deeply before handing it to Arthwyr and my close companions. After they had each quaffed from the cup, I then offered it back to Pawl. He and each of his chieftains drank from the cup in turn.

Suddenly the ranks behind Pawl opened to reveal my love, my Trynihid, swathed in a beautiful gown of silken green with flowers in her hair. Such a vision of loveliness I will remember to my dying day. As she stepped forward, receiving the cup from the hand of her uncle, she drank deeply.

"I drink from this cup of peace and union. I drink from the cup we will share all the days of our lives. Whatever God pours into this cup, we will drink together," she said solemnly as she handed the cup back to me and I drank again. "Whatever the all-loving God would deign to give I will drink with you, my love," I rejoined.

A priest, whom I later learned was her cousin Catwg, appeared at her side. He inscribed a circle around us with his staff as he prayed:

"May the Mighty Three your protection be.

The Mighty Three encircle thee.

God before you and behind, God above you and below,

God around your life, your love, your home,

Encircled be today and forever by the Mighty Three."

As he closed the circle in the turf he took his place before us. We simply and earnestly pledged ourselves to each other. Catwg bound our hands together with a silken cord and pronounced us bound together in the sight of God and man.

A great cry rose from the assembly … and we were man and wife.

CHAPTER 31

The following days were a flurry of activity as the army broke camp. My companions took care of everything so that Trynihid and I had time to ourselves.

A few more days and we were saying our goodbyes. With a heavy heart I relinquished command of my men, putting Morgan in charge. I did not know when I would see them again. Llew agreed to carry letters back to my mother and brother. I had no doubt they would be in good hands.

The next day we were on the road to Penychen. Over the next two weeks we travelled west through the heart of Britannia to arrive in the realm of King Pawl.

The lightning-fast courtship with Trynihid was the culmination of a longer process. It was like the sudden rush of water from a bursting dam. We had been thrust together by events beyond ourselves, each being carried along by the current. Our love had grown and pressure had built until finally the dam burst and swept us along with it into matrimony.

Those first few weeks with Trynihid were ones of tender exploration and sweet communion. To be united with her body and soul was a source of tremendous joy.

As we rode together toward a home I had never known we talked some about the past and how God had orchestrated events to bring us together. His sovereignty is a marvel.

One frosty morning our conversation turned to the future.

"What now, my good husband? Oh it gives me joy to call you that!" Trynihid's smile shone across the space between us as we rode side by side. "You have been a scholar and a warrior; what will you be now, besides my dearest love?"

"Oh, you spoil me with your love, my dear. What indeed? Your uncle has extended an invitation for the winter; so I suppose I will endeavour to be a good guest and then see where that leads."

"But will you be happy?" she asked.

"I will be happy by your side! Never you fear, I am sure there will be work enough for me when the time comes."

Later that day, I found myself riding alongside Catwg.

"I don't know that I thanked you properly for your words and your prayers. I am very grateful," I said.

"It was my pleasure. I was very pleased to serve my uncle and my cousin in this. Serving you was just a happy accident!" He grinned.

I grinned back and observed him for a moment. "You sit upon that horse more like a warrior than a priest, if you don't mind me saying so."

"As well I ought; I was raised to fight and to rule but God had other plans."

"What do you mean?"

"I mean that my father, Gwynllyw, eldest brother to Pawl, rules a fourth portion of the Kingdom of Glywysing. Pawl rules another portion and two other brothers rule theirs. My father is a man of the sword and shield. Many say he is a great warrior; he would certainly have me one. I hear you trained with Brennus the unconquerable," he concluded.

"The unconquerable is it?!" I smiled at that. "I've not heard him called that but I suppose the name fits. Yes, Brennus trained me in the ways of battle."

"Well, I had my own rough teachers. But one day a holy man, Tathyw, came calling. He requested that my father return a cow my father had stolen. My father loves to raid, and I am afraid he bears more resemblance to the chieftains of old than to a proper Christian king. In any event, Tathyw came demanding - more than requesting - justice.

158

My father would have none of it, claiming the cow as the spoils of a raid. My mother, always the quick one, devised a solution where both men could claim victory. Tathyw baptised me, and my father 'paid him' for the service with the cow."

"I think your mother and mine would get along famously!" I laughed.

"Well," he continued, "That was how I met Tathyw; and he became my tutor. I learned the ways of warcraft and kingcraft at the court of my father and the ways of Christ at the feet of Tathyw. To be honest, I preferred life at court."

"Well, go on then … what happened?" I urged him.

"Two years ago I was hunting in the forest on my uncle Pawl's land. I was stalking boar when a huge boar suddenly charged from the brush. I brought my spear around too late, and he snapped it with his weight as I leapt aside. He turned to me as I drew my knife, but I knew it would be of little use against this massive beast. He must have weighed 250 pounds. I thought, 'This is it … I'm dead.' As he eyed me I looked for a tree, but there was only scrub and bushes. As he lowered his head I knew he would charge. But then suddenly … he was gone. I don't know what happened. But I know what I did. I dropped to my knees and thanked our Lord Jesus Christ for sparing my life. I told him that my life was his to command."

We rode in silence for a few minutes as I digested his tale. Boar are dangerous quarry. I knew how evenly balanced the scales could be in battle or the hunt. Scales so easily tip from one side to the other. And what to make of his strange deliverance? I was still pondering these things when Catwg interrupted my reverie with a question.

"You are a commander of men, are you not?"

I nodded.

"Then you know how important obedience is," he continued. "If you command a man to do something you expect obedience. If you are commanded to do something you must obey; and you must obey without hesitation … without question."

"Of course," I agreed.

"Have you considered that you have a king in heaven who has every right to command you?" he inquired.

"Of course I have," I affirmed. "How could I not?"

"As I knelt on that forest floor, the heat of the hunt fading, I heard the voice of God." His eyes searched mine as he continued, "I knew his command on my life. I must lay aside my arms and devote myself to prayer and to making disciples, just as our Lord did … just as the apostle Paul did." He paused before continuing, "I went directly to my uncle Pawl who agreed to give me that patch of the forest to build a community of prayer and blessing. I then went back to my old tutor Tathyw who with all joy laid his hands upon me and consecrated me to the service of Christ. Tathyw gave me the tonsure that very day. My father, when he heard, wanted to lay hands upon me in an entirely different way!" He laughed, but his heart was not in it. "And so, raised a warrior, I live as a priest." He opened his hands to indicate the completion of his tale.

"A story with many twists and turns indeed … but a story that seems not half done," I countered. "You are but a young man as I am. Who knows what our journey holds for us? Our lives are not half over. At least, I hope not!"

"Who knows … indeed?"

CHAPTER 32

We left Catwg with his father – who was much as Catwg had described him – but not before enjoying his hospitality for a few days. He was keen to hear about the war against the Saecsons although was less keen to commit himself to the cause. When questioned about it, he would only say, "Each man sets tasks for himself."

I was not satisfied with the answer, but neither did I wish to antagonise my newfound family. So I kept my own counsel and enjoyed the feasting.

I also took long walks with Trynihid as she pointed out memories from her childhood. Her mother died on the day of her birth. Her father died at the hands of Scoti raiders when she was just a baby. After that she divided her childhood in the households of her uncles - her mother's brothers. The family was kind to her and she seemed to be well-cared for ... if a bit lonely. Eventually she settled permanently with Pawl, the youngest of her uncles.

She often took me to the huts and hovels in the hollows and the forested valleys, where she seemed to know every person by name. I could tell she was well-loved by all in those parts, not only by the highborn. She would often leave some small gift, in secret if she could manage it, to ease their burdens. I'm not sure she managed it quite as often as she thought she did, but I loved her heart. Didn't our Lord teach us to give so that even our left hand does not know what our right hand is doing? That was Trynihid's way - simple small acts of love and kindness to the least of these ... and she did it as unto Christ.

It was not long after that we arrived at Pawl's caer. It occupied an ample space atop a hill with unobstructed views down to the sea, not more than five miles hence. A fortress and a busy settlement, it was much larger but not dissimilar to my own home in Armorica. Trynihid was well-loved here - as everywhere - and as Pawl and his men spoke highly of me, it was not long before I felt at home there.

Soon after our arrival, Pawl approached me. "Illtyd, you have made a name for yourself in the wars with the Saecson. And you can have no illusions as to my esteem for you, having entrusted Trynihid, my treasure, to you." He clapped his hand on my shoulder affectionately, before continuing. "I am getting older and would entrust the war band to one I know will look after them well - and even more, to one I know they will follow. In short, I would like you to lead my war band. You will eat at my table and lack for nothing. You will be like a son to me, even as Trynihid has been like a daughter. What say you?"

I was surprised and deeply humbled by his offer. "I can only say that this is a great honour, and I am humbled you would bestow it upon me. But are you sure there is not one among your men who would lead them?" I asked.

"Oh, I'm sure there are some who would lead them, but none would lead them as I would have them led. We grow wild men here in these wildlands. The Silures were ever a thorn in the side of Rome. Why do you think they based a legion here in our midst?! Even after all these years of Roman comfort and Roman rule we are still wild Britons in our hearts. I would have a man lead them who would be good for them. They are strong and no doubt they will challenge you but I am sure you will lead them well. Treat them well and they will make you proud as they have done me. I dare say you will find them no more nor less difficult than your men from Armorica. So, it is settled then?"

I slowly nodded in reply. My mind flashed back to receiving my first position of command from my mother. Not quite a year had passed. What a tumultuous year it had been! Not two years had passed since Avallon. My hands were no longer the soft hands of a scholar. I doubt my students would have recognised the warrior I had become. Now I sat at table with a king and he offered to make me his battle chief. I was younger than nearly every member of his warband but had already led the men of Armorica on campaign. I hardly knew what to make of it all. I did not have long to wait to find out.

The next day, Pawl summoned his men to the courtyard. As I looked out over the war band of Penychen I saw thirty-odd faces. Over the months of fighting with Arthwyr, I had become familiar with these men, if only vaguely. The warriors assembled were those attached to Pawl personally. There were many more who gathered in time of need but these were the core and the most respected and seasoned of them all.

"You have made me proud as your king and as your sword brother," Pawl began. "You are a joy to my heart. From time immemorial our people have held this land and have held our heads high. Once more, we have gone raiding and have returned with the spoils of our adversaries. This year you followed me far afield to fight the Saecson scourge, but it will not always be thus. I will remain your king, hopefully for many more years ..." Here the men interrupted him with good-natured cheers and he waved them down before continuing, "but I will lead you to battle no more. It is time for another to lead." The men shifted restlessly.

A change in leadership is always a tricky thing. Trust is hard to build, easily broken, and even more difficult to transfer. Leadership in war is a matter of life and death. Pawl had established trust over many years, not only because he was their king, but because he had led them so often and lost so few. I understood their nervousness and shared it because I knew what was coming next.

"You will of course know Illtyd ap Bicanys, a prince among our cousins in little Britannia beyond the sea." He gestured for me to step forward alongside him. "You will remember him for his bravery and boldness on the field of battle and of course for his marriage to my niece. I can think of no better leader, no finer man, to whom I could entrust you." He fixed them with an iron gaze as he continued, "You will follow him as you would follow me. It is my will as your lord and king." He paused, letting his gaze sweep the assembly. "You will find him to be a fair and strong leader and a more energetic one than I am these days." He laughed, patting his stomach to comical effect. Turning to me, he added, "Illtyd, my men are yours to command." With that, he turned and walked back inside into the hall.

I felt their eyes boring holes in me as I stood before them. "You know me but little. I know you even less but I have marked your prowess in battle. I am honoured to be your battle chief. We have come from a long season of war and this winter provides respite; yet I would not have us lose our edge or become rusty. We will trade blows and train together; but this week let us rest and sample some of the cider I brought with me from Armorica." I waved the men into the hall, and we all went in together, where Pawl and Trynihid had set a feast to celebrate the occasion.

Pawl invited me to sit at his right hand. As I did he leaned over and said, "Well done, lad. Well done. You have made a good beginning."

CHAPTER 33

That evening as the drink flowed freely and tongues loosened accordingly, there were songs and tales of daring exploits. I carefully observed and listened even more so.

As Proverbs tells us, "Be diligent to know the conditions of your flocks." While I had been on the same campaign as these men for some months they had not been my concern. And although I had now been in their company for several weeks my attention had been entirely focused on my new bride with little energy left for other pursuits. This evening was my first opportunity to observe them closely.

They were, as you might imagine, a varied lot in size and temperament. They were rather bawdy and rough, but that was to be expected. These were fighting men who had ever lived on the very fringes of the empire. Even then, all they knew of Rome were legions and taxes. Few of the more refined benefits of Rome ever made it this far or were even desired. What need had they of glass or wine when they had horn and ale?

As the night wore on someone produced a harp, and the tales became songs.

We Britons are a happy and cheerful breed. The Romans came and conquered but the people remained. The scene playing out before me could have been from a thousand years earlier: meat and fire, drink and song, rough-and-ready men and women rooted in the earth and sturdy as oaks but bright and colourful as the meadow flowers … and as likely to laugh or cry as to fight. They were a people conquered but unconquerable. Now in these days when Rome was but a fading memory our people were still fighting and feasting. We truly are a people hard-pressed on all sides but not crushed, struck down but not destroyed.

Romans or Saecsons may come from over the sea and claim the land for themselves, their boots upon our necks; but I fear not for our people. Lord willing, we will endure. We will find a way to be who we are. We will be Britons no matter whose taxes we pay or who rules over us. Whatever the cloth covering us, beneath it all beats a Briton heart.

I sat among these people, and I confess I fell in love again. I fell in love not with a woman but with our people. I found my heart strangely warmed and moved to prayer. Barely knowing what I was doing I rose and a song of worship rose from the depths of my being. I do not remember the words nor the tune, but I know I sang of the love of God for the Britons. I blessed them, and I cried out for God's protection over them and his strength within them. I asked for grace to love and serve them well, and I prayed for God's presence and blessing to dwell in and among us.

Then as suddenly as the song came upon me it was gone. I collapsed into my seat like a wrung-out cloth. Silence hung over the hall. I remember the scuttle of the hounds under the table … it was that quiet. Pawl stood over me and pronounced, "Hear him my people. A war leader I brought you and a bard we have found. May his blessing rest upon us all!" A murmur of approval rippled through the crowd and the moment passed.

As I lay in bed later that night Trynihid asked me, "What happened tonight?"

"To be honest I scarcely know. Did it make sense? I only remember snatches of what I said."

"Yes, it was beautiful and powerful and frightening all at the same time. You were yourself, but more than yourself. You spoke with authority beyond yourself."

Although I barely dared to say it, I ventured, "Perhaps it was the voice of God. I felt suddenly that I must speak … and it was as if the Spirit of God was playing me like an instrument. Not that I was passive but that I barely had time to recognise the next words before they were coming out of my mouth. I was not constructing sentences as we were taught in oratory, but the sentences were coming unbidden and flowing from one to another like a river of words from a source further upstream than my own mind."

Trynihid took my hand in the dark, "Could it be what the prophets felt? Could it be that this is what Elijah, Moses, or Isaiah experienced?"

I couldn't tell if she was excited or frightened or both; I only know that I felt both. For this was all new to me then. At that time I scarcely knew the voice of God at all. I am ashamed to admit for all my years studying the Scriptures, I had almost no experience of the one who wrote them for us. For all my learning and theology, I had precious little practical religion.

That day, the day I took command of the war band, was a turning point in my life; but not as I had imagined it might be. I trace what came later back to then. Of course hearing my story you may be able to discover the hand of God back further … and more clearly than I. There is a limit to what any man may see of himself. After all, my eyes look out from my own face; while you can see my face clearly, I can only ever see a reflection of the same.

"I don't know, my love," I patted Trynihid on the hand and turned to curl closer to her. "I don't know, but I hope it may be God."

CHAPTER 34

Over that winter I split my time between training the men and becoming familiar with the terrain. I tried to combine those two activities whenever possible. One of the best ways to do that was to hunt. Much of Penychen is forest. The forests are ancient and like the people only get wilder as you go up into the valleys and the mountains beyond.

One of the obligations and joys of the warrior is to provide meat for the table. Pawl's warriors knew every hollow, every clearing, every rock and stream of their land even as I did of the land of my birth. I made a point of splitting the men into different groups and accompanying various ones as we hunted. Our main quarries were boar and deer, both excellent eating and fun to hunt.

Being out in the field with the men days on end was a joy and I got to know their various strengths and weaknesses. Some were better with a bow or a spear. Some were exceptionally strong and others stealthy. You might think that you could tell that by looking at them but I still remember watching Edrys, the most roly-poly man you could imagine, picking his way silently toward a deer without making a sound. I'm still not sure how he did it, but he was a quiet one!

I often find it better to learn through observation and to allow yourself to be surprised. It is hard to see the truth emerge in front of you when you have already decided what it will be - even harder when you have announced your foregone conclusion in advance. I believe this principle holds true whether the subject of study is a man, an animal, some natural occurrence, or even a scriptural or theological conundrum. Careful observation and prayerful reflection will generally lead you to the truth.

One of the truths that emerged during my time with these men - my men - was their unruly nature. In reality unruly does not go far enough. They were a rough lot. That did not surprise me entirely, as men often are. There is a rough comradeship among men in many settings. No, what surprised me about these men was their willingness to use their power selfishly and even cruelly at times.

I knew Pawl to be a man of faith and a good man. But as I got to know his kinsmen, his warriors … they seemed of a different cloth, more in line with the Catwg's father, Gwynllyw. He was famous for leading raids and for generally taking what he wanted when he wanted it. There is a rough sort of pragmatism there, I suppose; but I cannot truly respect it.

Kian's devotion to his violent and vengeful gods is detestable; but beneath it there is a deeper story. Myrddin's actions - wrongheaded as they were - sprang from a place of misguided faith. There were deeper drivers, a larger narrative. There were principles and forces at work. I did not agree with Kian. I grieved for Myrddin. But I at least knew they stood for something beyond themselves.

Brennus and my father had trained me to see a warrior as the wall around the people. They instilled in me an understanding of the warrior's place in the social order. Although my tutors Kian and Scapilion did not agree on many things, the most important things they both taught me was to respect and value the contributions of others. Kian emphasised the order in nature and the connectedness of all things. Scapilion stressed the different gifts that God gives to each person. We each have our role to play but we are all part of the one body. The hand cannot say to the foot, "I don't need you," nor the eye to the mouth, "I don't need you."

But the attitude of these men was something else. I was familiar with the bald pragmatism of men like Arthwyr. But even Arthwyr's pragmatism served the greater good of the people at least on some level. Of course, I know there are drivers in each of us that are not the best of us … drivers like fear or pride or revenge. I had seen these all too often in myself and in others. What I saw in these men was a sort of crass selfishness.

I noticed it in small ways. When we ate together they would squabble over the best bits of the meat or the most comfortable seat. They scarcely acknowledged the servants in the hall unless they were mistreating them. They openly scorned the farmers in the fields. They regularly displayed a mix of pride and selfishness.

There is in each of us a strong desire to be loved, respected, and admired. We want to turn the hearts of men and women toward us. I feel my own desire to make an idol of myself and want others to come and worship the idol that is me. The foibles of my sword brothers disconcerted me. Only later did I discover what troubled me most about them were the ugly parts of me I saw reflected in them.

But troubled I was. I watched as they gloried in the privilege and position they held as warriors. They were freed from many of the menial tasks of life and so they looked down on those who served them rather than gratefully receiving their service. They shamelessly took advantage of those weaker than themselves. They threatened and abused and took whatever they wanted whenever they wanted it, justifying themselves in their own minds with the maxim of the craven: The strong rule the weak.

This is not a new story, I know. This is a story as old as time. The tales of Greek and Roman gods illustrate this repeatedly. The Scriptures are full of similar stories - Judah with Tamar, David with Bathsheba. But the biblical stories also carry the theme of repentance. There are consequences when God's laws are broken. Yes, these things are bound up in the hearts of men. These are the sins that so easily entangle us. These are urges to be resisted, not to glory in.

As the winter wore on, I made it a point to train not only with weapons and hunting but also to weave the values that had been instilled in me into our training; however, to no avail. I saw the condescending smiles as I talked about being selfless in battle and life. I saw the superior looks and the raised eyebrows as I encouraged them to think of others as more important than themselves, to play their role in the tribe while also honouring the parts of others. I shared John the Baptiser's admonition to soldiers not to exploit others but nothing seemed to touch them. Nothing touched their hard hearts.

170

CHAPTER 35

Although I remained concerned by the state of their souls, I had no complaints about their responsiveness to my leadership. Seasoned warriors before I arrived, they needed little training in weapons. I focused on tactics and coordination. Although individual skills are essential, battles - and more importantly, wars - are won not by individuals but armies. The Romans taught us this.

The Romans may well have been the most pragmatic of peoples. The Greeks were great thinkers. The Celts great warriors. But the Romans mastered coordinated tactics like no other. They were also adaptable. They learned from each engagement and would adapt even their armour and weapons as they fought different enemies. The best commanders know that the battle will rarely go the way you plan or expect. You will have to adapt to survive and to win. But you cannot make up new tactics in the heat of battle; you have to drill many tactics so that your men can execute the right tactic at the right time.

My men already knew the basics of flanking, attack, and defence. But even during mock battles they often devolved into a mob rather than a disciplined unit. That was fine on a raid and would probably be good enough for skirmishes but was too risky for large-scale engagements. And given what we had seen the previous year there were sure to be more of those ahead of us. So I worked the men hard, arranging formations and then calling out commands or describing an opposing tactic and letting them adjust on their own.

For example, they might have assumed a covered defence like the testudo to protect themselves from archers before I called out to brace for a cavalry charge. They would then rearrange themselves and get their spears planted quickly, so as not to be mown down by the imaginary horse and rider. Once I even enlisted the help of Trynihid and the servant girls. I had hidden them behind a wall with a supply of pebbles and small rocks; then I had the men move past in formation. On my signal the ladies let fly with their missiles. Only after the first flight landed did the men realise they were under attack. "Slingers," I cried out, and they quickly raised their shields to cover themselves.

You should have heard the shrieks of laughter from the girls as they scored hits upon the hardened men! As the men formed up to attack their position behind the wall, quick as a flash the girls retreated to the relative safety of the kitchen.

Of course it was not all fun and games. We worked hard and the men put up little resistance. It was clear to them that these were not meaningless exercises but would bring real advantage on the field of battle. Once a man understands that you are trying to help him he often becomes easier to teach. Of course, getting to that point is usually the problem.

As the feast of the nativity of our Lord approached, Pawl and I made ready to attend the council in Dumnonia. I looked forward to seeing Arthwyr again but Pawl was none too sure of what awaited us. I tried to dispel his fears, but I should not have bothered.

We arrived to find fewer than we expected, and less goodwill as well. It was good to see Arthwyr again, but he was already hard-pressed.

It seemed that the battlefield successes of the previous years had only increased the machinations of the kings of Britannia. For all of the taxes and troubles with Rome, centralised power did keep the peace. Without an emperor or the threat of the legions coming down upon their heads, the princes and kings of Britannia nipped at each other like ill-tempered hounds. The kings of the south were wrangling over lands recently reclaimed or scheming to use the combined arms of the Britons to clear land so that they might claim it for themselves. The kings of the north were demanding that the Dux Bellorum lead the army north in the spring. There were demands for the troops to be everywhere and serve everyone.

I wondered what would become of this braying pack of men. I would just as soon have left them to their own devices but for the people they ruled. If these men kept biting and devouring each other the Saecson would never be defeated.

When this was raised, some openly counselled peace. It became clear that some had already made treaties and even given their daughters in marriage to Saecson leaders to purchase peace. Others, following the example of Vortigern, had taken wives from among the Saecson. They argued that the Saecson were here and some of them had been for generations. Better to make peace with them than to fight them.

I couldn't believe my ears! What had happened to these men? I thought I was going to jump out of my skin!

Finally Arthwyr rose to address the assembly. "My lords, perhaps during this peaceful winter, you have forgotten - we did not choose this fight! It was not we who sought out new lands to conquer. The Saecson has not come as our guest. He has not come as a settler nor a supplicant. They have come, and they keep on coming, to take our land, our treasure, our homes, and our women for themselves!" His eyes swept the room angrily before continuing.

"When the Romans came the tribes thought they could negotiate. They tried to use the legions to settle old scores. We chafed under the Roman yoke for hundreds of years! Are your memories so short? Think not back to the Romans then … think only of Vitalinus the unlucky. He styled himself the High King Vortigern. He took a Saecson bride. He thought he could make peace with them, to use them. Is that too far back still?!" His voice rose further. "Have you forgotten the betrayal and slaughter at Anderida? Have you forgotten treacheries so recent!?"

Silence fell over us as we remembered. Then more quietly, his voice husky with emotion he continued, "You cannot negotiate with a wolf when your head is in his mouth! I don't speak to you now of vengeance. I don't speak to you about glory. I don't even speak about justice. If you want peace you want no more than I want. But the way to gain peace is through strength. We may yet have peace, but not until they ask for it. Not until they know we are too strong to pillage. Not until they know that the cost of their pillaging is too high to contemplate. They need to be defeated. Only then they may ask us for peace. Even then I would not trust them. I would see them driven into the sea. I would see the backs of them once and for all. We did not drive the Romans out, but they are gone. Can we not rule our land for ourselves? Can we put aside our small ambitions while we face this common foe?" Arthwyr sat down.

Immediately Pawl was on his feet, "My brothers, we are gathered to celebrate the birth of our Lord Jesus. Did not our Lord say, 'a house divided against itself cannot stand'? Let us not be divided. Let us band together again this year and see what may be done. Let us not resign ourselves to be prey. We are not sheep to be slaughtered, waiting only for the wolves to attack again. And they will strike again! Arthwyr is not wrong. I am older than many of you, and I have seen this unfolding. My lands are safely in the west and yet we have fought at your side. I have lost no lands to the Saecson but I know in here," he cried as he thumped his chest, "that they must be stopped … and we must be united to do this. Otherwise they will pick off one settlement, one fortress, one kingdom at a time. Just a mouthful each time … and soon the plate will be empty."

I would like to tell you that the conversation was over at that point, but it went on for several days more. Eventually it was agreed that we would renew the campaign in the spring, and that we would muster the army in the northern Kingdom of Elmet. Nearly everyone agreed. Some of the southern kings felt they could not spare troops for the campaign as they were already under threat. I understood their plight but feared for the future of Britannia.

As we rode back to Penychen, Pawl and I discussed all this. "Is it possible that we will have to make peace with them? How could we even contemplate that, knowing their history of proud treachery?"

"I do not know what the future holds, but I know that God holds all things in his hands," Pawl responded. "I cannot imagine He would honour these pagans nor allow them to triumph … and yet … No … I simply do not understand the ways of God. The Romans were not godly people and God allowed them to conquer the world. His ways are not my ways. But I know I must stand for my people. My purpose is clear. I am a shepherd of my people and I would not have them food for wolves; so we must do what he bids us do, eh Illtyd?" He smiled at me.

"Yes Pawl, we must do as he bids …" I spoke the words with little conviction. I knew I had to submit. There just no effective opposition to the ruler of the universe. I could kick against the goads but it would not change the outcome - like Jonah, inexorably journeying to Nineveh no matter what direction he travelled. There is nowhere to hide from the all-seeing one. My obedience signified resignation, not delight. To learn to delight in submission is a long hard lesson; at least it has been so for me.

CHAPTER 36

We rode home through wild weather ... snowing one day, raining the next. The rivers were swollen and our route home was longer for it. A cold and challenging journey makes coming home all the more welcome. The evening was falling as we approached the caer, looking forward to the warm embrace of home once more. With joyful hearts we rode in ... but immediately knew something was wrong. Instead of hearty greetings from our loved ones there was a deathly silence punctuated by quiet weeping.

Trynihid came from the hall to greet us. "What is it? What has happened? Surely no raiding at this time of year!?" Pawl asked.

"Nothing like that ... well actually it was a raid of sorts, but not what you might think. Come in and sit. I'll tell you." She set warmed spiced mead before us as we shook the rain from ourselves before sitting on a bench near the hearth.

"Ten of your men went raiding last night, but they did not all return," Trynihid began.

"What!" I cried and was on my feet.

"Sit down and let me tell you. There is nothing to be done right now. Everything is being seen to." She gently pushed me back toward the bench.

I resumed my seat and she continued. "They were drinking and enjoying themselves yesterday evening. Someone started singing one of the old songs about raiding. Then someone else said they were hungry for some pork. As you know, we don't keep pigs; but then someone remembered that Catwg keeps famously tasty swine at his llan. That was all it took. Some laughed and cursed them, but ten headed off in the dead of night. There was no stopping them."

I shook my head slowly. I could picture the scene too easily.

"As you likely know, the weather was terrible last night. We thought surely they would come to their senses once they were soaked by the rain and lashed by the wind. We expected to find them safely abed this morning with sore heads and bruised pride. But it was not to be. They made their way to Catwg's place and snuck into the stables just before dawn. As you can imagine, stealing pigs may start quietly but it was never going to end that way. Catwg and the brothers were roused, burst forth, and set after the men. In their drunken haste, they drove the pigs and themselves right into bogs swollen by the river. They must have been too drunk to recognise the danger. Five have returned alive and they brought Aled's body back with them, but four are still missing. The rest of the band is out looking for their missing brothers. The women are preparing the body and his wife has been sent for. I expected her by now." Trynihid looked around as if she might have missed the new widow's arrival.

"The fools," Pawl whispered. "Such waste ... and for what?"

"I will go and join the search for the bodies." I made to rise.

"No," Pawl took my arm. "Night is falling. The men are searching for their brothers. There is nothing you can do to help them this night. You are weary from your travels. The men will return soon. We will wait for them here."

I reluctantly resumed my seat, wiping my disbelieving face with my hands. "All this for what?!"

We did not have long to wait until we heard men entering the yard. We went out to meet them.

In rode the bedraggled remnants of the warband - heads hanging low, soggy from the rain, exhausted from the ride, and grieving the loss of their companions. Four bodies they carried with them, each slung across and tied on his own horse, not mounted and riding as they should have been. We waited in the rain, watching as they dismounted and untied the bodies, gently caring for them as if they would wake if jostled too roughly.

Later, as they warmed themselves by the hearth, it was my turn to bring the warming mead. I sat with them as they told their tale. They found the bodies scattered downstream from Catwg's settlement. Catwg and his students had helped them in their search. This surprised me, but only a little. I could imagine his anger over the raid giving way to compassion for these foolish ones. They said that Catwg had gone home once the bodies had been retrieved but that he was coming to us on the morrow.

They apologised to their king and to me. They knew they bore some responsibility for the deaths of their brothers. I let them pour out their hearts. They were a sea of grief. That sea changes colour with the sky and tides as any other. Sometimes it is the flat slate grey of denial and reserve ... then the deep green of sadness and regret ... then the white foam of angry waves crashing on the shore as if their crashing could bend the shore to their will. I loved the honest hearts of these men even in my anger.

I too bore some of the blame. These were my men, after all. As their leader I was responsible for their actions. This is one of the heavy burdens of leadership. It is not a tangible thing, but it weighs on you all the same - the responsibility for their well-being, the knowledge that your decisions will impact their lives and that their choices will affect yours ... and the second-guessing of yourself after the fact. Now that this deed was done the stone was cast and the ripples would move outward no matter what. But I was caught in these ripples because I was in fact their leader.

I was tempted to shirk and blame. In my heart I confess I did blame them. They had brought this disaster on their own heads and on all of us. Even as I accused them I felt conviction. Had I been there I would have stopped them; I do not believe they would have openly defied me. I did not second-guess my decision to attend the council, but I wondered if I had been too lax with them before my departure.

I watched Pawl, and I knew similar thoughts were going through his head. He had known these men for years. He had drawn them to himself and established them as his war band. He knew their wives and children, and many of their parents he counted as his friends. This would weigh heavy on him.

Neither of us looked forward to Catwg's arrival in the morning.

CHAPTER 37

My dreams were troubled that night. I dreamt I stood at a fork in the road. One way led into a forest with bodies hanging from the trees like spoiling fruit. The other path led into a valley so dark that the darkness seemed liquid … almost a living thing. I could not choose between them. I felt dread rising in me. I wanted to climb up to gain a vantage where I could see further to know which one to choose; but for some reason I could not climb the tree before me. All the while I felt the dread and knew I must choose. The earth beneath my feet began to shake and pitch and I was afraid I had missed my chance and was damned for not choosing.

I awoke to find Trynihid shaking me, a concerned look on her face. I was drenched with sweat and troubled in heart. I shared the dream with Trynihid and she too was disturbed. We settled down again. I took comfort in her nearness but struggled to sleep.

The next morning after breakfast, Catwg arrived with a few of his students. We exited the hall to welcome him as he arrived. As he came through the gate, he greeted the warriors in a stiff but not entirely unfriendly manner. He asked where the dead had been laid. He disappeared into the building where they had been laid out, blessed them, and left his students there to pray. He then made his way across the yard toward us.

He was not smiling.

Pawl stepped forward, "Please come in nephew, and accept my hospitality."

Catwg gave him a hard look but said nothing as we went inside.

Trynihid brought the welcome cup and we sat together near the hearth.

Pawl began, "Catwg, I apologise for the attack upon you and yours. Tell me what I can do to make restitution and I will do it."

179

Catwg nodded, "I expected no less, uncle. You have always been a good and wise king … but your men much less so. I have to wonder that you have kept such men in your service. You know what comes from strife such as this. Last night it was me they raided. The lives of half the fools are forfeit, and I expect the others will not do something so foolish again … or at least until the pain of this memory is less keen. But what if they had raided my father's people? Then, brother or no, you would have had war and many more would pay for their foolishness."

Pawl bristled at the rebuke from his nephew but did not respond quickly. After a moment he nodded. "You are right. Many a lasting quarrel has started among our people over less. Lives are precious and honour perhaps even more so. I am sorry my men have dishonoured you; and in doing so they have dishonoured me. Tell me what I can do to make it right."

Catwg held up his hand toward Pawl. "We have found the sows alive but lost most of the piglets. A year's worth of meat we have lost because of those fools. You will provide meat for a year, after which your debt will be considered settled." Pawl nodded. "But there is one thing more I require." Turning his eyes upon me he added, "You, Pawl, were their king and bear ultimate responsibility; but Illtyd was their leader. I require Illtyd to come to me each week. I know his duties of command will require him to be elsewhere; but whenever he is available he will bring your payment of meat and do whatever I require of him."

Pawl looked from Catwg to me and back again. "The meat is easily agreed and more than fair. The other …" Pawl looked at me again.

"I will go, for you are right. I have reproached myself already and I will do what penance you require for their sins and my own."

Catwg nodded, and just a hint of a smile was visible on his face. "The terms are agreed then; let us drink to our reconciliation," he said as we passed the cup around again.

And so it began. Each week I would take the agreed ration of meat to Catwg's llan and do whatever task he set for me. I delivered the meat to the kitchen and typically received my assignment from one of the brothers. In the beginning, it was mucking out the barn or the stables or spreading the muck in the fields. I was not happy with my work, I freely tell you. Six days a week I spent honoured in a king's court and one day a week labouring in filth, being smirked at by Catwg's young students. It was humiliating. Humiliations should breed humility, but they did not in me. I soon forgot the wrong my men had done and felt I was hard done by. I grew angry.

Several weeks went by, and I scarcely saw Catwg. Then one day, having delivered the meat, the cook asked me to come through to the dining area. When I did so Catwg shooed the students out and beckoned me to come sit with him. "Have you never wondered why I asked for you?" he asked.

"To do penance," I replied.

"Is that all?" He smiled as if to himself before continuing. "I see two roads before you Illtyd. One road leads back to the wars. You have been a prince among the Britons and you may yet be a king. You can ride to the wars against the Saecson." Then, adding under his breath he murmured, "At least they will start against the Saecson …" Then turning back to me he continued, "You can ride to the wars and you will win fame and glory. You will become great in the eyes of this world."

As he spoke I felt an almost physical exultation in my spirit, as if my chest were inflating and I was growing taller as he spoke. What he described was my dearest wish. Greatness! Was I not born to greatness? Everything in me told me that I was meant for something great.

"Or you can take the other road."

"What other road?" I asked.

"I see only the beginning of that road. I see the purpose of it but do not know where it will lead in the end. The other road is the road of service to an even greater cause, but I expect it leads to obscurity. Take the second road and none will sing of your exploits, none will know your name … none except the one who will write your true name on a white stone."

"Why would I choose that road?" I protested. Even as I said it I felt my skin aflame and a strange movement in my chest as if a bird were fluttering there.

"I cannot choose for you. I will not try. I can only tell you what I have learned on the way, for I walk the second road." He looked off into the distance, nodding slowly. "I have chosen to serve my people by devoting my service to the King of kings. I look to build the Kingdom of God, to make his blessings known on earth. There is a much deeper and more difficult battle being waged … one of eternal significance. There will always be wars and rumours of war - the Romans one day, the Scoti another, the Saecson the next. Even if no foreigners assailed our shores, we would fight each other."

I nodded. I knew the truth of what he said.

"No - there is a deeper war, a longer campaign to which I have been called. It is more satisfying to fight an enemy you can see. The rush of the fight and the heat of battle are exhilarating, as is the moment when the battle is over and you look your sword brothers in their glad faces and rejoice you are alive once more. The clash of arms and the risk of death make victory and life that much sweeter!" His face flushed, and I was reminded that he too was a warrior once.

"But the battles we fight here in this fortress of prayer are harder. No one sees and few appreciate the war we fight on their behalf. We battle for our souls. We battle for the souls of our people. We battle the spiritual forces of wickedness in the heavenly realms, the powers and principalities of this present darkness. We use spiritual weapons to demolish spiritual strongholds. No one knows and no one sings our praises.

"The war we fight is subtle and secret. We fight for those who do not ask nor even want us to fight on their behalf. We fight for the souls of the men who raid us. Because even when they raid us we would see them delivered from the sin in which they revel, from the wickedness in which they delight. We fight to free them from a slavery they have

182

grown to love. You see, we too are engaged in life and death struggles … eternal life and eternal death.

"We too serve a king. Pawl is a good king, but he does not hold a candle to the king of the universe. I invite you to serve the King of kings and the Lord of lords. Lay aside your weapons of earthly warfare and come run the race set before you. But I cannot make this decision for you. I can issue God's call, but only you can choose your answer. But choose you must. You will know."

My heart leapt within me, but my will was strong. I remembered my dream, but I did not share it with him. I did not want it to be true. Something in me told me that I must choose the second road - the road of service, the path to darkness; but I was not ready. I could not imagine it could be worth the cost. I feared all that I would lose. I longed to be great and Catwg offered me lowliness. I longed to be known and he offered me obscurity. I could not embrace it. I would not.

With my heart churning and my head swimming, I lurched out of my seat. "You cannot ask this of me!" I protested.

"I do not ask it of you," he said quietly. "I merely tell you what I see before you. There are two roads. You choose."

Shaking my head, I turned to leave; then remembering my penance I asked, "What task have you set me this day?"

"Your task today has been completed. I will see you next week." He made the sign of the cross over me and I made haste to get out of his presence and end my agony.

CHAPTER 38

My children, you who have known me only in my later years may find my lack of understanding surprising. You have seen the results of many years striving after obedience. You know me now in the twilight of my life; but I was not then who I am now. I am probably not even who you think I am now. My heart still wanders and I am startled still at how easily my faith evaporates in the face of temptation. You may not see it, but I know the inside of the cup is still dirty even if the outside looks clean. But I digress ... where was I? Oh yes ...

I rode home slowly that day, wondering at what had transpired. I did not ride straight back. I needed time to think, to clear my head. In truth I needed time to bolster my defences against the direction I felt compelled to go. I steeled myself against the road into the darkness. I would gladly choose war and death when faced with the faceless darkness. I knew battle. I knew how to deflect a spear or parry a sword. I knew many ways to kill a man or win a battle. But what did I know of this spiritual war Catwg described?

Even then, though, I saw through my hastily-erected arguments. Had I not seen the direction Kian wanted to lead the people? Had I not seen and felt the darkness in the grove Kian called sacred? I had seen the blood and detritus from his sacrifices. I knew the old stories and I knew better than to think they were just quaint tales. Kian and others would bring those old ways back if they could.

What if Catwg is right? What if the most important battle is not against flesh and blood, not against enemies we can defeat by force of arms? I felt he was right. I feared he was right.

Eventually I made my way home. Trynihid greeted me cheerfully, "What ho! My love returns looking fresher than usual from my cousin's stable!" Then, seeing my face, she drew me aside. "What's wrong?! What has happened?"

I scarcely knew what to say. I was still unprepared to talk about the conflict raging within me. "Later," I tersely replied. As you can imagine, this did nothing to alleviate her concern.

I was miserable company that evening in the hall. I kept to myself and made my way to our bed as soon as I could. Trynihid followed me. As she lay down beside me she gently touched my shoulder, "What is it, my darling? Tell me!" she implored.

"I'm afraid," I whispered. "I'm afraid that God is calling me …"

Trynihid patiently waited.

"Do you remember the dream? The dream of two roads one of blood and one of darkness?" I asked, turning towards her to see her face in the dim light.

She looked disturbed as she recalled that night. "Yes, I remember."

"What if it was more than a dream? What if it was a sign?"

"A sign of what?" she looked confused.

"I am afraid God was showing me, speaking to me, preparing me for this very moment." She watched me closely across the inches between us. "Catwg has invited me to lay aside my arms and leave this world of war behind … to leave this life I know behind. But what I fear is that it is not Catwg who invites me; it is the God Catwg serves." I burst into tears.

It was a real ripping and tearing going on in my heart that night. I felt my head would split with the pain in my soul. I wept and cried and had no words. And Trynihid, sweet Trynihid, held me and let me cry. She stroked my head, held me, and joined me in my tears. We wept together for I know not how long.

With my face still wet I pulled back from her. "Pray for me! I would oppose God but I know it would be of no use! But oh how I do not want to follow him into the pitch dark! I do not know where that road will lead me!"

"Us," she said quietly but firmly. "Where it will lead us. For I pledged to drink from our common cup whatever God would pour into it and I mean to honour my pledge!" she said fiercely.

"Oh, my love! Us. Yes … I mean us. Would you walk into the darkness hand in hand with me? I do not know what lies on that road," I cautioned.

185

"I confess my fear of what lies ahead, but I will face what comes by your side." There was an air of finality in her tone.

"Oh Lord, have mercy on us!" I cried. "Oh Lord Jesus, you know I have pledged myself to you and I would not be faithless now; but you also know I don't want this. I don't want this call. I like the life I have, the life you have given me. I know this life and I am grateful for it. I don't want to give it up. And for what?! What is this new calling … to give up everything and follow you into darkness, the valley of the shadow?!"

With these and many similar words I poured out my heart to the Lord, as Trynihid and I held each other tight.

In the end I knew I had to follow the King. I knew I had to obey; but oh my children … obedience is often costly. To obey a call to ease and joy, to lie down in green pastures beside quiet waters may seem easy; while to follow the call into the valley or into the very presence of your enemies may seem frightening. I had known fear and courage on the field of battle. But this was different. The real battle was within.

Looking back I can see that God was preparing me for this spiritual battle even as Brennus had prepared me for the physical ones. The war in the soul is one of self-will and submission. I knew the battle had started but I did not know the next steps. The ferocity of my defences surprised me. My will and my pride fought like a cornered boar slashing at my mind and my spirit.

"What now? Are you decided?" Trynihid asked. "As for me, my decision is made; I will walk this journey with you, no matter what comes."

I pulled back slightly to fix my eyes on her face. Such beauty of spirit! Such strength of soul! Once again, I counted the blessings God had given me in my wife. "I will follow this road; but as to what is next, I do not know …" Then, in the quietness of that moment, a wave of exhaustion hit me.

Trynihid gently stroked my cheek and whispered, "Let us sleep now my dear, and wake to see what God has planned for us."

CHAPTER 39

I awoke the next morning to find my bed empty. Trynihid often rose before me, and this day was no different. The sun was already well up.

As I entered the hall, Pawl called to me, "Oh, there he is! It's nice of you to join us at last, young prince. I hope you slept as well as you did late!"

I smiled at his good-natured jest. "Yes, old king … I have slept late indeed." Glancing outside I added, "It seems a glorious morning as well."

"Afternoon you mean!" Pawl was enjoying himself immensely.

I just shook my head and smiled as I approached the table where they were just finishing and sat down to break my fast with bread and cheese. "I am glad to find you still here, as I had an eventful day and a fitful night."

Pawl quizzically looked at me but his jovial spirit remained. "What befell you, my lad?"

I told him about my conversation with Catwg and the portentous dream. I shared my fears and my uncertainty about what lay ahead. "And so I come to you and ask you for your counsel. What say you to all of this?"

Pawl sombrely stroked his beard for some time before replying. "I have known you were touched by God. That does not surprise me. In fact this drew me to you. I have observed you - at first from afar and now more closely - marking Christ's influence in you. Your Godward inclination is one of the things I love about you and one of the reasons I gladly gave Trynihid to be your wife. And yet …" He shook his head. "… and yet this is another matter. I saw in you a husband and a war leader and hoped perhaps even a king; but to lay all that aside would be a blow …" He paused again. "It would be a blow to me and to all Penychen. You know I sought to retire from war. I entrusted my men to you. And yet, I would not choose to oppose the purposes of the Almighty. His ways are not our ways …" his voice trailed off.

"I would say this to you, Illtyd," he continued. "Don't be hasty. If this is God's calling on your life, it will be his calling tomorrow the same as today. He does not change like shifting shadows. What seems so urgent today may not seem as important tomorrow. Such are the passions of youth. Take your time. Say your prayers. Seek and you shall find. Knock and the door will be opened … only … only don't be hasty."

I nodded. "Believe me when I tell you that I would have this call ring untrue. This is not a call I desire; but if it is from God I dare not refuse. With your permission I would go more frequently to Catwg to learn from him about the road he walks."

"That is a good course," Pawl agreed. "Go to him as frequently as you like. I will see to the men. We have several weeks yet before we are due to set out to the north and join Arthwyr in Elmet."

I chose my next words carefully, "My king, I entered your service willingly and gratefully. You have been kind, just, and generous. If this calling is not fancy nor delusion but is from God, I would ask you to release me from my pledges. I will not be able to accompany you to the wars."

Pawl nodded before replying, "I know, my son; but we are not there yet. Let us take each day as it comes as a gift from the all-wise Father. Until then, let us remain as we are."

I readily agreed, rose, and went to find Trynihid. Not too surprisingly, I found her nearby. She was pleased to hear how my conversation went with her uncle and sped me on my way to see Catwg. We were both eager to find our way through the confusion and tumult. If this was to be the path, we wanted to be on our way.

As I rode to Catwg's llan I found myself praying again, asking the Lord for guidance and clarity. If I was going to upend our lives I wanted to be sure it was God's doing and not mine.

How many times have I seen men falsely claim God's direction or blessing on endeavours wholly other?! When a man claims to speak for God he must be careful. As James warned us, not many should aspire to be teachers for they will incur a stricter judgement. The laws of the Hebrews also contain many warnings about false prophets. We must remember - as Paul warned us - to test every spirit, to test everything and hold onto the good.

But therein lies the problem. How do we test? How can we tell the difference between the urgings of our heart and the urgings of the Spirit? How do I discern between the thoughts coming from God and the thoughts coming from my own mind ... or even from the enemy of our souls?

Of course, the clearest standard against which all supposed revelations must be measured is the Scriptures. God does not change and shift. His Holy Spirit who inspired the authors of the Scriptures dwells in us. Even then I knew these things. After all, I had been trained at the feet of Scapilion. I had been a teacher, if a minor one, in the school of Germanus in Avallon. The ways of the Scriptures were familiar to me; but at that time the ways of the Spirit remained a mystery.

As I entered the llan I found Catwg enjoying some late winter sunshine while lecturing his students. He looked genuinely surprised to see me. Dismissing the students with a wave, he turned to me cheerfully. "Back so soon? Come inside; let us find someplace warm to sit."

I gladly agreed. Although the weather was dry and the sun was out, I was chilled from my ride.

We found a place near the fire in the small hall that served the community for lectures and dining. "I did not mean to disturb your lessons. I wanted to speak to you." He motioned for me to continue. "I have not yet made a definite choice, but I would speak with you about discernment. I will follow God's lead ... and I believe he may be calling me to leave the road I am on for the road you walk; but I must be certain before I choose. I must be certain it is his will. Can you help me?"

"I believe I can help you. But certainty is not something I can provide." Catwg paused before continuing. "The road I journey is often dark. I

189

rarely have certainty, but I generally have direction. You know the Scriptures well I imagine, perhaps even better than I. Tell me, do you think Abraham had certainty when he took Isaac to the mountain?"

I pondered his question for a few moments. "Hebrews tells us that he believed God could raise Isaac from the dead; but in Genesis God made no such promise. So, no, I suppose Abraham did not have certainty; but he knew God's command. If God would speak to me as he did to Abraham, then I would believe and obey without hesitation. But God hasn't done that."

"Hasn't he?" Catwg raised a quizzical eyebrow. "How did God speak to Abraham when he told him to kill his son, the son of promise?"

"I don't know. It isn't clear in the text."

"So it isn't clear ... interesting ..." Catwg grinned. "I agree. ... The text says that God spoke to Abraham; but we don't know if it was in a dream, a vision, a physical experience, an impression in his mind or emotions, or an audible voice. Scripture gives examples of God speaking in all these ways to his people. The passage involving Abraham is unclear as to the means but clear as to the message. How clear must it have been to Abraham for him to have staked the life of his son upon it? He must have been sure about the message!

"This was not the first time Abraham had heard God's voice. He had been walking with God for many years. At times he even entertained God at his tent - or an angel of the Lord at least. When you first meet someone you may not be able to pick them out of a crowd. As you get to know them you learn their tone of voice, their attitude, their turn of phrase. Over time you may even see the end of their sentence before they are halfway there.

"I believe Abraham had learned the voice of God - the language of heaven if you will. You have learned Latin, I assume."

"Of course," I replied.

"But you did not learn it at your mother's breast. You had to study and work at it. In the beginning it was foreign to you in sound and structure. The words were on the page before you or floating in the air around you but you could not make sense of them. The revelation was there to be had and yet it was beyond you.

"In Hebrews we find a fascinating passage about discernment. Paul tells us that he would like to give the Hebrews solid food but he can't. Although they ought to be mature and teaching others they still require milk. They are spiritual infants. Then he says that solid food is for the mature who by continually training themselves have learned to discern between good and evil. He does not fault them for being young. He points out that they have not trained themselves to discern. Do you see?

"When you first learned to fight you did not know how to properly do so. You were trained. Brennus was your master because he knew how to use the weapons of warfare. He guided you, but you had to practice and master the weapons for yourself. Do you see?"

Heaving a sigh, I responded, "I remember those years of training. That was hard work, but the lessons of those years have become a part of my very sinew. I hardly think - I just know how to read my opponent or the flow of battle. I remember too the years of studying languages in Avallon. My muscles grew soft, but my head worked hard. Both kinds of training were difficult, but I found them very rewarding. Catwg, would you teach me to discern? Would you be my spiritual battle master?"

Catwg held both hands up toward me. "Wait! No! I am humbled by your trust in me but I am just a learner myself. However, this I will do - I will share with you what I have found and what I am finding. We can walk this journey together. As you see, I have students; but I do not have a sword brother to stand with me and fight alongside. Let us take our place together in the war band of our God. What say you?!"

"I say you are too modest. I crave your help, and I think you have more to offer than you know. But I will take what you offer and gladly. Where do we start?"

"Let us start with what you already know. Tell me how God has spoken to you in the past. How has he led you to this place in your life?"

CHAPTER 40

I told him about my dream.

"When did you have this dream?" Catwg inquired.

"The day I returned from the council. The night before you came to Pawl's llan."

"Hmmm. Interesting." Catwg stroked his beard. "I wonder that you didn't mention this before."

"I didn't mention it because I was afraid. I did not want it to be true," I admitted.

"I appreciate your honesty. Yes, it is one thing to desire to hear from the Lord - many eagerly pray for it - but when he speaks fewer are keen to heed his message. One of the keys to discernment is honesty. You must be willing to be honest about what you experience, as well as what you desire. Do not be too quick to interpret. Better to take note of all the particulars before you rush to judgement about the significance of them, singularly or as a whole. Honesty is key.

"Another key is awareness," Catwg continued. "A man who is unaware of his thoughts, feelings, and desires is at the mercy of them. You must cultivate awareness of the inner workings of your heart and mind so that you might check their influence on your discernment. It is all too easy to interpret signs and experiences through the pattern of what we wish to find. Only by being aware of your predispositions and feelings can you counteract them and hold them at bay while considering what God might be saying. Awareness and attentiveness to everything around you are equally important … attentiveness to the world and everyone in it, knowing that God may speak through anyone or anything. Remember, God spoke to the prophet Balaam through an ass!" He chuckled to himself.

"A third key is faith." Catwg paused before continuing, "By which I mean the belief that there are important aspects of our world that are rarely visible or tangible. The world that is real has two main components: the world as we see, taste, and smell it; and the spiritual

192

world. A man who denies the reality of the spiritual world rarely if ever encounters it. Not because it isn't real but because he will not allow himself to see. He is like those who heard the voice of God at the baptism of our Lord but said only that it thundered. To interact with God, you must at least entertain the idea that he might exist. This is perhaps the simplest act of faith. And then we can pray like the man who brought his demon-possessed son to Jesus - 'I believe, help me with my unbelief.'

"But perhaps the most essential key for discernment is humility. You must be willing to hear not just what you desire … not just what you already think is best. You must be willing to surrender to the Father. You must be prepared to be directed. Jesus Christ said it this way - 'Unless you change and become like little children you cannot enter the kingdom of heaven.' Small children do not question the wisdom or direction of their parents; they are content to be carried wherever their mother will take them or to slip their hand in the hand of their father and be led wherever he would go. But as we grow our wilfulness increases and we are far more challenging to lead.

"Adding to these is the importance of knowing the Scriptures. Of course, in this you are already well-prepared." Catwg fell quiet, then lightly added, "I suppose I may have some things to say after all."

I chuckled, "Yes you do, and I am grateful to hear it. I like to think I am honest. I do have some knowledge of the Scriptures. And I believe I have at least a small measure of faith. It will be awareness and humility that trip me up."

"I believe you may be right in your assessment. But let me ask you this … have you never felt God move around you or speak to you? My sense, from the beginning of our friendship, is that God has been at work in and around you for some time. Perhaps you have not seen it because you were not looking for it?"

"I do not know for certain. That is part of my dilemma. I do not want to be too hasty to attribute my experiences to the spiritual world. I have felt the evil of the spiritual world in a druidic grove. Yesterday when you were speaking to me I felt my skin hot like a flame dancing on the surface. I felt something in my chest … a fluttering feeling. I have sung a song I did not know. I have prayed prayers I did not compose. But dare I name these things as divine visitations?" I queried.

"You are wise to be cautious. I do not say that you name them as divine. The first step is to be aware of them. You have mentioned a variety of experiences, and many of them have the ring of the Spirit about them. But before we burden these phenomena with divine authority we would need to weigh them … to test them and see if they are right. We compare them with Scripture. We look at the fruit of them. We consider alternative explanations. But most of all we pray.

"We pray for divine guidance. Jesus gave us the Spirit of truth to live in us and to guide us into all truth. James tells us that if any of us lack wisdom we should ask of God and he will give it. Jesus taught us that the Father loves to give good gifts to his children; but most of all, he loves to give himself to his children.

"Discernment is not just about knowing what to do. It is not a search for information. Discernment is about growing in relationship with God. The God of the universe desires to be known by all! He has chosen you and is speaking to you. Ask him to open your eyes and ears and heart to receive all that he would give you … most of all himself!"

Oh, my heart thrilled at this conversation with Catwg. I felt so encouraged. Here was a man I could learn from, a man whose passion for God and knowledge of God far outstripped my own. I was eager to join the race toward the throne of Grace. Catwg had a head start but I was keen to catch him. By running in his footsteps my journey would be quicker and easier. But that is the way of teachers - we teach others so that they might not only follow but surpass us.

In that conversation and the ones that followed, I began to recognise the ways that God had been at work in the sovereign foundations of my life. I knew the path Catwg trod was the road I must choose.

CHAPTER 41

In just a few weeks I was confident I would not be returning to the wars. Or rather, my part was shifting. I knew I must lay aside physical battle for spiritual, even as my understanding of this was still quite dim. Trynihid agreed and prayed for me as I went to talk with Pawl.

Pawl took it well. He was, unsurprisingly, disappointed ... not least because he would be riding to the wars again himself. I was sorry to have raised his hopes; but he held no grudge and freely released me from my position and pledges.

He was one of many I knew would be surprised at my decision. Without making too much of myself, I think it is safe to say that I had made a name for myself as a warrior. Changing direction made little sense to me; I could only imagine what others might think. I knew I must write to my mother and share the news of my new vocation. I did not know how she would take the news. I wondered about Brennus, Rhodri, Morgan, Cai, and Llew. I wondered most about Arthwyr.

When one comes to a fork in the road of life and chooses his way, he must face the lonely reality of parting ways with his compatriots. Sometimes the choice is made for us, as when I was taken to Avallon by my father. Other times it is thrust upon us by circumstance. But sometimes we must count the cost and turn our own feet onto a new path. I do not miss the blood or the killing, but I miss the rough camaraderie of the cohort. I miss my sword brothers even now.

Does that surprise you, my children? In the many years you have known me I have spoken little of these things. We have walked many roads and faced not a few perils of our own. I always carry you in my heart, even as I always carry them. We have shared a holy vocation to serve our King. In some ways the grisly work of fighting the Saecson was a holy vocation as well. But then I did not know you. I turned onto another path and turned away from my band of brothers for a future I could not then imagine.

With Pawl's blessing Trynihid and I made arrangements to move to Catwg's llan. Catwg was only too glad to have us both join his community. They set to work and soon built a small cottage for us. We moved in and went straight to work. Trynihid, having managed the household of a king, found it easy to manage the affairs of the llan. Catwg had known Trynihid from their childhood; she quickly found her place in the llan. The younger students were instantly smitten with her, and I sometimes caught the older students admiring her as well. She had such a natural grace about her and made all feel loved and cared for. She became a mother to many and a sister to the rest.

Trynihid could be fiery and feisty, but she was so full of joy and love. I loved her so much. She was such a gift to me. I don't know if I could have made the move from Pawl's hall to Catwg's llan without her. Sometimes I wonder if I loved her too much. God blesses the love between a man and a woman, but he is also a jealous God who does not endorse rivals to his affection.

Catwg quickly made use of me as a teacher, and I was only too glad to resume that work. The students were not all the sharpest, but they were eager; and I would take eagerness over innate talent every day. I drilled them in the rudiments of logic, writing, sums, and Scripture to lay a foundation for their mental worlds. We sang the Psalms, read the Scriptures, observed the sacrifice of Christ, and prayed often … both individually and communally.

Added to this life of scholarship and prayer was the practical work of building a community. Catwg was determined that ours would be a community of blessing. We were to care for our own needs and to bless those around us as we had opportunity. The llan itself was built on a small rise, but much of the land around it was marshy. So there was much to be done.

It was there in the practicalities of life that Trynihid proved her worth again and again. She would have made a great queen. She missed nary a detail as she looked after the llan as if it was her personal domain. Catwg was only too glad to leave the running of things to someone else so he could focus on prayer and the care of souls.

Nowhere was Trynihid's practical nature better expressed than in the effort to turn the marshes to useful purpose. She directed ditches to be dug in precise locations and angles to drain the bogs effectively. She put the bigger students to work trenching and the smaller ones to work collecting all the stones they could find in the fields. The ditches were then filled with the rocks so the water could drain easily into the river. It was ingenious.

Not only would we have more arable fields; the removal of the stones would make the ploughing that much easier and the ploughshares last much longer. Soon we would have fields of fertile soil ready to be ploughed and planted for barley.

Trynihid made arrangements for Pawl to provide seed for planting in lieu of the meat he was due to supply. I can't say that all in our company were happy with the trade, as we saw markedly little beef already; but Catwg knew it was a good trade. I suspect that some of the poor souls near the llan ate at least as well as we did, once Trynihid began looking after the kitchen. She was always generous to a fault. We never went hungry and neither did our neighbours. We didn't complain too much.

As the winter receded and spring arrived, Trynihid and I began to feel settled in our new home. Catwg, long like a brother to Trynihid, was fast becoming a brother to me as well. Whether working side by side in the fields or with the students, I saw much to be admired in my new brother. But my favourite part continued to be our conversations.

CHAPTER 42

Often in the evenings we would sit at the hearth and talk. We talked about the activities of the day and the progress of the students. Trynihid often joined us as well.

"How go the wars against stone and water, queen of the fields?!" Catwg called out as Trynihid made her way toward us across the hall one evening.

"We will batter them into submission soon enough. I have the right troops for the job," she called back while ruffling the hair of a young student still at table. "Don't forget to help clear up when you're finished, my dear," she whispered into his upturned beaming face. "These young warriors have yet to meet a challenge they will not master, am I right?!" she called out again.

The boys in the hall roared in response to her praise. They would charge through fire and rain for her and she knew it. Our people have long respected the strength of women in a way that neither the Roman nor the Saecson have. There is a strong argument to be made that the real strength of the Britons is the power of our womenfolk. I have often wondered at the ability of our women to bring out the best in us. I don't know which is stronger or more intimidating - a Briton armed for battle or the woman who sends him there with fire in his heart. From Boudicca to Brigit, Celtic women are not mere bystanders in history; they exert tremendous influence over events. Trynihid was one of these women and we were all happily in her thrall.

I fell more in love with her with each passing day … her power and her competence even more beguiling than her natural beauty. I frankly admired her as she made her way toward us across the hall; she smiled back her beatific smile and settled herself next to me, entwining her arm in mine and taking the offered cup.

"A few more weeks and the war will be won. We have turned our stony adversaries into allies. The stone-filled trenches will help to move the water and keep the field drained. The water, properly managed, will serve rather than afflict us. Then it will be ploughing and sowing. I dare say the fields will yield more than enough for eating and we should be able to keep enough to seed our fields next year and even more."

Catwg nodded, "I have no doubt. You have managed all this admirably, and we are indebted to you, Trynihid. You have fed this community not just today, but for years to come. You have blessed us and we will be a blessing to many because of you."

Now it was Trynihid's turn to beam and blush.

Catwg continued, "In all we do, I would have us be a community of blessing. We sow and reap and tend our animals to feed ourselves and bless those around us. It is right that we do so, but there is a blessing we must bring that is deeper and more needful. There is a famine for the word of God. Souls are hungry for the bread of heaven. It is good and right that we build our community in all the physical ways required. But we must also build our community spiritually; we must arm ourselves for the spiritual battle and use the divine weapons God has given us to demolish spiritual strongholds."

He paused, then looking at us with tenderness and passion he said, "I'm sorry my friends if I seem ungrateful. I tell you frankly again, I am glad you are here. You have served us in so many practical ways. Without your gifts we would not survive. And because of your labour and leadership I have been able to devote myself to prayer and the ministry of the word. There is a fire in my soul … an impatience that I fear is not from God. I so desperately want people to taste and see that the Lord is good! I want to know him and to make him known!" He paused again. "There I go preaching again. You didn't know you were going to get a sermon this night," he chuckled.

"I hear you brother. I do," I said, clapping him on the back. "I know God did not call me here to merely feed the bodies of men. He has called me to fight for our people … to fight spiritually. I fear I do not know how to wield the weapons of this spiritual war yet. But I am eager to learn. I can't say I share your passion as of yet, but I am hopeful and feel even now that perhaps the Lord is readying the hearth of my soul for such a conflagration. I feel his movement but do not yet know what it means."

"My husband and my cousin," Trynihid interjected, "May it not be that we each have our roles to play? You, Catwg, may preach. You, Illtyd, may teach. I can pray and love and lead. And we can all pray!" she added with a twinkle in her eye.

"I can feed our people and in so doing, play my part in showing the love of God in tangible ways. After all, didn't Paul write that the body of Christ has many members? We are not all mouths or eyes or feet or hands. The body needs various parts playing various roles. We will reach maturity when each part does its work, connected to the Head that is Christ. So, we may each appreciate and encourage each other in our contributions. Each of us has a way to express the heart of God."

"Truer words were never spoken," Catwg agreed. "I say you preach as well as you pray!"

"But what of these spiritual weapons to demolish strongholds?" I asked Catwg.

Catwg pursed his lips and paused before responding. "I have been thinking about that and scouring the Scriptures to see what I can discover. I am sure discernment is key. Our Lord Jesus Christ never did anything except that which the Father was doing. He never spoke any word except that which the Father gave him to speak. The impression is that he was doing miracles every day, but I don't think that is true. Over his three years of public ministry only 37 miracles are recorded. Now, John says that Jesus did more than that … but still, that is not many. We also have numerous examples of Jesus teaching. But Luke tells us he often withdrew to lonely places and prayed. Jesus lived a life of constant communion with the Father and the Spirit. He cultivated that life through lonely prayer. I do not think the weapons of divine warfare depend on technique and training, like a sword, spear, or shield. I think divine power is just that … divine."

"I think I see," I responded. "Paul said that God's power was made perfect in his weakness and that we carry around God's power and authority and presence in our jars of clay so that no one will wonder if the power is from us or from God. So these weapons are not things we can own or techniques we can master. They are expressions, manifestations of the power and presence of God through us but not by us. So then, his power is translated through us ... like the power of the horse is translated through the warrior to the spear and all that combined force carries the tip of the spear through the enemy; but the real power driving it is the horse, not the spear or even the warrior."

"Perhaps," Catwg ventured. "But in that case I would say the horse is the Father, and the warrior is the Spirit of Christ, and we are but the spear. But I would not want to push that too far. We do have choices and God has given us real power, where the spear has no choice in the matter. Paul says we are God's ambassadors and that God has entrusted to us the ministry of reconciliation. He is the one who is at work reconciling the world to himself; but we are real actors invested with real authority on behalf of his kingdom. Our choices matter."

Trynihid chimed in, "I agree. But if our choices matter, could we not then thwart the hand of God? What if God called you to do something and then you were disobedient? A warrior may be told to charge but then baulk at the order and run away. What then?"

We stopped to consider her question. A weighty silence filled the air as we searched for an answer to her honest but vexing question.

"In truth," Catwg said, "I do not know. I am sure I have failed many times, but I do not doubt that somehow the God of Heaven has things well in hand. He is working all things together for good and knows the end from the beginning. What I do know is that I would do my part. I want to know and do the will of God. I pray that when called upon I will not be unfaithful or unworthy of the calling I have received. Even then, I must throw myself upon his mercy and trust his grace to give me what I need."

"Yes, brother," I responded. "First I must know the call. I cannot obey the order until I perceive the order. But before I can understand the order I must learn the language of heaven. I suppose Jesus spoke that language natively, but it is foreign to each of us."

"Or perhaps it is the language we were born to speak but we have been avoiding the lessons all our lives. The invitation has always been there but we ducked the lessons because we didn't see the point or we just wanted to do something else," Trynihid offered.

"So we must devote ourselves to our lessons then, no less than our students must. The Spirit is our teacher and he guides us into truth. He will guide each of us into the work he has planned in advance for us to do if we will but hear and heed his voice," Catwg said.

"Yes, but that is where the difficulty lies. We circle back around to it. How to rightly discern the voice of God?!" I cried. "That is where my impatience may exceed your own."

"Have you considered the words of Luke I mentioned? 'Jesus often withdrew to lonely places and prayed.' Often. Withdrew. To where? To lonely places. He was alone. Right after his baptism he withdrew to the desert for forty days. Would you consider the same?" Catwg inquired.

"I would consider it. I will consider it."

"What might that look like?" Trynihid asked.

"I do not want to direct. I merely ask because that is what comes to mind. I have been reading Athanasius' 'Life of Antony'. He tells the story of an Egyptian Christian who gives up everything in obedience to the Spirit and lives in the desert. There he finds struggle and temptation but also Christ. Think not that a life devoted to prayer will be a comfortable life. In the wilderness Antony faces his own weaknesses and inner struggles unmitigated by the distractions of living in community. He also faces down demons. Don't think that we retreat from the world to avoid conflict or war; we retreat to fight for the world. The devil does not want people of prayer, and he will not fail to note the steps we take here. We can expect to be attacked. But fear not - we can also expect God's deliverance … whatever form that might take." Catwg looked grim.

"I have already given up so much!" I protested.

"Have you?" Catwg queried.

"You know I have!" I cried. "I am the eldest son of a noble house. I know I am young, but I know my worth. I have studied with the finest scholars. I have commanded a thousand men. I have sat at council with kings. I am a prince and could be a king, but I have left that all behind to come here. I am here in this llan and not in a place of power. I have left all that behind!"

Catwg sat mulling my words before responding. "There is something in what you say. You are a prince, as am I. But in truth what have you really lost? You have given up dreams and visions of your future. You have abandoned a future you never had for the future to which your king invites you. You craved glory. Did you not?" He looked into my eyes. "The Lord seeks to deliver you from your little dreams and invites you into a larger life of union with him. What you now experience as loss you will come to see as gain. But you have a lot more dying to do. The Lord is clearing the stones from your heart and draining the swamp of your desires. He is preparing you for planting but must drive the rough plough across your back to do so. Follow our Lord into the wilderness and see what you may find there. That is my advice."

CHAPTER 43

As Trynihid and I lay abed that night, I could not sleep. I knew even then that there was something in Catwg's challenge. But I just could not imagine how to start or what to do. As I tossed again I heard Trynihid's drowsy voice. "Sleep still eluding you, my dear one?"

"Yes, I'm sorry to disturb you."

"Is it Catwg's words that deny you sleep? Would you like to talk about it?" she offered. "Or perhaps your argument is not with Catwg but with another?"

As usual, Trynihid touched the heart of the matter. I rose from our bed and began to dress. "Yes, my love; my struggle is not against flesh and blood after all."

She turned and propped herself up on one elbow, her hair falling across her face. "I suppose it rarely is," she said with a smile. "Tell him I said hello," she added playfully before rolling back over.

Wrapping my cloak tightly about me, I left our room. Carefully latching the door, I made the short walk to the chapel. It was dark and cold inside but I was glad to find it so. I went in, lit a rush and approached the altar.

I knelt before the altar and started to pray, "Jesus, Son of David, have mercy on me." Before long, tears began to flow. I didn't even know why. There were feelings - powerful feelings - roiling inside me but I had no words. I found myself lying before the altar, my forehead on the cold stone, trying hard to listen … trying hard to hear something … trying hard to make some clarity emerge from my swirling heart.

A picture … a picture and a word formed in my mind. The word was "west," and the picture was of a small river - a brook really - running through a valley. That was all. I asked, "Was that you, Lord? Tell me more." But I had only the memory of the word and the picture burning bright in my mind's eye … no more than that.

"Surely not, Lord. Surely you must give me more than that," I muttered in the darkness.

But even then I knew it was enough. I knew it was more than God had given Abram. God called Abram to leave his people with only the vague instruction to go to a land God would show him. We don't even know how Abram knew which way to go when he set out. But we know God met him along the way.

The truth is that I knew even before I left my bed that evening. I fought against the knowing. I did not know because I did not want to know. I resisted admitting the truth. I had given up my dreams … Catwg was right about that. I had traded one form of community for another and God was calling me to follow him into the wilderness. Catwg was right about that too. I had known it from the moment he said it.

I knew I must follow the path that my Lord took into the wilderness and trust he would meet me there as he had Abram and Jacob and Moses and Antony and so many others before me.

I had walked many paths before, but each path led from one community to another. This path I knew I must walk alone. I did not know what would happen or what I would find in the wilderness.

I returned to bed sometime before dawn and settled myself down to sleep beside my beloved. I felt her shift and thought she woke, but as she said nothing, I nuzzled in and went to sleep.

When I woke the next morning, she was already gone.

I soon found her fluttering between the kitchen and the hall, looking after our rowdy band of students. Only fifteen in all, of various ages, but they were a noisy bunch. This morning the sound was not extreme as they ate their porridge and bantered before setting out early to the fields.

I watched Trynihid in the kitchen, instructing and encouraging her young charges. When I caught her eye I saw concern flit across her face as she searched mine. She motioned for me to wait, turned to take stock of the situation and confident it was all in hand, made her way over to me. Throwing her arms around me she kissed me and then pulled me into the corridor.

"I can see in your face that you did business with God. Tell me, what he said to you," she said eagerly.

"He said only one word but he showed me more. He showed me my own stubborn heart and my resistance to revelation. I saw a picture of a brook in a beautiful valley and heard the word 'west.' I know that I must leave you and go into the wilderness as our Lord left everything and went into the wilderness."

She bowed her head but kept her arms around my neck and drew me toward her. "Oh, Illtyd! I love you. I knew he was calling you and I thought it would be thus. I am so glad you are listening to him, and I want you to obey. And yet, I will miss you. God brought us together, and we have come so far so quickly. We have had only these few months together. When will you go, and more importantly … for how long?"

"I think I should go soon … very soon. Now that it is clear I feel I must. As to how long, I don't know that yet; but I would think not less than forty days."

She looked sombre as she considered. "Forty days is not that long. I suppose I could live without you for that length of time," she added playfully. There was a crash in the kitchen and young voices raised. She turned quickly toward the kitchen. "Grab your breakfast; we'll talk more of this," she called back over her shoulder as she ran back to her charges.

I found Catwg at table and settled down beside him with my porridge. He acknowledged me but made no move to speak, nor did I. We ate our oats in comfortable silence for a few minutes.

"So," I began, "with your blessing I will follow Jesus into the wilderness."

The corners of Catwg's mouth drew up for just a moment before he replied, "Has God confirmed this to you?"

"Yes, I believe so." I then recounted my experience in the chapel.

"Yes, I believe he has. That sounds like him," Catwg was grinning broadly now.

"I am concerned about Trynihid. I assume she can stay here and you will look after her?"

"She is most welcome to stay, but my guess is she will do more of the looking after than I." We both chuckled at that.

We discussed my plans and agreed that it would be better for me to leave soon rather than to delay. You see, my children … when the way is unclear it is often best to delay. But once God has given you direction any delay is disobedience. As James tells us, if you know the good you ought to do and do not do it, that is sin.

God had made it clear that I should leave the llan and head west. I supposed that the valley was either a metaphorical place, like the quiet waters in the twenty-third Psalm, or a real place I would find in the west. I did not know how far I would have to go nor what I would discover in the wilderness. I only knew that I must go without delay.

CHAPTER 44

I spent that final night in the sweet embrace of Trynihid. Not knowing when we would see each other again, we loved each other well. We held each other and whispered words of love and encouragement. We prayed together and finally fell asleep in each other's arms.

We awoke together early the next morning. Accustomed to life as a warrior, I took little time to gather what I would need and sling it over my shoulder. I took precious little with me.

Word had spread through our small community that I would be leaving, and I was somewhat surprised to find the whole llan turned out to see me off.

Catwg looked me up and down. Observing my shield on my back, he reached out and touched the spear I leaned upon. "I don't think you'll be needing these," he said gently.

"I trust I will not, but one never knows."

He paused before answering, then added, "Trust is the operative word. If you would walk into the wilderness in the footsteps of our Lord, I would encourage you to lay aside your earthly weapons and entrust yourself fully to his protection. He will not fail you."

"I trust he will not. And yet I will take them," I replied stubbornly.

"As you wish," he replied. Then he pulled me into an embrace before placing his hand on my head.

I knelt before him to receive his blessing.

"Go with our blessing and the blessing of our Triune God. May you find all the Father would show you. May you hear all the Spirit would tell you. May you feel the very presence of the Son as he walks this journey with you."

That done, I rose and walked west.

I scarcely knew where to go nor how far I would have to walk. I took no food with me, trusting in the Lord for the fast or food as he would provide. I knew water would be plentiful as it always is in our beloved but somewhat soggy land.

Taking my time, I worked my way down toward the sea and then west along the coast. There was no denying the beauty of the land. As I made my way across the tops of the south-facing sea cliffs I pressed into a crisp wind blowing off the sea. It wasn't long until the rain came … more a mist at first. I barely felt the drops but was wet through before long. Still I walked on. I was not too miserable, as I was accustomed to the weather and life in the elements.

As I marched on I reflected on other marches I had made. I remembered the faces of my sword brothers and wondered after them. Where were they now? Were they marching together through the weather toward yet another battle with the Saecsons while I marched alone?

I saw no one as I walked that day. Toward evening I could trace the outlines of the long-neglected ramparts and ditches of an ancient fort. It seems as good a place as any to find some refuge for the night. I knew then that I was drawing near Cor Tedws. Although I was not well-versed in the topography, during my time with Pawl I had heard of the ancient fort and the old Roman villa long since abandoned. The Scoti had raided the place many years before, finally destroying the last vestiges of Roman society in this area. They stole what goods and people they could carry and burned the rest. Since that time the area was considered cursed and no one inhabited it.

I turned over the long, sad history of the place in my mind as I made my shelter beneath the underbrush in the ancient ditches that evening. I stretched my cloak out among the branches to keep off the rain and channel the runoff away. I made sure to keep my shield and weapons to hand, just in case. I had no real fear in this deserted place but knew caution to be the best defence. I decided against a fire but cut some springy branches and arranged them for my bed to keep me off the damp ground. This done, I settled down for the night.

I remember praying a lot that evening. I wondered about the people who had built this ancient fort. These must have been my people. That whole area was ruled by the Silures, although rarely as a whole. The Britons are quick to unite against outsiders, but no sooner are they dealt with than we begin to divide against and among ourselves. The Silures were no different in this regard than the rest of the Britons. Would they be pleased that after all this time a son of the Silures found refuge under their ramparts once more?

I also wondered about the presence and pleasure of God. Was he pleased with me? Had I begun this pilgrim wandering as he wanted? How would I know if he was pleased? What - beyond obedience - was the point of this exercise?

I had walked west. Was that enough to make him smile? I prayed for a sign of his pleasure or blessing - a word or a picture. All I received was a steady drizzling rain. At least down in the ditches I was free from the worst of the wind.

I lay down and tried to sleep as best as I could.

CHAPTER 45

I awoke the next morning to sunlight and birdsong. The rain had stopped sometime during the night. I rose from my den and walked to the top of the old ramparts to survey in the sea and the valley before me.

The tide was high and flowing in below me, making it more tidal estuary than river valley. I noted old timbers peeking their heads above the waves. It looked to be the remnant of a ruined quay or sea wall. From the headland I could see distant land lying low across the Severn Sea. I wondered if anyone stood there looking at me. Turning my back to the sea and looking north I could see some way up the valley.

I prayed, "Oh Lord, bless me this day and guide my steps. I want to please you in all my ways. Teach me your ways that I may walk in them. I am a pilgrim in this wilderness. I would meet you here."

After my simple prayer, I gathered my things and made my way along the eastern ridge of the valley. It was slow going, as the ancient wood was a tangle of undergrowth, mostly bramble. I could understand why some counted this land as cursed. In Genesis, when God cursed Eden thorns and thistles grew where paradise had been. If this had once been a paradise, it was no more. I saw no fiery angel, but I met many a thorn that day and was none too happy as the day wore on.

Eventually I found my way down toward the river and discovered a track, most likely from wild pigs, through the brambles and bracken. I had to stoop, but at least I was no longer caught and torn by the thorns around me. I pushed further north up the valley. As I did I came out in a meadow - a small clearing really - beside the river. The water was cold and clear and flowing over the rocks into a small pool. It was a tranquil scene, and I paused to pray and to thank God for delivering me from the thorns … at least for the time being.

I drank from the river and washed my scratched face and limbs, then settled down next to the river. I lay back in the tall grass enjoying the sunlight on my face, unsure of how to spend my day. Away from the rhythms of life in the llan I found myself with no responsibilities. I didn't entirely like the feeling. I didn't know quite who I was with no obligations or expectations.

I was beginning - just beginning, mind you - to learn the lessons God had for me in the wilderness. Naked we come from our mother's womb and naked we will return to the earth. But there, lying next to the river, I found myself bare before the Lord. Without the status of a warrior or the leadership of a prince who was I? Who was I, just me alone before God? This is a question we all must face. Who am I really? When all is stripped away, who are we?

I had no clear answers, only more questions. I prayed again for guidance. I asked the Lord for help. I lay there in the sunlight and drifted off to sleep with the sound of the brook in my ears.

I awoke with a start and an awareness that I was not alone. Just on the other side of the river was a huge stag frankly staring at me. I do not know how long he had been there. Judging by the sun, I could not have been asleep long. I lay quietly, watching him watching me. After some time I slowly sat up. He lowered his head almost imperceptibly for a moment and then turned and bounded upstream. He went only about a bowshot before stopping and looking back over his shoulder at me.

I stood up and he was off again, disappearing around a bend in the river. I had no particular plans for the day so I decided to follow him. I knew I couldn't effectively track him in the stream, but if I was attentive I should be able to find where he left the river. I was not hunting; I did not know if I could fast forty days as our Lord had, but I knew my fast had just begun. I had no need of meat. I sought to be attentive; and considering that God might speak to me in any way, I decided to track this lord of the forest.

I made my way up the brook, sometimes on the bank, sometimes in the flow. It was neither deep nor rapid, and I made quick and silent work as I stalked the stag. As I went farther up the river the branches started to close above and I found myself walking through a tunnel. The sun penetrated the leafy canopy and sparkled off the water, painting the ceiling with shimmering light. The brook itself looked a mix of emerald, gold, and silver. For just a moment I lost myself and imagined I was walking on the heavenly streets of gold. Could they be more beautiful than this?

I walked on in this reverie enjoying the sounds and sights, contemplating the joys of this world and wondering how they might compare with the glories of the next one; when, following a bend in the river, I found myself in a familiar place.

CHAPTER 46

Before me stood the image I had seen in the chapel. All thoughts of the stag fled as the picture merged with the image in my mind. Every part of it aligned … from the water tumbling over a small fall, to the way the light caught a moss-covered tree spanning the banks … even the willow branches hanging down to the surface of the small pool beneath the waterfall. Everything before me exactly corresponded to the picture - the vision - I had seen in the chapel.

Yes, my children, I call it a vision now. In the chapel I saw only a picture, as I could not trace the source; but now I call it a vision. How else do you explain that I saw something I had never seen and had it burned into my mind with such precision?

I stood there in rapt wonder for I do not know how long before slowly moving forward into the scene. Reaching out just over my head, I touched the massive log spanning the brook, feeling its wet, rough bark with my hand. It was real as I supposed, but something about touching it helped to ground me in the reality of the moment.

God had led me to this place. There on the banks of the brook I knelt in prayer and thanksgiving. "Who am I that you should show me such grace, should give me such gifts? I am just a man, and you have condescended to speak to me, to show me things, to lead me here. Oh Lord, I want more. I want more of you. Show me your glory. Lead me in the everlasting way. I want more of you!"

I prayed and sang and worshipped there in that holy place. I found myself beside a pool beneath a small waterfall. Looking to the western side of the brook, I could see something up the bank. The bank sloped steeply up for a short distance before ending in a rocky escarpment covered with growth. But there in the cliffside was what appeared to be an opening obscured by some vines. I crossed the brook and found myself looking into the mouth of a cave. The entrance was narrow before broadening to a smooth floor. It was just tall enough for me to stand in comfortably, and about three times as deep as it was tall.

I knew the Lord had guided me to this place, although I was still not entirely clear why. Whatever the reason, it seemed he sent me to this cave. I set about making the cave habitable. I cut branches and used them as a makeshift broom to sweep the floor and clear the cobwebs. I gathered stones from the river and constructed a small hearth. I gathered firewood and cut branches to arrange at the rear of the cave for my bed. After a few hours I had a rustic but serviceable dwelling place. I prayed and consecrated this place to my Father's work and pledged myself anew to his service.

"Now what?" I wondered. I sat down on the edge of the cave looking over the river, listening to the sound and drinking in the shifting colours as the dusk came on. The beauty of the place was undeniable; there was a deep peace about it. I knew I had come to meet with God, and I knew he had drawn me to this place at this time but I did not know what to expect nor what to do. Precisely what does one do in the wilderness? What did Jesus do? The Scriptures tell us only that he withdrew to lonely places and prayed … and that he was tempted.

So I prayed. I poured my heart out to the Lord about my wife, my family, my friends, my experiences, and my desires. I soon ran out of words. I prayed the Psalms and Scriptures I had committed to memory. When I opened my eyes again after what had seemed many hours, I could tell from the light that very little time had passed. I must admit I was discouraged and bemused.

Prayer is both the simplest thing in the world and a skill to be developed. The smallest child can do it … the newest of new believers can do it. The essence of prayer is conversing with God - talking with the Father, Son, and Holy Spirit. Then, I still thought of it as me talking to God; I scarcely knew how to listen. True, I had heard things from him, but those were rare occasions. These divine offerings of grace came not because I had attained discernment but because he intervened and bridged the gap.

I was still but an infant, spiritually speaking. Infants make a lot of noise and communicate their needs to their parents but understand almost nothing of what is said to them. The nursing mother may coo over her babe and speak comforting words but the babe receives none of it.

The babe is only comforted when he has the teat in his mouth and gets the milk he is after. The mother knows this and is not stingy to offer herself, her nearness, and the very life she carries within her. She is not frustrated that the babe does not understand; and yet she speaks to the babe so that he will learn to understand and associate her voice with her love and her care.

So are we when we first come to believe. We understand very little and feel our needs very great. We cry out to God for rescue from our besetting sins and trials. He comes to our rescue, although we perceive very little of his voice or his purpose. We are grateful for his presence and his rescue but we are still like infants who soon forget they are cared for. As soon as another need presents itself the babe wails and demands to be fed or changed or held. There is nothing wrong with this behaviour in an infant; but God would not have us remain infants forever.

So there I sat by the riverside, praying as well as I knew how, but soon realising my lack of skill. I was reminded of my early days with Brennus, learning to fight. I readily picked up the wooden sword but did not know how to wield it. Only after much toil and effort was I prepared to take up a real sword and join the ranks in battle. I wondered how long it would take for me to wield the sword of the Spirit in prayer.

I pondered these things in my heart and mulled them over in my head as the light faded on my second night in the wilderness with only my God as my companion. I lit the fire, banking it for the night and lay myself down to sleep.

CHAPTER 47

The next morning I awoke full of purpose but still lacking direction. I knew I needed to learn to pray, but I had no teacher. Where was Scapilion when I needed him?

All those years in Avallon with Scapilion now seemed wasted to me. I know he tried to teach me more than knowledge; but I had not been ready. I took in only what was of interest to me. I loved learning but cared not for the life of the Spirit. I learned and taught the Scriptures as I learned the ways of nature from Kian or the ways of the war from Brennus. I drank in knowledge but missed the nourishment contained therein.

Nevertheless, the mental training of Kian, combined with the scriptural immersion in Avallon meant I now carried around significant portions of the holy texts within my mind. The Scriptures had been yet another realm to conquer … a tool to be mastered, not a source of spiritual enlightenment much less an invitation to intimacy with the Almighty. I found it stored away in the library of my mind. I had missed the opportunity to be tutored into intimacy with God, foolish child that I was.

I prayed that morning, but my prayers seemed useless and powerless. Disgusted at my wasted youth and squandered opportunities, I decided to spend the day exploring my surroundings.

I knew there should be an old Roman villa somewhere in this valley and I went looking for it. As I headed north along the river the forest thinned and I found more open meadows. I reasoned that these must have been fields for the villa and continued north looking for ruins, not knowing exactly what I was looking for or even why I was looking.

I had always been a man of action. Having come away into the wilderness I found myself adrift in my thoughts and feelings. Feeling the inadequacy of my prayer life and becoming aware of my squandered opportunities was hard for me. I found the silence and solitude oppressive and uncomfortable. I know now that I was searching for something to distract myself. The search itself became my distraction.

As I walked I noted the plants and signs of wildlife. Although I was fasting at that moment, I knew that would not last indefinitely. It was good to know there were food sources available. Roots, leaves, and food in abundance: pignuts, sorrel, meadowsweet, ash, elder, and the ubiquitous nettles. There were also plentiful fish and signs of deer and boar.

I continued to move north and the land continued to level out. Then I spotted a rise of ground and what appeared to be some walls. As I made my way toward it I could see it more clearly. Here had stood a villa of considerable size. It was in ruins now and looked as if it had been burned. The roofs were gone but the rooms and two large courtyards were still clearly visible. The beautiful floor mosaics were now overgrown, as grasses reasserted their claim to the land once more. I wondered after the lives of those who lived here. They must have been prosperous - even wealthy - to have had such a large house with fine floors.

They may have been very like my own family. We might even have been related. I had heard tales that those who lived here had been Christians and had spread the gospel from this place to the surrounding areas. Perhaps the faith of my family had roots in this place. I did not know, but I wondered as I wandered in and out of those ruins.

I must confess I grew even more depressed as I contemplated all this. What was the point of building a villa or a community if it was all to end in death and fire? And doesn't it all just end in death eventually? We fought the Romans, the Scoti, and now the Saecson ... but what difference did it make? We would all be food for worms in the end. The grass would grow over us all.

But just then a flicker of hope - of knowledge - flared somewhere deep inside: But it doesn't all end here. There is a Kingdom that never ends, and this world is not our home! The long and winding ways of this world always end in death, but death is not the end. Death is just a transition point, a doorway by which we enter the next world. What we do in this world matters because it matters to the one who rules all worlds. His kingdom is an everlasting kingdom; and though I may not see it fully realised in my lifetime, I will see him reign and I will reign with him.

As I pondered these things, I found myself praying for those who lived in this place. God have mercy on their souls … I did not know if they knew God but prayed for his mercy upon them. These long-dead souls may even now be sitting at the heavenly banquet, and I may join them there before too long.

As I prayed for them I was moved to pray that this place, Cwm Hodnant, might once again become a place where the kingdom of God would manifest. Perhaps this might be a thin place, a place where the veil between heaven and earth would be pierced and God's very presence and power would be made manifest. I prayed his kingdom would come, and his will would be done in this small corner of the world as it is in heaven.

These prayers did not feel powerless or useless. They felt infused with power from beyond me. I felt carried along in my prayers that afternoon. As I walked back down into the valley toward my cave abode I felt renewed.

I did not know then what I know now. I could not have predicted how those prayers would be answered. But I felt something shift in me, and possibly in the world. I felt God with me, and I knew that I must take up the shield of faith and the sword of the spirit and learn how to pray.

Over the next few weeks I devoted myself to prayer. I continued to fast and to drink only water. I felt my body but little as I focused on my soul. I felt carried along as if I were caught in the flow of a mighty current, and it was my joy to let the current take me where it would.

I did precious little beyond praying during those weeks. I did make a simple door for my abode from old man willow's long hair and affixed crude hinges and a latch to cracks in the walls with whittled pegs. This kept out most of the rain and made it feel more like a home and slightly less like a cave.

Without the need to eat and all the assorted domestic chores that come with community, my time and energy were freed for prayer. Sometimes my prayers were formal recitation of prayers from the Psalms or other Scriptures. Often I prayed prayers found in the Gospels, either those of our Lord Jesus Christ or those of others. One of my favourites, then and now, is the prayer of the blind man, "Jesus, son of David, have mercy on me." Other times I found myself wandering up or down the valley, walking along the shore, praying God's blessing on all I would see or allowing my mind to wander in the current of his love as my feet wandered over the land. These meandering times of prayer became ever sweeter to me.

With each day and each encounter my confidence grew, as did my discernment.

CHAPTER 48

Some days and nights were sweet and I enjoyed the peace and presence of God. Others were spent in bitter struggle, but I was making a start of it.

As I did I was grateful for the years of training with Scapilion and Kian. Because of these two men I found my mind was full of knowledge to use in my new endeavour. But knowledge alone is not enough.

Wisdom is the application of knowledge to life. Distilling observation into truth is a primary step and one to which we often pay little attention. Seeing things as they are is not as simple as it may seem. What we take in through our eyes, our ears, our noses, and our fingertips is the beginning of knowledge; but all of these experiences become part of our world when we integrate them. We label them and fit them into the larger story of our understanding. This sorting and labelling can only be accomplished by using the tools we have previously developed or constructed. We have these constructs in our minds, through which the river of life runs like water through a weir. The weir only catches the fish it is designed to trap, but other things flow through it uncaught.

I have come to understand the importance of discernment to the life of every Christian. It is not enough to pursue deep learning or esoteric knowledge. The knowledge of the Scriptures is of course important, and I do not mean to disparage education. I myself am a teacher and mentor to many. But this knowledge, this information, must be integrated and applied to be truly grasped. This integration takes place within us and in dialogue with the Spirit.

The longer I have lived the more I have come to realise the importance of understanding ourselves. What do I notice and why? What bothers me and why? What am I afraid of? Why do I think or act or feel the way I do? I don't have to answer all these questions but I have to at least ask them. It was during this, my first time alone in the wilderness, that God graciously awakened me to these questions. I began to pray like Augustine, "Lord, let me know myself that I may know you."

The knowledge of oneself is not an end in itself; it is another step in the journey of eternal life. Jesus taught us that eternal life is to know God. To know God, I must bring the real me into relationship with the real God. I must work hard to get to know God in and through the Scriptures first and foremost, and also through prayer. I must also work to know myself; and God alone knows the human heart. Jeremiah says that the heart of man is deceitful above all things, and only God knows the heart. God alone knows all things, and he alone can guide me into right knowledge of myself. I would not be like the man James describes who looks in a mirror and walks away immediately forgetting what he has seen. I want the Lord to show me an accurate reflection so that I may take action and live in light of what I have seen. I want to live in the light, not stumble in the darkness.

My mind was filled with the knowledge of the world and the Scriptures, but I was a novice in understanding myself. Of course I knew that I wanted things, as does any man, but my deeper motivations were unexplored, even well-defended. God gently but firmly laid siege to my heart in those weeks of silence and solitude.

As the weeks wore on and I pressed into prayer, I found myself tempted in surprising ways. I found myself angry or distracted. I often felt my desire to escape from my hermitage and return to the blessed noise of community. At times I found my loneliness to be bearable, even as I became more accustomed to the presence of God.

I missed Trynihid sorely from time to time, and often I would awake in the morning keenly aware of her absence. A few times I would have sworn she visited me in the night; but I always woke alone. On these mornings I found it hard to begin my prayers. I was tempted to believe all of this was folly. I was tempted to leave my refuge and to fly back to the comfort of community and the arms of my beloved. Once or twice, I confess I began to pack up my meagre belongings to return.

But each time as I began to do so something would call me to endure … to resist the temptation to quit or be distracted … to stay alert because the devil prowls around like a lion looking for someone to devour.

Sometimes in the night I would awake suddenly and would have sworn there was someone in the cave with me. My hand would dart for my sword or my spear, which I still kept close to hand in those days; but I could find no foe. And yet in those moments I would be seized with a violent terror that would not be reasoned away. I have felt the rush and terror of battle, but this was worse. I have seen men cleaved wide open and have done the cleaving myself, but this was worse. This was a terror that could not be seen or opposed by arms. As long as my enemy could be seen and my weapons were to hand I felt a fighting chance; but what to do when your foe is invisible but every bit as real as a Saecson warrior?

In those moments, I cried out to Jesus to save me … to have mercy … to fight for me. I was reminded of the words of Jude, the brother of our Lord, and I rebuked Satan in the name of Jesus. Sometimes the relief was immediate but other times I sat shivering in the dark and praying with wide eyes until dawn. I knew Jesus made a public spectacle of his enemies when he triumphed on the cross; and I knew that I had to resist and stand firm, and after I had done everything, to stand. I was learning how to stand and resist. I was pushing the spirit world as Brennus had made me push the rock all those years before. I am not sure how much I moved it, but I know my muscles were strengthened and my courage grew as I fought each battle against invisible foes.

And so God began my training for the spiritual war. That training continues to this day. Over the years I have found dealing with the devil and his minions quite straight forward. I searched the Scriptures and learned from Christ how to wield the divine weapons of Scripture and prayer. It would be easy to blame my trials and temptation on foes without, but the invisible enemy within was perhaps even more difficult as he would slip from my grasp. But my soul was a well-oiled wrestler in the night. No sooner would I lay hold than it would slip from my grasp and spin away into the darkness.

I also found I had little stomach for the fight. The truth is that I was comfortable with my way of life and did not really want to change. I had not done poorly for myself in this life, and I was content with things the way they were. I often found myself moaning at God and asking to be left alone. It seemed the world was full of people who were content in their sinful ways. But even as I prayed these prayers I recognised them to be lies.

Praying aloud in solitude and silence has served me well. As the words exit my mouth and come back through my ears, they seem to rerun the weir and can be caught. I heard the honest prayers of my heart and knew my heart was lying. I asked God to never leave me alone, not really … even as a part of me still desired it … perhaps it still does. I also knew enough to know that even the lords and kings I knew were not genuinely content. They were all seeking something … something beyond themselves - more land … more power … more. Their actions and attitudes exposed the true nature of their discontent.

Oh my children, may we be like Moses who forsook the sinful pleasures of Egypt because he knew there was a better treasure to be found - greater and lasting pleasure to be found - in the presence of God. The path into that presence goes through many seasons, some more pleasant than others.

The experience of God's presence is fantastic. I pray many, if not all of you, have tasted of the river of his delights. Taste and see that the Lord is good! As nursing infants we taste the sweetness of our mother's milk and enjoy the warmth of her nearness. But there comes a day for every infant when, because of the love of the mother for the good of the child, the weaning arrives. The mother denies the child what he has rightly known because it is time for the child to grow and to move onto other foods.

Similarly, the child's every cry and whim is no longer catered to. No loving parent will immediately give them everything they want when they demand it. The child must learn to move and to walk to obtain what they desire.

And so with us, God meets us first as infants and meets us as our Saviour. He nurtures us until we are ready to learn to walk. In those weeks in the wilderness God nurtured me, but also moved some distance to teach me the necessary perseverance and endurance for the spiritual journey.

As I neared the end of my forty-day fast in the wilderness, it became clear to me that I was only scratching the surface. I felt the call of God to the life of Antony. I wanted to live in the desert - the wilderness - and devote myself to him alone. I could not go back, not yet.

CHAPTER 49

I could not leave my hermitage and return to the wider world, but neither could I continue my fast.

I still felt strong enough but was aware that my body was leaner than when I had set out. I broke my fast slowly with mushrooms before adding greens, fish, and whelks to my diet. The whelks and limpets were easy to collect upon the beach, and I constructed a simple weir in the river for fish.

I no longer carried my weapons with me. Aside from a knife for daily use I had no need of weapons. I lived simply and the Lord met my requirements from the forest, river, and shore. I carried on my life of prayer and struggle in the valley I came to think of more as my home. Over the next days I felt my strength returning and ventured farther afield on my daily prayer walks.

Some weeks later as I stood upon the headland near the ancient trenches of the old fort, I noticed a currach on the sea below. It appeared to be carrying ten or twelve Britons. I raised my hand and prayed God's blessing on their journey. They must have noticed me, for they turned their boat toward shore and laid on their oars. I made my way down to the beach and arrived along the banks of the river just as they were leaping ashore and tying up the boat. As they brought their craft ashore, I counted eight warriors, four sailors, and a somewhat green-looking but finely dressed older man.

The warriors initially greeted me warmly and I them, but the green-looking man, once he had the firm ground under him again, fixed me with an officious-looking glare. Overlooking his rudeness - which was not easy for me in those days - I welcomed them and offered what hospitality I could. "I confess I have but little, but what I have you are welcome to. I have not yet checked the weir today, but I suppose God knew you were coming even if I did not. I suspect he will have furnished all we shall require."

The official, whose pale green tinge was looking slightly pinker at this point, found his voice, "And who are you to offer us hospitality? Who gave you permission to fish this river? Who are you, and who is your master?"

"I am happy to answer all of your questions. Shall I take them in order?" I replied with a grin. He did not return my smile but I could see the warriors and sailors over his shoulder and they were smiling, if cautiously. "I offer you hospitality as one child of God to another. The Lord Jesus Christ himself has invited me to this valley, and I presumed the fish were included in his invitation. As to who I am, I am Illtyd ap Bicanys, servant of the High King of Heaven, and I am pleased to make your acquaintance. And who might you be?"

"I am Cyflym, steward of King Meirchion of Gorfynydd upon whose land you stand. I have never heard of you and am quite certain you have not been granted permission to build a weir nor eat the king's fish. The king has entrusted me with the management of his affairs, and I have granted you no such permission. I command you to dismantle this weir and be gone from these lands, gods or no gods. You can serve your 'king' elsewhere," he sneered.

The warriors shifted uneasily. I could tell they did not like this man, but they did recognise his authority. And yet they seemed troubled for some reason. I decided to test the man.

I looked him boldly in the face. "I will serve the High King of Heaven wherever he directs me. I have served him on the battlefield with Arthwyr and I now serve him here. He has directed me to this valley through visions and words. I have resisted trials and temptations you know nothing of, and I will not be so easily be blown off the course he has set for me. As to the weir, I see no reason why it should trouble you or your king, but I am happy to dismantle it if you wish." I moved toward the river and made to pull out the stakes forming the weir, but as I approached I was surprised to find many fish within. "Well!? Come and see!" I gestured for them to look into the weir.

The official didn't move, but his men did not so easily suppress their curiosity. They rushed over to the riverbank. The weir was fairly teeming with fish. "I have never seen it so full. Truly the God whom you mock must love you to provide such an abundance for your visit.

I tell you, I have used this weir for weeks and have never seen it thus. It has furnished me with a fish or two each day, but never like this. Here, come and help me."

One of the sailors grabbed a net from the boat and with the warriors help we soon had a fair pile of fish on the bank. "Please take these fish back to your king as a gift from Illtyd ap Bicanys. Tell him I mean no offence." I turned and began to dismantle the weir, pulling up the stakes and throwing them into the river. I knew it would take me only a few hours to make another one should the need arise.

"You cannot give a gift you do not own!" Cyflym barked. "These are the king's fish, and I seize them in his name. As for you, I command you to leave this land, or we will seize you too and take you to the king."

I turned toward the obnoxious little man. "Will you now? You would haul me bodily before your king for what charge? What crime have I committed that would give you the right to arrest a freeborn Briton on the land of his ancestors?" I knew he had overreached himself.

"Will you leave or won't you!?" he demanded.

After pausing to pray once more I replied, "I will go. God himself called me to this valley but he called me here to talk with him, not to debate with you. I will return to Catwg's llan. If you or your king wish to charge me with any crime you will find me there. I give you my word."

This seemed to satisfy him. The warriors gathered the fish into baskets as the sailors turned the currach and prepared it for running. Within but a few minutes they were on their way. I prayed a blessing on them - most of them anyway - with a heavy heart. Before they reached the sea I was making my way back up toward my humble abode.

It was too late to set out that evening. As I lay down to sleep I thought about the strange and sudden end to this season. God called me here, and I had resisted every temptation to leave. The vision of the river near the cave came again into my mind. I can still see it in my mind's eye, even now. It is burned in my memory. Surely God's direction had been unequivocal.

But now I felt a deep peace about leaving. God had met me here and I felt he was not done with me or with this place. Even so, the time for my departure had come.

CHAPTER 50

I awoke the next morning to see the sun shining through my woven willow door. I had grown to love this sweet and simple life. It was not without some sadness that after these many weeks I prepared to return to Catwg's llan and my dear wife, Trynihid. I had set out for forty days of fasting, and that had stretched into nearly four months in the wilderness.

I swept and closed up my little hermitage, lashing it shut against I knew not what. I made my way down to the sea along the now-familiar paths, better marked by many days of use. I wondered how long it would be until I returned. It really was an unspoiled paradise of wilderness to me now. The brambles and thorns were still there but it had become a place not only of trial but also of sweet fellowship with God. Perhaps it was just my folly, but it seemed the very atmosphere had changed during those days.

It took me the whole of the day to make my way back east then north to the llan. It was dusk as I crested the rise and laid my weary eyes upon the community. The southern fields came into view first, and I was pleased to see the crop already well along. I noticed new barns had been built to receive the grain. I also saw beehives. It seemed that my wise Trynihid had been busy in my absence, using all her gifts to bless.

I suddenly found myself aching for her arms again and knew it now as no sin or distraction. I hurried along and found the community at table in the hall. I spotted my sweet Trynihid among them but as I made to sneak up behind her, holding my fingers to my lips to silence the boys who had spotted me enter, something gave me pause. Something in her shape seemed different.

One of the young boys let out a whoop and pointed at me. Trynihid spun around, spotted me, threw her arms wide and hurried toward me. I pulled her to me and felt the warmth of her body pressed against mine. Something was definitely different. Holding her from me I looked down to discover her swollen belly. My eyes swept up from there to find her nodding at me with tears in her eyes. My own, my love, was pregnant and well along by the look of things.

Trynihid's belly was not the only part of her that had swollen in my absence. She was rounder in every regard and full of life. She was beautiful! As I took in this new form of beauty, my eyes rose again to hers. She was happy, but there was a question in her eyes.

"Oh, my love!" I exclaimed. "You are with child! You are so beautiful! Look my friends, we are to have a baby!"

They all laughed. In my exuberance I had forgotten that this was hardly news for them. They had watched the slow transformation of my love from maid to matron while I had been away. It now seemed I had been gone too long and missed too much.

"Oh, my darling! I am sorry I have been gone so long. If I had known …"

Trynihid placed her hand over my mouth and drew me into the corridor. "Shhh. You have returned and you are glad. That is all that matters now. I was afraid you might be displeased to find me … so … like this."

"Displeased?! No, my love! Never! God has blessed us with a child and I am all gratitude and happiness. And you have never looked lovelier."

"Really? Do you think so?"

"I really do. You are the most beautiful woman I have ever seen. Your pregnancy changes your shape but not your beauty."

She kissed me then, and I knew I was home. But I did not know how to reconcile the home I felt in the hermitage with the home I felt here. I seemed to belong in both places.

We went back into the hall and my sweet love served me while I told them about my time. They were surprised to hear that my hermitage was a mere day's walk to the west. They had discussed it in my absence and thought perhaps I had walked all the way to the western sea. I had been gone for a long time.

In my absence, the llan had continued to grow. There were a few new faces among them.

I remember the wheat was nearly ready for harvest when I returned. It had scarcely been planted when I went. My wife was heavily pregnant and I had not known her to be so when I left. She must have been, for I had no doubt of her faithfulness and she was far along but not nearly ready to birth.

Later that evening she shared with me about her life while I was gone. She had suspected she was pregnant before I left but was not sure and did not want to trouble me. A few weeks after I left, she had consulted with Rhiannon, a wise woman who often served as midwife to those in the area. Rhiannon confirmed her suspicions and congratulated her. Rhiannon had been visiting and looking after Trynihid ever since.

Rhiannon lived in a nearby settlement and frequently came to help or to request help. She was an old woman to my eyes but I suppose she was younger then than I am now. Interesting how our perspective changes over time. Rhiannon was widely respected and I recognised in her some of the craft I had learned from Kian.

Once when she was visiting to check on Trynihid and obtain some lard she needed, I admonished her to invoke no ancient gods in the care of Trynihid. She just shook her head and responded, "You have nothing to fear from me, young Illtyd. You pray for her and me both. I believe in Christ the same as you, but that doesn't mean there isn't something in the old ways worth remembering."

I agreed with her, and we talked about my training in the old ways at the knee of Kian. She nodded slowly and seemed pleased. I then shared the dark path he had taken. She frowned and nodded. "You'll have no trouble from me. Come, bless me. I welcome your blessing." She grabbed my hand and put it on her head. I smiled and blessed her. Then, beaming up into my face she made one last rather emphatic nod, turned on her heel with deceptive alacrity and made off toward the kitchen, leaving Trynihid and me both laughing. Just before she was out of our room she turned and said, "Oh, and I believe you are carrying a boy. Just thought you might want to know." She was gone before we could reply.

I wrapped my beloved Trynihid in an embrace. She smiled and asked, "Would that please you, my love, to have a son?"

"It would … but then it would please me to have a daughter as well," I answered, then added, "I do not pray for a son. I pray for our child and for you. I pray for God's blessing on our family and our future together. Beyond that I am content."

Chapter 51

After four months on my own it was good to be back in the community, but it took some getting used to. The simplicity and silence of my hermitage were replaced by the noise and activity of the students. We worked in the fields, studied in the hall, prayed in the chapel … and did all of it together.

Catwg and I spent many evenings discussing my time with the Lord in the wilderness. He encouraged me. "You are on the right track, my friend. God is revealing himself to you and is drawing you ever onward. You have experienced the trials of solitude and silence. You have faced your demons but now you must put your lessons to work in community. We may think of ourselves as more holy than we are until we are faced with the frustrations and foibles of others. Although, I am pleased to hear how peacefully you responded to Cyflym. That must have been a rude interruption to your silence."

He shook his head slowly, gently laughing to himself as he imagined the situation. "Sometimes I think God has a wicked sense of humour!" He clapped me on the shoulder then added more seriously, "Meirchion is my uncle, and Cyflym is an obsequious little man who lords what little power he can find over everyone around him. But he is a more learned man than my uncle who is more naturally a warrior than a king. Even as a child, they called him Meirchion the wild."

"I wonder he did not join the wars," I commented.

"There is no wonder there. Meirchion did not go because he saw no personal profit to be gained. You will find many of the kings here in the west are the same. They look to the defences of their own lands and fear the Scoti more than the Saecson. Maybe they are right. Time will tell. No, Meirchion did not go for the same reason my father did not go. Of the four brothers only Pawl answered the call."

Catwg and I had many conversations about many things. But most of them were about the Lord. It was in that season that Catwg laid his hands upon me and gave me the tonsure. I became a priest in the church of God.

Over those months, although revelling in my happiness, I observed a change coming over Catwg. He seemed ill at ease … almost restless. When I questioned him he put me off, often asking after Trynihid and the child growing day by day inside her. He frequently expressed his gratitude for our presence in the llan.

We brought in the wheat in mid-summer. We had the right combination of rain and sun to plump the heads of grain and perfectly dry weather for the mowing. It was a glorious harvest. We felt blessed by God in every way.

As August approached the weather grew even warmer. The bees grew drowsy and it was time to harvest their delicious honey. Trynihid and Rhiannon oversaw the collection of the honey and the making of the mead. A few young hands made off with bits of the comb but the women pretended not to notice. They were always careful to insist that the combs when empty were returned to the bees. That fed the bees and cleaned the wax, which we then used to make candles for worship.

While the bees enjoyed the heat, Trynihid did not. I remember my sweet wife being as cranky as an old badger as she tossed and turned, unable to get comfortable in our bed. There were times in the night when I admit I wanted nothing more than sleep and our bed seemed much smaller than I remembered it. And my bedmate seemed less pleasant than I might like. I was filled with compassion … but not always. The combination of her swollen belly and the hot weather made her miserable. I could only imagine what she was going through as I marvelled at the miracle of life and the strength and perseverance of my sweet love. It is no small thing to submit yourself to pregnancy.

Finally the day arrived. Trynihid's water broke one morning and Rhiannon was sent for. She came with a few other women in tow. The boys were shooed out into the fields and told not to return until they were sent for. I'm sure they didn't mind.

Catwg stayed with me in the hall. We could hear Trynihid crying out from time to time. I have seen brave men in battle, but there is a bravery in women as they struggle and fight to bring life into this world that astounds me. I spent hours that day praying and fretting and praying some more. I was filled with a strange mix of excitement and anticipation, mixed with fear. The most precious person I knew was sweating and labouring to bring my child into the world.

As the morning wore on I did not know what to think. Rhiannon occasionally appeared and offered encouragement. "Don't you fret now. This is her first baby; it sometimes takes time. You keep praying and she'll do the rest."

As the afternoon moved toward evening, my excitement and anticipation gave way to fear. Catwg suggested we walk over the chapel for prayer. Sitting in the hall was doing us no good, so I readily agreed.

Rhiannon found us coming out of the chapel as dusk was coming on. "You better send for the boys and see them to bed." Catwg quickly left with a nod. "I don't know how much longer this is going to take." She looked me square in the face and said flatly, "And you better pray. Unless God does something, we may lose them both. Trynihid is a fighter, but something is wrong and she has started … well, never you mind. Just pray."

I had never felt more powerless. Rhiannon is not a woman easily perturbed, and she had delivered many babies in her time. I saw the fear in her eyes. If she was concerned, I was terrified.

I don't remember exactly what happened next, but I do remember laying on my face in the chapel and begging the Lord Jesus to intervene. I begged the Father to deliver my wife and child from death. I begged the Spirit to breathe life into both of them and to guide Rhiannon and the women. I dare say I never prayed with more fervour, before or since. I do not know how long I prayed.

The candles burned down and night had fallen. I only remember the light coming in when the door was opened. I heard footsteps approaching and I raised my head, rubbing the tears from my eyes. Rhiannon kneeled beside me. She placed her hands on my shoulders and tears fell from her eyes as she said, "They are gone from this world, dear heart. The struggle is over." Then she pulled me into her embrace, and we wept together there on the floor in the darkened chapel.

CHAPTER 52

It wasn't just my wife and child that perished … something in me died that night.

I don't remember much about those days. I remember stroking her face, the face of my beloved. She looked so very tired. Peaceful but exhausted and pale. So pale.

I remember someone trying to place my dead son in my arms. Yes, Rhiannon had been correct. But my son never breathed the air of this world. He was tangled in the very cord that should have brought him life. They were bound together even in death. I would not hold him. My heart had no place to cradle death. I wanted no dead son; I wanted my son alive.

I remember we buried my wife and my son. They tell me many came from far and wide to honour her memory. As a princess in a royal house she was widely known. As a woman and a servant of God, she was dearly loved by all who knew her … none more than myself. I had no time, no interest in greeting the people. Some may call it rude, but my heart had no space for anyone.

Oh, that broken heart of mine was excruciating! My children, be kind to the broken-hearted. There are more of them in the world than you may imagine. Surely we rejoice with those who rejoice; but we must also weep with those who weep. I had no patience for those who issued platitudes. How could I sit and exchange pleasantries with kings or princes or endure the gossamer words of priests?

I often woke from sleep with the feeling that I had just drifted off, and my pregnant wife still lay beside me. I reached for the warmth of her presence but found nothing. My bed was cold like my heart. In those first few days I felt nothing … or nearly nothing. But with each new morning came the realisation hardening within that this was indeed happening to me. It wasn't just a bad dream; this was a nightmare from which I could never escape. As this terror hardened into reality my heart hardened with it. It hardened and burned as the nothing was replaced with rage.

Catwg was my constant companion in those days, Catwg and Rhiannon. Rhiannon cared for me like the lost child that I was. I could not have asked for a better mother in those days of blinding grief. Everything in those days was a haze, but I remember Rhiannon and Catwg and their silent but caring presence.

After all the guests had left, life in the llan began to resume its rhythms. I stomped around the llan furious that life should just carry on for anyone without Trynihid.

One day I found myself standing in the kitchen screaming at a boy who had dropped a dish. It was only an accident, but my pain flared out at his momentary clumsiness. I fear I would have beat him had Catwg not been close to hand and restrained me. I nearly turned on Catwg as well. I was not in my right mind. I reached for a nearby rolling pin to vanquish my foe. But Catwg propelled me through the door, into the corridor.

I rounded on him with my fists balled up, prepared to beat him into submission. But Catwg stood tall and firm in the door neither cowering nor threatening. His face was set like flint for whatever storm might blow his way but his eyes were full of compassion. It was the eyes that saved us from something we would both have regretted.

I howled with rage and ran outside. At first my feet carried me toward the chapel, but I refused them. I would not go in there! The place reeked of death to me. Suddenly the whole llan felt like death. I knew I could stay there no longer.

I made my way to our cottage and began to gather my things. I paused, surveying the room and wondered about the life I would never have. Everything around me called out her name. Her scent still clung about the place. Her clothes still hung in the corner. Things for her hair, her rings and bracelets lay on the table where she had left them. The flowers and herbs she had hung for drying dangled from the rafters. The rough-hewn cradle for the baby still sat in the corner. It took all my self-control not to smash it all to bits. I knew then that I was leaving and I was never coming back.

Before too long, Catwg appeared at the door. He watched me in silence as I shuffled about the room gathering my belongings. "Don't be hasty, my brother."

I dropped my chin to my chest and replied, "I don't believe this is haste. I simply cannot stay here. The life I thought I had is gone. This llan reeks of death to me now. I cannot stay."

"I understand. I thought this day would come but it feels too early to me. I would that you stayed but a bit longer and we could break this silence of death together."

"I am glad for your friendship and for what you have done for me and for my family," I responded, my voice made husky by the raw emotion in just pronouncing the word "family." I struggled to lay hold of my feelings for some minutes before continuing. I dashed the tears from my eyes with my fists and added, "I must go. I will go. Please don't try to stop me." I moved to return to my packing.

"I will not stop you; but before you go there is something you should know." He paused. When I looked into his face he continued, "I will not be here when you return."

I was frankly shocked. "What do you mean?"

"I will go to Scotia; I have been planning it for some time. I had intended for you and Trynihid to care for the llan in my absence. But that is not to be. The church of Christ is growing; I feel a burning in my heart and an itching in my feet. They are building great communities of faith … communities of learning and blessing. I did not have your years at Avallon, and I have envied you. I feel I must go and learn from our brothers and sisters all the Lord would teach me. Would you stay and provide leadership for this little flock?"

"You know I cannot. How can you ask me this?!" My anger flared up again.

"I understand, but I had to ask. I see no one else." He raised his hands gently before him to pacify me. "I do not understand what God is doing," he added sadly.

"It seems everything is dying." I found my fists at my side again. With great effort, I forced my hands open, shaking them as if I could fling the anger from my soul like water droplets from my fingers. "I will stay to help you until you go if you need me," I offered weakly.

"Thank you, but that will not be necessary. I will make arrangements with Pawl's household to see the boys home, and provide for them. We have animals and grain. They will return with more in their pockets and their heads than they brought with them. I trust God has worked in their hearts as well."

I made no reply. I did not want to speak of God.

"Pawl has sent word. As you know, he is away with Arthwyr. He wants you to know you are still like a son to him. You are always welcome, always a part of his family. He requests you to return to him if you will, when you will."

Dear old Pawl … he was such a good man. I smiled as I replied, "Please thank him for me. The day may come when I will enjoy his hospitality again, but not now. I cannot return to that world and I cannot stay in this one. I will flee into the wilderness like Moses. Perhaps I will find the Lord there as he did, or perhaps I will find only more death. Whatever it may hold, I know that is where I will go."

"Then go with my blessing and my heart." Catwg embraced me and I was glad for it. Then he slowly turned and walked out the door, leaving me to my packing.

As I turned back to the task at hand, I discovered how very little I needed or wanted to pack. The best of Trynihid's jewellery had been buried with her. From our life together, I took only the cup we shared at our wedding. The beautiful cup had been gifted to us by Pawl, and we had pledged to drink whatever God would pour into it.

I wrapped it and put it in my saddlebag as the one memorial to my beloved and our shared life. Everything else connected to her I left to be distributed as Catwg saw fit. I took only my personal possessions - clothing, bedding, weapons, tools, and utensils. I found myself thinking in terms of what I would need on campaign ... what I would take if I were going to war.

I stacked my bags outside and turned for one last look. My heart was breaking as I reached in and closed the door for the last time.

CHAPTER 53

I saw Catwg once more that day. After saddling and loading my horse Glew in the stable, I found our little community assembled outside.

I went over to the boy from the kitchen and apologised for my temper. I asked his forgiveness, which he freely gave, and kissed him on the head. He was not more than five or six. I then said goodbye to each in turn. I knew - although they did not as of yet - that this was the last time this particular community would ever be together. Trynihid's death brought the end of many things.

As I mounted they began to sing Psalm 23. Such a beautiful blend of voices and message. I have never forgotten the way it wafted over the hills to me as I rode away west. We are a people blessed with music and faith, and when those come together it is a balm to the soul.

I arrived in Cwm Hodnant while the sun was still high in the sky. There was no room in my cave for a horse, but there were small clearings near enough with plenty of forage in the late summer. After leading Glew through the river to the cave and unloading, I led him to the nearest clearing and set to work. I knew he would not want to go far from me, but neither did I want to search for him in the morning. I walked around the meadow with him and then hobbled him in the middle of the field before making my way toward my new home.

It was good to be back in my cave. I was pleased to find it much as I had left it. It appeared that no one had disturbed it in my absence. I had returned with all I would need to make it into a more comfortable abode. I decided to focus first on creating a shelter for the horse. Improvements to my house could wait. I wanted to build a stable and paddock for Glew before the weather turned.

The next morning I rose early and found him as I had left him. Glew was pleased to see me, and I was grateful for the simple companionship of my trusty horse. I took off his hobble and let him wander a bit as I worked. The meadow I had selected was the nearest to my cave. The river ran close to the escarpment on one side with the field on the other side. I supposed the area might flood in the winter or early spring, so I decided to build the stable away up the bank on the steep side of the river. This would mean it would be on the same side of the river as my hermitage and accessible to me in every season.

Over the next few weeks I split timber and built a simple but sturdy shelter using the cliff as the rear wall. I dug out a flat floor and drove the timbers into the ground like the wall of a palisade. I wove willow and hazel then coated it with a mixture of mud, hay, and dung to make solid walls able to withstand the rains that were sure to come.

That done, I cleared a pathway through the forest from the stable to my door and then went to work to fence the meadow near the stable as a paddock. I used the trees around the pasture for my posts and used saplings and branches to create simple rails all the way around, leaving just a small opening that I closed with a woven willow gate. It was little more than a bowshot from my abode.

Then I set to with my sickle to store up fodder for the horse for the winter, cutting it and leaving it to dry in the meadows before bundling it and storing it in the rafters of the stable.

The truth is that I was happy for all the work. Working hard and solving problems allowed me to ignore myself and my God. I was tired enough most nights that I had very little time to think before sleeping. Occasionally, when I found myself staring into the fire or lying in bed, I felt the pricking of the Spirit … the gentle invitation to talk to him about what had happened. But I turned away his advances and kept my stony silence.

I did not want to talk with him. I did not want to feel at all.

As summer turned toward autumn the weather continued to be unseasonably warm. I took to riding Glew on the shore. The sea, which in high tide rushed up and banged itself against the cliffs, receded a bow shot or more exposing the sandy bed of the sea. One of my few joys in that long dark season was to ride down the shore as fast as possible. The rush of wind and water, horse and man, almost made me entirely forget myself. Almost.

It was on one of these rides along the shore that I spotted the currach. I made good speed back to my hermitage, not knowing if I had been spotted. But not wanting to be thought to be cowering, I bedecked myself for battle and rode slowly back down the valley to see what would come. In truth, I relished the idea of a fight.

The currach must have spotted me, for by the time I reached the shore they were already pulling up onto the sand. I rode slowly down to meet them but did not dismount.

I was greeted somewhat apprehensively by a small party of three warriors and two boatmen. As they clamoured out of the boat I recognised one of the warriors from their previous visit. He was a tall man with dark hair and a savage scar from his right ear and down onto his neck. He stepped forward to address me. "Illtyd ap Bicanys, I see you have returned to the lands of our king. Are you perhaps riding through?" he offered hopefully.

"I am not," I firmly replied.

He shifted his weight back and forth, seeming to weigh his options while testing his footing on the sand. "I see you are armed for battle. Do you expect trouble? You will have none from us this day. I remember the way your God provided a feast of fresh fish on our last visit. I have no doubt you are highly favoured by the Christ."

"Am I!?" I scoffed.

He studied my face for a moment. Glew, sensing my anger and desire for battle reared up, but I soon brought him firmly under control.

"We have heard of your loss, my lord. Trynihid was kin to our king, and we grieve with you; but I must report your presence to Cyflym and the king. I do not know what they will do. What will you do? What shall I tell them?"

"Tell them I am in Cwm Hodnant, alone but for my horse. I request the king leave me to my grief. I mean to trouble no man; but neither will I be troubled nor driven from this place until God himself releases me." Then, thinking perhaps more clearly for a moment, I removed one of the golden armbands Arthwyr had given me on my wedding day. "What is your name?"

"I am Owain ap Mor, battle chief of the king's household."

"Owain ap Mor, take this to the king for me." I flung the armband to him and he caught it deftly in one hand. "Tell him that I beg he will grant me to live upon his lands in peace. I make no other claim upon him nor his land. This valley lies fallow and unused. Surely he can allow a man to find solace in this wilderness. Ask him to remember Trynihid his niece fondly as I surely do."

I could stand it no more. My heart burned in me at the mention of her name. I turned and galloped away up the beach once more. I had to lose myself before I turned my rage against those men. I would not be a murderer. Of course I had killed in battle; but to run men down on a lonely beach when unprovoked would be another matter. Glew and I galloped along the beach until my anger had calmed and he was worked into a lather. "I'm sorry old friend," I whispered into his ear. "I'm sorry."

I turned his head toward the cwm and allowed him to set his own pace. I leaned down upon his neck and wept.

CHAPTER 54

I wept for my love. I wept for my child. I wept for myself. I wept bitter, angry tears and felt the raw pain of her death again as if for the first time.

When I came to myself, Glew and I were standing in the paddock. Glew, my one remaining companion, had faithfully brought us back … back to where we belonged. I swung down from his back and busied myself with his care, muttering to myself as I rubbed him down. It felt good to care for him, to be rooted in the feel and smell of his living presence. I cursed myself and apologised again for my callous use of him on the beach. It is one thing to ride hard when needs must, but another to drive an animal to exhaustion for no good reason … or for a selfish one.

After feeding and watering him I made my way back to my hermitage and threw myself upon my rough bed. I reached out for sleep but it eluded me. I didn't care to eat. I didn't care at all. I just wanted to sleep, to find the nothingness, the respite that sleep provides.

"Will you not even give me that!?" I huffed. "Having taken everything from me and driven me into this wilderness, will you even deny me the rest of sleep!?" I spat the words toward heaven.

It was the first time I had consciously addressed God since Trynihid's passing. It was not much of a prayer, but even my harsh questioning was a beginning.

I have often found the hardest part of prayer is starting. Overcoming the barrier to begin conversing with the one from whom we have been estranged seems insurmountable until it is done. Then, once the talking starts the conversation can continue on whatever line it follows.

I took the conversation no further that night. I could almost feel God's presence in the room, waiting for me to speak, patiently waiting for me to turn towards him. I refused. Like a petulant child I turned my face to the wall and clenched my jaw. I lay there refusing to listen, refusing to feel, refusing to respond to the gentle invitation. Finally I was wrapped in the quiet arms of sleep.

But I had no rest that long night. Every time I slept I dreamt. I had no sweet dreams. I do not remember them all, but some of those dreams stay with me even to this day. I saw Trynihid shaking her head at me, disappointed. I saw an infant reaching out for me across an abyss. I was tossed in a stormy sea with waves crashing over me. I was surrounded by foes on a battlefield. No matter how many I slew they rose again. All hope was lost as they crushed in against me. All night long rest eluded me even when sleep did not. When I awoke once more from one of these tortured tableaus I was not sad to find the pale dawn light creeping in.

I rose from my bed as tired as I had begun. A sense of fate or providence hung over me. I knew I could find no rest apart from God, and yet my heart rebelled. I just did not want to talk to him nor hear from him. But my emotions got the better of me and I found myself speaking aloud the feelings I had not dared to feel.

"What is the point?" I softly ventured. "What difference does it make? They're dead. Nothing I say or do will bring them back. I begged you to save them. I begged you. You are supposed to be a good father, but what father allows his children to suffer and die when he can do something about it? All that I know about you now tastes like ashes. I want to spit you from my mouth. But here I am talking to you all the same. What do you have to say for yourself?!" I challenged.

Nothing.

No thunder. No lightning. Nothing.

Just the sound of the creek and the soft rain slowly soaking the land.

"I know you are real. I have seen too much to deny you. But I don't trust you. I did not seek or even ask for Trynihid. You gave me this sweet gift only to dash it from my hands and shatter it before my very eyes. What kind of man does that? What kind of God does that!?"

Still only silence.

"Have I displeased you? Oh, I know I have. I am all too aware of my failings, but for which one did she have to die … did they have to die? And if not because of me, then for what? Explain yourself to me!" I screamed into the heavens.

"Here I am," I continued, "trapped in this wilderness. I know you have brought me here. I know I cannot be anywhere but here, but I do not know why. I do not understand! If I but knew your purposes … if you would just explain to me your reasons. Show me the plan, the pattern. I acknowledge you as King of kings and Lord of lords. I cannot go forward, and I cannot go back."

But there, at that moment, a thought started to grow in me. I could go back. I knew Pawl would take me back. Catwg's last words to me assured me that the path back to Pawl … to Arthwyr … to arms, lay open to me. I had but to turn my feet on to the road and I could resume the life of a warrior. There is great clarity and a kind of simplicity in the life of a warrior. It is a rough and dangerous life but it is grounded and solid. The rules are clear. You will fight. You must kill. You may die. You feel the heft of your weapons and you test your mettle against your enemy. It is blood and sweat, iron and wood. In the rush of combat, there is precious little time for reflection or wonder.

Is it simpler … or does it only seem so?

I renewed my assault. "So, High King of Heaven, shall I serve you once more as a warrior amidst the host of Britannia? I see nothing for me here. What am I accomplishing in this forgotten valley in this neglected land?"

I heard movement outside of my cave. I silently reached for my sword. Quietly pushing open the door, I peered out into the morning light.

The soft rain misting down, and the babble of the brook greeted me. Then I heard it again - movement in the brush just upstream. Now something moving in the water. Hooves on stone. I lay aside my sword and grabbed my spear. The antlers came into view first - a huge rack followed quickly by the head of the proud lord of the forest. I readied my spear as the stag was close enough now that I could smell his musky presence. He must have scented me as well because just at that moment he turned and fixed me with his princely gaze.

We looked into each other's eyes, neither attacking nor defending, for I do not know how long.

I slowly lowered my spear and lay it gently beside me. We solemnly regarded each other. I moved slowly out of the cave, grabbing a fist full of grain as I did so. I sat just on the lip of the entrance, cautiously extending my hand to offer a palm-full of grain. He regarded me coolly, looking from my face to my hand and sniffing. I rose slowly from my perch and inched closer until we were nearly touching. I poured out my handful of grain on a smooth stone before him and slowly retreated. He eyed me again for just a moment before lowering his grand head and nibbling the grain. After a moment the food was gone.

He raised his head to me again as if to ask for more. I grinned at his boldness and reached back into the cave, retrieving another handful. This time I placed it further up the bank, closer to my cave. He took a few tentative steps toward me before lowering his head and helping himself to the grain. I reached out an empty hand towards him as if to stroke his nose, when suddenly he leapt to the side and was gone, into the forest again.

CHAPTER 55

Oh my children, life is full of mystery. I long for clarity and understanding, but the longer I live the more I am forced to make my peace with mystery. There are so many things that are beyond our ken. Everything in creation naturally aligns itself with our all-good, all-wise Creator. The heavens and the seas declare his majesty and power. Only for humanity - and perhaps the angels – is there a choice. We can obey or disobey. We can choose to glorify God and worship him. We can also choose to disobey. The stag has no such choice.

I sat there at the entrance to my cave, looking up the river and waiting for the forest lord to show himself again. I found myself wondering after his life. How did he understand our interaction? I tried to imagine how I must appear to him. What was he thinking or feeling about me? But a gulf stood between us. I might feel affection toward him but I could never understand him. I could never inhabit his experience.

As I pondered these things, I felt a subtle change in the atmosphere … something tugging at me. I recognised it as the Spirit. It was almost as if someone was gently pushing thoughts into my mind as if putting flowers in my hair, tenderly and kindly.

There were no actual words but the message was something like this: "Yes, there is a huge gulf - an uncrossable gulf - between us. But take heart … I have crossed it. I came to bridge the gulf between us." God's gentle invitation beckoned me to cross the bridge of Christ and to be reconciled to him once more. I had become alienated from him again. I had not lost my faith but I had lost my way. In the depths of my heart I still believed; but I was confused and angered by his failure to protect my wife and son.

I struggled even as I felt his presence. I was afraid to let go. I was afraid to trust. The gentle probing continued. There was no condemnation. He seemed to be acknowledging my questions and affirming my feelings without answering them. It felt like a warm embrace … but one I did not return. I noticed my fists clenched tightly in my lap. I felt tension throughout my body. I tried to shake it off, intending to rise;

but I sat there still, conflicted. I acknowledged his love but did not yet fully return it.

And so it began. The visit of the stag that autumn began a long slow time of healing. God patiently loved and revealed himself to me. My external life continued much as it had. I made small improvements to the cwm of various kinds. I planted a garden and ploughed a field. I made basic furniture - a table, a chair, a bench. With little effort on my part the forest provided most of what I needed. I thanked God again for the deep knowledge of the natural world Kian had transmitted. I often prayed for Kian's soul.

Over time, prayer became natural for me again. I found myself conversing with God and grew increasingly sensitive to his presence.

Don't misunderstand me, his presence is always with us. But our ability to perceive him can grow. He is always at work, our Lord Jesus perfectly obeyed his will and even he did not always understand or want to do the will of his Father. I continued to grow in discernment - a never-ending process. I made a start then … and now I am a little farther along.

I missed community - my family, the school in Avallon, the warband, Pawl's household, Catwg's llan … each one a particular kind of community. Living alone in the cwm with only animals for company was trying. Having loved and lost, I felt it even more keenly. My previous time in the cwm was a temporary absence from others. I still belonged somewhere. But this time was different. I had nowhere to be. No one was waiting for me or missing me. I was just alone.

In that loneliness, I found myself hungry for relationship. I questioned God's wisdom. I questioned God's care. I questioned his commands for my life. In that solitude, I wrestled with God more than ever before. I demanded he explain himself to me.

I have such an inquisitive mind. I'm always trying to predict the outcome before any action is taken. It would be irrational to do otherwise in this life. But God did not, does not, submit to my questions. He is not unresponsive. He communicated with me, and I became more adept at understanding his ways. In that time of solitude

I gained greater clarity about the subtle moves of his communication with me. There were external circumstances like the miraculous catch of fish or the arrival of the stag. The stag became a regular visitor during those months. In time I fed him from my hand, stroked his nose, or patted his fine flanks. I was amazed that a creature as wild and strong and free as he would be drawn by my care and loving respect.

There were also sensory experiences that assured me of God's presence. Have you ever felt someone's eyes on you before you saw them? Or had the hair on your arms stand up before you turned to catch a glimpse of someone sneaking up on you? I learned to be sensitive to the way my body responded to God's presence. Of course he is always with us, but sometimes he reveals himself in extraordinary ways. He spoke to Abraham and Moses as a man speaks with his friends. They saw him with their eyes, and Abraham even broke bread with him. I did not share such exalted fellowship, but I did grow keen to know and experience his presence.

But the most common way he communicated with me was to gently whisper things into my soul, more often than not drawing me back to Scripture. I cannot tell you how many times I was working on some sort of domestic improvement or labouring in the field or fishing, and a story or a simple word of Scripture would suddenly intrude upon my consciousness. At first I didn't realise these were evidence of the Spirit … nor do I believe everything coming unbidden to my mind is from him. Over time I grew in my ability to understand both the movements of my heart and of his Spirit. And yet I have not perfected this skill; even now I am growing still. Oh how I love to live in constant communication with him, even though I do not always like what he has to say.

Does that surprise you? That I, even after all these years, am not always happy to hear what my Lord says to me? Perhaps I should not say such things, but I will not have you thinking me more - or less - than I am. Exaggerating my personal holiness or relationship with the Father would serve no good purpose … none at all. I want you to know the truth and I hope that you will take from my life some wisdom, some hope, to help you on your own journey.

I tell you truly ... I do not always want to hear what he says. Sometimes he asks me - often he asks me - to do things I would prefer not to do. Submission is a hard thing ... perhaps the hardest thing for me. My mind is prone to ask questions and solve problems. This has served me well in life and I believe my ability to do so is itself a gift from God. However - and this is important - submission has been and continues to be my greatest struggle in relationship with God.

You may call it pride, my children, and you would be correct. The struggle with pride manifests in different ways. In me it is my intellect. The gift that God gave me is the very thing I turn against him. I believe I know best. I refuse to trust that he knows best and that he is trustworthy. I naturally reserve judgement on whether to submit to him until I can see how it will play out.

I was not aware of this at the time, but it became clear during those months alone in the cwm. I had no one else to argue with, no one else to blame. I knew God had called me to that place but he refused to tell me why. I felt my gifts, my abilities, my skills were being wasted.

At first I didn't feel like this at all. At first I was glad there was no one to trouble me in my grief and pain; but as my healing continued and my loneliness increased I looked for reasons to leave the cwm and re-join the stream of humanity. I found myself grumbling and complaining in my conversations with the Lord.

When I would complain of being alone, he would remind me of his presence. I countered that it was not good for man to be alone. Even in Eden man required a human companion. Throwing his own words back at him, my only sense of his response was of his goodness and his loving heart toward me ... a general feeling that this loneliness must do its work in me. He never explained his purposes.

Late that autumn, after the wind had turned cold but before the first snow, my isolation was suddenly penetrated by the sound of riders crashing through the forest.

I was rubbing down Glew in the paddock near the stable when suddenly the stag leapt into the corral. He lowered his head, and I feared my old friend might charge. But just as quickly he lifted his head

253

and bounded across the stream and straight into the stable. A moment later two massive hounds sprang into view followed rapidly by a hunting party on horseback. The dogs, perhaps confused by the scent of my horse and finding me before them shied back, growling. One of the men called out to the dogs while another kicked down the simple railings I had tied to the trees.

Riding through the gap, a tall man who bore a striking resemblance to Pawl called out, "You there! Where is my stag?!"

CHAPTER 56

I regarded him frankly before replying. "Your stag?" I asked.

"Reign in your impudent tongue before I cut it out."

"I meant no disrespect King Meirchion." My use of his title and name both surprised and calmed him. "I only mean that a stag is one of God's most noble and free creatures. Once it is killed and roasting, it may be rightly yours, but until then I am not sure it may be called so."

Meirchion scowled at me long and hard before beginning again, "Illtyd ap Bicanys, I did not recognise you in the heat of the hunt. Cyflym told me you were here and Owain," he paused to gesture over his shoulder, "brought me your gift. Shall we call it rent? We will speak later about you living on my land, but for now I ask you a simple question." He paused momentarily before continuing with urgent agitation. "For the love of God, where did the stag go?! He could be leagues away by now! You and your horse have thrown my dogs; will you at least help them back on the scent by pointing them in the right direction?"

"I am afraid that will do you no good."

"Why is that?" he growled.

"Because where he went, you cannot go without invitation."

"Is that so?" I could see the colour rising in his cheeks. "I am losing patience with you, Illtyd! Where is the stag?"

"The stag is enjoying my hospitality, and I will not let you eat my guest. Indeed there are no customs or laws among our people that allow for the eating of guests," I added with a smile.

Meirchion was angry now. "Where is he?" Then, noticing the stable across the brook he called to his men, "Will someone not bring me my stag?!"

Two men rode spurred their horses toward the stable.

"Stop!" I commanded. The men paused, looking from me to their king and back again. "You will not violate the laws of hospitality, stag or no stag! This is my land, the rent fairly paid as you have just acknowledged. I invite you all to join me for a meal. You are welcome as my guests, but none of my guests will be allowed to eat another. Perhaps some other day, if you meet in other circumstances you may do so, but not today. Not while under the sacred bonds of hospitality."

I could see that Meirchion was conflicted. He was unaccustomed to being contradicted, to be sure. And then there was the issue of the rent. He might not have liked that I was there - and he was hungry for venison - but in acknowledging my payment he had bound himself. He knew as well as I did that by law and by custom, hospitality was a duty and a privilege not lightly to be cast aside. I watched his jaw clench and unclench as he chewed over the situation. Finally he swung down from his saddle - with considerable ease for one so old, I might add.

"Well, let us see what your hospitality is like then," he challenged.

Relieved that the moment of tension seemed to have passed, everyone relaxed.

"I regret to say I am ill-prepared, as I expected no guests today, but what I have I am more than happy to share. Please make yourselves comfortable; I will be back presently." I started to walk away and then thought the better of it, turning back to say, "Owain, if you and a few of your men would help me, I would be most grateful." Meirchion nodded and while a few men saw to their horses and dogs, Owain and two of his men followed me toward the stable.

I wasn't exactly sure what I would find when I entered. I gestured for them to wait outside as I cautiously entered to find the stag, legs tucked under him like the most docile creature, on a bed of straw in the corner. I quickly retrieved some grain and fed him from my hand, patting and cooing over him. He started, and I stepped back quickly to find Owain staring slack-jawed in the doorway, "It's true then … he … he is your guest." Hearing his voice, the other two crept gawking into the stable, but I pushed all three outside.

"Let us leave my guest in peace for the moment. He has enjoyed his repast; now let's get to work on yours," I suggested.

"The truth is we have provisions enough with us for the day. There is no need to trouble yourself." Owain looked at me, still puzzling over what he had just witnessed.

"It is no trouble. I have seen to one guest and he did not refuse my hospitality, as you have seen for yourself. I have offered hospitality to you and your king and I will not fail to feed you heartily." I led the men along the path to my cave, and they helped me retrieve various things for our impromptu meal.

"Please take all these things down to the paddock. As you can see, I have no room to entertain you indoors; but as the weather is fine, we will enjoy what God has given us under the azure dome he has provided." We started down the path together. "Oh, and start a fire when you get there, will you? I have something else to retrieve."

I continued downriver, basket in hand, returning a short time later with plenty of fish and not a few limpets and winkles. Meirchion had claimed the lone chair and small table for himself. I smiled at this but only nodded politely at him. The rest of the men had spread a cloak upon the ground and Meirchion sat upon it while they arranged themselves around. They were already talking among themselves with the ease of men with deep bonds.

I quickly cleaned the fish and placed them on spits for roasting. The winkles were set to boiling with leeks and herbs in a pot on the fire. I put the limpets carefully on the coals at the edge of the fire to roast in their upturned shells. From the provisions Owain had helped me retrieve, I set nuts, apples, and berries before my guests. I noticed they had retrieved flatbreads from their bags as well. Once this was all arranged I turned my attention back to my guests. "My lord, I trust my humble fare will not trouble you. I regret I am not adequately provisioned for guests so many and so eminent. I have no wine nor mead, nor even cider or beer. But I have fresh water aplenty, and God has provided fish and the bounty of his good earth."

"It may be God's earth, but this is my patch of it. All that you have, you have from my hand, from my streams, from my coast," Meirchion responded haughtily.

"And I thank you for letting me settle here." I bowed my head slightly. "I believe God has called me here, and I am grateful for your permission."

"About that," he interrupted as he raised his hand toward me. "How long have you been here now? It seems you have settled yourself rather permanently," he gestured to the paddock and the stable. "How long do you intend to stay? This has been a favourite hunting ground of mine; and as you well know, the deer seem to favour the woods here about."

"Yes, I have noticed that … one stag in particular," I replied with a smile. "As to how long I will be here, I do not know. I have been discussing that with the Lord at length."

"Have you now?" It was Meirchion's turn to smile. "And what does he say to you?"

"He says many things, mostly about his love and his goodness, but very little about the future. I am afraid he has kept me in the dark. I only know that he has called me here."

The smell of roasting fish was wafting over us now. "Excuse me, my lord." I turned back to the meal preparations.

Before long I had prepared a plate for Meirchion. In truth, I only had one plate. The others had to make do with their flatbreads and whatever they could find. The conversation mostly ground to a halt as we enjoyed our meagre feast.

"Well I must admit that was tasty!" Meirchion offered, licking his moustache and wiping his hands. Having eaten, he seemed in much better spirits.

"Simple fare, my lord," I apologised.

"Yes, but we are not too grand to delight in the simple pleasures of life. Are we lads?" He asked his men. Their responses were enthusiastic but muffled by the food still in their mouths. He turned to me seriously. "You know, you could come with us. I know how Pawl esteemed you, and I have heard of your service in the wars with the Saecson. We are far from the Saecson here, but the Scoti trouble our shores and the bastards have even settled in the west. I fear they will push into our lands before long, or die trying. I won't trouble them if they don't trouble me, but I'm not sure they feel the same. We could use a man like you with us. You are clearly a resourceful and educated man, and I know of your prowess in battle. What say you?!"

CHAPTER 57

My heart leapt at this invitation. I was hesitant about Meirchion …
but, I reasoned to myself, God did call me to this place and perhaps
this is what he had in mind.

"Nothing would please me more," I responded. Meirchion looked
both surprised and pleased. But no sooner were the words out of my
mouth than I felt I must decline. My head dropped to my chest as I
gritted my teeth and sighed. Looking back up into Meirchion's now
troubled face I added, "But I must decline."

"Why?" he asked with furrowed brow.

"I don't rightly know. I only know it is not what God would have me
do. I seem nailed to this spot. He has not released me."

"And what if I released you from this spot? What if I forbade you to
live upon this land? What then?" he ominously inquired.

"I have no easy answers for you, my lord. I only know he bids me stay.
I would serve you gladly as my kinsman and king, but the King of
Heaven will not allow it. I am no less frustrated than you, I assure
you!" I added.

Meirchion looked at me darkly for some time before rising suddenly.
"It seems you will not ride with us; but we will be off. My quarry eludes
me today on all fronts. Please give my greetings to your other guest
and tell him I hope to have him for a meal at my hearth before long."
He grinned grimly as he gestured toward the stable.

As he swung into his saddle he added, "Perhaps your king will have a
change of heart. We are not done with this conversation. Winter here
if you like, but know a warm hearth and goodwill await you in my hall."

Those words troubled me through that long cold winter. In bouts of
cold or fits of loneliness his invitation beckoned and tempted me. I
sometimes dreamed of myself in the company of men, around the
hearth, enjoying the warmth of human connection only to wake and
find myself alone.

I continued to knock on heaven's door through those dark days and darker nights. The more I did, the more I knew the companionship of God. His presence comforted me, and I grew ever more aware of his subtle movements. He met me in that season and assured me of his love and care. He also made it clear that he required my absolute surrender. As my commander and my king I owed him nothing less. He had purchased me back from slavery and I owed him everything … but oh the struggle to submit!

Alone in that valley I found my ears and my heart reaching out for connection. As I did so I touched God, but I also came into contact with others. At first these other voices seemed indistinguishable from my internal dialogues. I know my heart is deceitful and wicked but sometimes unbidden thoughts would suddenly rise up in me … ideas and temptations. Sometimes these were directly contrary to God, like the temptation to leave the valley and find solace in the company of men when God demanded my presence there. Other times they were more subtle.

Like the serpent in the Garden when he asked Eve questions about the trees, I found questions rising in me. "Did God really say you have to stay here? Why would God say that when he also said it is not good for man to be alone?" They were subtle questions intended to drive me away from God. When pushing a boat away from a quay, you don't shove it with all your might. You softly and steadily push and the water parts before the gentle push, even though it resists the thrusting heave.

In that long dark winter, God reminded me again of the spiritual war. Whether we choose to acknowledge it or not, we are embroiled in a long, drawn-out campaign against a wily and powerful enemy. Satan and his demons are arrayed against the kingdom of God. They have been fighting this war for millennia and have many strategies and tactics at their disposal. We, however, must come fresh to the fight in each generation. This war plays out most often through deception - for when Lucifer lies, he speaks his native tongue. He and his minions have mastered the arts of their long cold war, and they prey upon us all.

One of their greatest deceptions is to lull us into disbelieving their existence. We cannot fail to recognise the difficulties we face in this life, and we look for an enemy. When the demonic is removed from our reckoning, we are left to see others as the enemy. We bite and devour each other, which delights the demons. Satan knows he was defeated at the cross of Christ. He knows his time is short, and so he prowls around looking for those he can devour and drag with him down into the fiery pit. When we leave demons out of the equation, we demonise others.

Another deception demons use is to reveal themselves in another guise. They are real and they can move and work and show themselves. When they do so they mask their hateful and destructive intentions by promising to enter into agreements with us. They call themselves gods of water, earth, birth, and death. They feign control over the things we need, the things we desire … and promise them to us if we will but bow down and worship them. Did not Lucifer, the devil himself, do as much when he tempted Christ in the wilderness? And so we find Kian and Myrddin and many like them led into a captivity they welcome as they readily serve these so-called gods who only want to destroy them. Many are fooled these days and learn only too late - in this life or the next – that they have been deceived. May God have mercy on their souls.

Those months in isolation showed me I must spend my life in the heavenly warband and fight for the King of Heaven. As I grew more attentive, I grew more adept at discerning between the voice of God and the voices of demons. But not all the voices leading me astray were external. I recognised some movements of my heart were simply me, and I struggled to more fully grasp the struggle within myself.

My pride was my constant companion. Strangely, I found it easier to submit to Brennus, Pawl, or Arthwyr than to God. But as the Lord pointed out to me that winter, the appearance of submission is not the same as true submission. I prayed so many times that winter, "Lord, I believe - help me with my unbelief." I wanted to want to submit to God. I knew the stories of his faithfulness in the Scriptures. But still I found it hard to surrender my will, to believe that he was for me. I knew his promise to work all things together for my good, but it was, and still is, hard to exchange my definition of good for his. I knew I had no choice but to submit. It is foolish to resist. A sailor does not fight the wind nor sail against it. He must accept the wind that is and learn to work with it. The Spirit, like the wind, blows where it will and we are but sailors who can move with it or vainly attempt to row against it.

In the long, slow conversation that winter, God reminded me of Antony of Egypt. My wet, cold cwm was a far cry from the desiccated sands of Egypt, but it was deserted enough.

God reminded me of my dreams and of my calling to lay my arms aside and take up spiritual weapons. I knew I must foreswear arms forever. My time in the warbands of the Britons was truly finished. It was many more years before I could part with Guielandus' gifts, but that is another story.

I realised I had resisted Meirchion without weapons or the threat of violence. Upon reflection, I wondered at my boldness to defend the stag from the hunt and to stand unarmed, commanding men with nothing but will and words.

In the absence of human companionship I pressed deeper into my prayers. I had no choice but to seek a companion that would never leave me or forsake me. That seeking led me to a rhythm of prayer and work that has marked my life ever since. I sought to become ever more aware of when I was obeying Jesus' command to remain in him, and when I had slipped away or wandered off.

Even though I knew the call of God and the reality of the spiritual war, I struggled to see prayer as real work - work that mattered. I have always been a man of action, a man who delights in a hard day's labour. It is easy to look back on a day spent in the field and admire what has been accomplished. What do you have to show for a day spent in prayer? The spiritual war is real and yet intangible. A smith, a miner, a farmer, a warrior ... each reaches the end of their day and see what they have wrought. The work of prayer is secret and the outcomes are a mystery.

God does not allow us to treat prayer like a recipe. He will not be reduced to a transaction. Prayer is a relationship with a living being. God is a free and very great king, the king above all kings to whom we may not dictate, with whom we cannot bargain. Of course we are free to try … men often do. But Christ is not like the gods of old whose favour may be bought or who may be threatened or cajoled into action. No, he has already made the sacrifice. He purchased us for himself. We are his children and we must approach as little children with innocent boldness, utter trust, and humble submission.

This is the lesson I had to learn that long cold winter … a lesson repeatedly learned but never mastered.

Eventually the spring came, and with it a new season of my life began in earnest.

CHAPTER 58

While the winter had been cold and wet, the spring was marginally warmer, though just as wet. The daffodils were just sprouting when my first visitors arrived. It had been months since I had seen another human face.

On a wet and windy day I heard horses and made my way out of my cave and across the river where, during the winter, I had cleared a small area in an ancient grove on the edge of the main trail through the cwm. After the impromptu feast in the paddock, I realised the need for a more convenient place to receive people. I had not expected to need it so soon.

Just as I walked into the clearing, two horses entered from the other side. The warrior seated on the leading horse called out to me cheerily. "Ho there Illtyd! You're still here after all! It's good to see you."

"It's good to see you as well, Owain ap Mor! Come and warm yourself by my fire."

Owain dismounted and turned to help a young boy down from the horse trailing behind him. But the boy pushed his hands away and leapt down himself. "May I know the name of my other guest?" I enquired.

The lad marched right up to me and looking up into my face - for he was no more than six years of age - said, "I am Pawl ap Aurelian and I am to be your student. You are to teach me all I will need to know to make my mark upon this world." As he finished his little memorised speech he nodded and seemed quite pleased with himself. I could not suppress a smile.

"Am I now?"

"Yes, you are. King Meirchion told me to tell you that, and you are his servant." The boy pronounced.

"Am I really?" My smile broadened.

Owain looked aghast and snatched at the boy, trying to push him behind him. But the little scamp leapt and spun away behind a nearby tree. Peeking out, he pulled a face at Owain. Owain sighed, and turning to me said, "I believe what the boy means is that King Meirchion would be grateful if you would take upon yourself the tutelage of his nephew Pawl."

I nodded. "Come inside, and we will discuss it over a fire and a hot drink. Do not worry yourself. I suspect the lad's version is closer to the words of the King."

As we settled around the fire in the cave, I had another chance to study my young guest. He had a head of dark curls that reminded me of my brother, Sadwrn. His quick eyes and bold face told me that teaching him might be a delight and would definitely be a challenge.

As they warmed themselves and I prepared our meal, Owain caught me up on the happenings in the wider world. The wars with the Saecson continued and Arthwyr was still Dux Bellorum. He had been wed to Gwenhwyfar and allied himself with the kings of the south. There was talk of granting him lands of his own from those recovered from the Saecsons.

Eventually the small talk subsided and Owain brought up the matter at hand … the matter seated across the fire from me, Pawl. "His father, Aurelian died in a Scoti raid," he said bluntly. "Meirchion has taken him in. You are a learned man, and Meirchion can think of no one better to teach his nephew. The king permits you to live here as long as this arrangement continues."

"Ah, so we come to it." I knew that old dog would be up to something. But I also sensed God's will behind the selfish designs of the king. So I agreed.

That long hard winter was the prelude to a fresh spiritual planting … a rich planting that continues to yield fruit and seed to this day, a fertile planting that sent seed out to fields far and wide resulting in harvests that continue to this very day. Even here in Little Britannia, land of my birth, there are fertile fields freshly cultivated.

I awoke that morning a solitary man, alone with God in the cwm he had ordained to me and went to sleep that night as a teacher. From that simple beginning, over the next months and years the llan grew. Even that first night I knew that my cave, which was quite comfortable for one, would not be sufficient for two.

The next day Pawl and I began the first of what would become many buildings.

Over the years you, my sons, joined us and then many more as our llan grew to include seven colleges. As more students were added and more mouths to feed, we needed more land to cultivate. It was muddy and herculean work to reclaim land from the sea.

As our community increased we sought to bless others with God's bountiful blessings. People needed a safe place to labour and live in those troubled times, and we were happy to have the help.

Catwg returned from Scotia and Rome bringing copies of the sacred texts. I am forever indebted to him and to our brothers and sisters in Scotia who cultivated and carefully preserved the knowledge of those who have gone before us. Without their bookish ways much wisdom would have been lost.

Of course the presence of Christ is not the absence of conflict. Even among Christians there are struggles and fights. How could there not be until that day when all strivings will cease?

CHAPTER 59

Pawl, you were the first ... and what a joy you have been to me. Do you remember? Do you remember the day you came to me? Who knew when I agreed to take you in all that would follow? God alone knew.

As forthright today as you were then, you were there when Dewi arrived. You witnessed the arrival of Samson, Gildas, Lenoris, Teilo, Tudwal, Baglan, and all your brothers.

I know many stories remain untold but I will leave that to you, my sons, my brothers. The rest of the stories are yours to tell.

Come now, let me bless you ...

Pawl, my son - you were the first to come to me. You have never lost your boldness ... and may you carry that with you to the day when you will see Christ face to face. In your confidence, have care that you do not snuff out the smouldering wick. Be sensitive to those you may bruise as you audaciously proclaim the good news about Jesus.

Dewi, my son - you are so hard on yourself. I admire your tenacity and your eagerness for holiness, and yet I fear you may push yourself and others too hard. Do not cease your preaching or your striving, but do not forget the tender love and effervescent joy of God. I know you fear the degradation of the body and the soul, but do not let your pursuit of perfection allow you to miss the grace he has for you.

Gildas, my son - you have a gift for words and I know that well. You have far surpassed your teachers in oration and writing. Your passion brings to mind the prophets of old who spoke the truths of God without consideration to high and low alike. And yet, in your zeal might you not be in danger of pulling up the wheat with the tares? Have a care that in your judgement you do not forget mercy.

Samson, my son - thank you for your hospitality. Even here in the land of my birth I find myself in need of that. Foxes have holes and the birds have nests; I have nowhere to call my own. But Samson, with all your success in spreading the faith and building communities of blessing and prayer, beware of pride. Beware of allowing others to put you upon a plinth and make an idol of you. Always be careful to give glory to God.

Teilo, my son - in your zeal for truth and righteousness, do not forget compassion. I know you are fervent for the truth. You would have our people set free. You fear the rise of the old ways as do I; but be careful. You cannot overcome fear with more fear. You cannot overcome the darkness in dark ways. In your eagerness to stamp out evil, do not forget compassion for those who have been deceived. Remember that our battle is not against flesh and blood.

Oh my children … indulge me but a little longer.

That the God of the universe, the High King of Heaven should stoop to us is a delightful mystery. He alone knows the end from the beginning. He alone sees all and works all things together for good. And yet, our stories matter. God himself has measured out work for us to do and a time and place in which to do it.

The story of my life is drawing toward the end and yet there are chapters in the life beyond that I cannot imagine. But you my children … your lives are not yet poured out to the dregs. You have many stories yet to live and work to do. I pray you will surpass me in holiness and productive labour for God's kingdom.

I fear my tale has become a lengthy one, full of digressions and details that may not feed your soul or your mind. I spoke the words as they came to me. I have tried to tell them plainly, without artifice or embellishment. I wanted you to know; I wanted you to understand - or at least to hear my confession.

It seems I was born to battle. It seems my life has been one battle after another. No enemy has been more fierce or persistent than the enemy within. This has been the most ferocious battle of my life … a fight against an enemy as strong as any Frank, as wily as any Saecson, as bold as any Briton: my own wandering heart.

The longer I have lived the more I have grappled with my own darkness. Too often, even in my service to God, my motives were mixed. My greatest struggle has been to know myself, to master myself, and to drag my recalcitrant carcass to the foot of his gracious throne. There, because of the cross of Christ, I find grace day by day.

May this grace - the grace of our Lord, Jesus Christ - the love of God, and the fellowship of the Holy Spirit be with you now and always.

Now I will close my eyes and rest a bit. I am tired and ready to go home.

Epilogue

And so it was. My master, Illtyd ap Bicanys, drifted off to sleep that night.

Sometime during the night he slipped out of his bodily tent, crossed the Jordon and entered the promised land, finding peace at last. His striving ceased and he entered his rest. He lived and loved in the time he was given. He cannot come to us but someday, Lord willing, we will go to him.

He was a scholar and leader, a man of incredible wisdom and ordinary miracles. He fed the hungry and clothed the naked - a contemplative revolutionary who lived his faith in unsettled times. He taught those of us who would listen and was unwaveringly patient with those who would not. Some would say too patient.

My master did not choose the day of his birth but it seemed he chose - or at least knew - the day of his death. I have never known his equal. His mind was a rare treasure, his knowledge esoteric, his service great. Not all have his gifts of wisdom or foresight, but to all who would receive it, the greatest gift is yours for the taking.

I, Gildas ap Caw, have recorded Illtyd's confession. You have read how he lived in the time and place God measured out to him.

I pray you may find all you seek, and may you grow in the knowledge and love of God.

Author's Note

In 2009 I moved to Wales. At the time, I knew almost nothing of the history of the area or peoples, including the Welsh. I've always loved history. My first degree was in ancient history with a particular emphasis on late antiquity. Before we moved, I came across a town called Llantwit Major in the Vale of Glamorgan. "Llantwit Major" is a bad anglicisation of the Welsh: Llanilltud Fawr, which roughly translated means "The large (great) enclosure (community/church) of Illtud (Illtyd)." I later discovered many other places in Wales and Brittany that bore his name.

This immediately provoked the question: Who is Illtud? The investigation that started with that question eventually led to this book, with all the joys and challenges it brought.

Illtud (I prefer the older spelling of Illtyd) was a truly pivotal figure in Wales and the British world of his day. His students include Saint David (Dewi in Welsh), the patron saint of Wales, Saint Gildas, the author of the earliest surviving documents of British history (and one of the few from a distinctly British/Welsh perspective, as opposed to those of English/Anglo-Saxon outlook), Saint Samson of Dol, one of the patron saints of Brittany, and Paul Aurelian, another founding saint in Brittany. Testimonies to Illtyd's importance exist in place names, genealogies, and local histories as well as later legends. This was a person who lived large in the imaginations of those who knew him … someone with whom those who came after wished to be identified.

Convinced of his importance but confounded by the idea that a person who had once been so important could virtually vanish from the historical narrative, I was intrigued.

I dove into this research with abandon. The deeper I dug the more interesting veins of history, myth, and legend I discovered. I found myself falling in love with Wales and the Welsh. I also found personal resonance with some aspects of Illtyd's life and my own. My quest for understanding fuelled my desperation to pick the grains of the truth scattered through the various, often contradictory sources.

Part of the problem I faced was the dearth of documentary evidence for this part of the world and this period of history. The ancient Britons and their progeny, the Welsh and Cornish, were educated peoples but more given to reciting poetry and telling stories than writing them down. Many of the Welsh and Latin sources are only snippets of the original or much later copies of copies containing quite a bit of interpolated information.

One clear exception to this is Gildas. His extended sermon "On the Ruin of Britain" was a primary source for me. The fact that Gildas was one of Illtyd's students made his writing even more interesting. Writing roughly two centuries later, the Venerable Bede used Gildas as his primary source for the history of Britain before the arrival of the Anglo-Saxons. The life of Samson of Dol, written a full century before Bede, was helpful as well. But these were only the tip of the iceberg where historical documents and artefacts were concerned.

History is an art as much as a science. It requires us to look back into the past to trace the tributaries that flow into our present, in search of meaning. Place names are an important part of tracing those tributaries, particularly in cases where documentary evidence is lacking. Poems, accounts of the lives of the saints, and the genealogies of the kings are useful as well. However, medieval documents cannot be considered historically accurate in the sense we would mean today. They were generally written centuries later by men seeking to advance their personal and/or political agendas. They simply did not think about historical facts as fixed in the way we might today.

Living in Wales also allowed me to visit many places relevant to the stories in this book. In doing so I came across many maps, genealogies, and artefacts in small museums and displays in churches dotted around Wales and England, all of which helped to reconstruct Illtyd's world in my imagination.

Illtyd's world was a world in transition. We like to think of our world as stable with clear categories and we often push this quest for stability and clarity into the history we curate. Our histories help to tell us who we are, how we got here, and what it all means. Illtyd lived in a monumentally turbulent time … a time between times, to borrow a Celtic phrase.

The Roman Empire was fading but it had seen hard times before and had bounced back. From our perch, we can see it would not recover, but they had no such clarity. The Pax Romana was fading and no new order had yet arisen. When all seems chaos, how do you live? Who do you trust? Where do you find your identity? How do you tell friend from foe, "us" vs. "them"? These were critical questions facing Illtyd's generation.

The rise of Christianity is another stream that may seem inevitable from where we sit but was not a foregone conclusion in Illtyd's day. There are nearly as many pagan shrines scattered around Wales and England from this era as churches. Many tales of the revitalisation of druidic worship, as well as the continuation of Roman paganism, survive from this era. The rise of Christianity in the Roman Empire was a relatively new development as the empire was crumbling. The status of Christianity in Britain was even more tenuous. There was a monumental conflict between competing world views.

Illtyd's era saw a huge clash of ethnicities and people movements. "Strange" peoples suddenly mixed with those who had historical claims to the land – people who had themselves settled among and/or displaced even older inhabitants in previous generations. There was an increasing tendency toward tribalisation as centralising/unifying forces lost their power and prestige.

All of these realities struck a chord with me. I wondered … could it be that Illtyd's era might have lessons for our own? This was brought home even more with the rise of Covid in 2020 because (although I don't explore it in this book) Illtyd's world was repeatedly buffeted by waves of pestilence and plague.

I have long been intrigued by the confluence of culture, identity, and faith. All of these themes swirl through the life of Illtyd and his contemporaries. As I studied and reviewed my copious notes, a story began to take shape around the questions: How can we live well through our tumultuous period of history? How does a saint become a saint? How can the seemingly contradictory stories about Illtyd be woven together into a narrative that honours his life and times and might be helpful in our own?

I voraciously devour historical fiction but am not a fan of books that serve up posthumous character assassination against those who cannot defend themselves. As I began to write I continued to research, trying to compose the most historically accurate version of events while recognising that imagination would be necessary to fill in the details.

I should probably mention the Arthurian inclusions. I believe the later Arthurian legends to be almost entirely fictional propaganda for subsequent English rulers. That said, in my research, I concluded that a British war leader named (or nicknamed) Arthur existed. I have chosen a more obscure spelling of his name in an attempt to create some space between the character I invented and those invented by Geoffrey of Monmouth and others.

Trynihid, Illtyd's wife, is my attempt to make sense of the conflict between some sources which have Illtyd married (and place names associated directly with her) and the later monastic treatment of her (either by ignoring her entirely or by him sending her away because he is repulsed by her). The history of the British church and of Celtic Christianity in general during this period was almost entirely independent from the form of Roman Catholicism that was developing on the European mainland. The Celtic church had recognised many women as leaders and did not forbid the marriage of clergy or monks. Roman Catholic practices began to exert more influence over the Celtic stream of the church after the Synod of Whitby. But during the time of Illtyd, Roman domination of the church did not exist.

A few other specific character notes (See character list for help with pronunciation):

- ❖ Kian is based on the legendary last druid of the Britons.
- ❖ Myrddin is based on the character in Welsh mythology, not Arthurian legends.
- ❖ Scapilion is based on a legendary scholar and priest in France and specifically at Avallon.
- ❖ Guielandus is based on a legendary smith and a deep dive into historical metallurgy.
- ❖ The names of Illtyd's families and the kings of the day are drawn from various genealogies.

I have chosen to default to older spellings (i.e. Saecson instead of Saxon), as these were more common in Illtyd's day. It has been interesting to discover much of our standardisation in spelling has come so late, particularly in English. Incidentally, the term Saecson was widely used to denote all the Germanic invaders of the time. Modern historians tend to distinguish between them as Jutes, Friesians, Danes, Angles, and Saxons … all of whom were progenitors of the English. While the Brythonic tribes shared a common language and general culture, they were not a unified nation. The Welsh and Breton are the primary nations carrying this rich historical mantle in our day. I have used some Welsh or Brythonic terms (i.e. Llan) where I felt they best brought out the distinct local flavour without losing my readers. (You can thank the early readers of the manuscript that many other Welsh words were removed!)

My ambition has been to write a story that would honour the historical personages and portray them as accurately and generously as my research and imagination would allow. Of course, I have resorted to invention where the history left gaps requiring explanation or the narrative invited elaboration while also telling an engaging and entertaining story. Below you will find a timeline of relevant historical events (as near as I could tell) and events I have invented to make sense of the intersection of history and story. Much of this involved judgement calls. Some historians would agree with my choices while others would not. There are a lot of dates and other events where there is not entire agreement during this era.

I have always found it fun to consider the "what-ifs" where the lines of history and myth converge. I hope this story educated and informed, even as it entertained.

I hope you enjoyed reading it as much as I enjoyed writing it!

Blessings on you and yours,

D. A. Stewart

Llanilltud Fawr

16 October 2020

NOTES ON LANGUAGE

Languages are not static things. They constantly evolve and change through exposure to social, historical, and geographical events. Over time languages (and language groups) influence each other and borrow words from one another. Language is often a key line of demarcation of identity and culture.

Illtyd's native language was a Celtic language most closely related to Welsh. He would likely have been exposed to a form of Gaelic from another branch of the Celtic language family, as it was spoken by the Scoti (Irish). He would have been educated in Latin. He would also have had contact with various Germanic invaders (Goths, Franks, and of course Saxons).

Latin was the language of the Roman Empire and remained the language of education and the church until its relatively recent decline. Latin languages remain with us as Romance languages. Two modern examples are Italian and Spanish. You may have noticed several places and names related to Latin, as it would have been common at that time.

English is a Germanic language and came into Britain with the invading Germanic tribes including, but not limited to, the Angles and Saxons.

Pronunciation

Welsh is a phonetic language, so you pronounce every letter and most letters have only one possible pronunciation.

Rather than providing a general pronunciation guide (you can easily find those online), I will provide a suggested pronunciation for native English speakers, with just a few quick notes that will be of particular use:

1- The "ll" (double l) is a single Welsh letter that has no English equivalent. It is roughly like aspirating a "th" as in "the" and "l" as in "tell" together or with the "l" sound immediately following.

2- "w" in Welsh is a vowel, like an "oo" in pool.
3- "f" in Welsh is like a "v" ("ff" is the "f" sound in English).
4- "dd" in Welsh is like "th" in "the."

There are only three specific Welsh words I included (besides names):

- Llan (*Thlan*) A community (and/or the enclosed/defined space where the community is located, often with a boundary wall/fence)
- Cwm (*Koom*) A small valley
- Caer (*Karè*) Fortress or stronghold

Character List

In Illtyd's time there were no surnames as such - they used the name of the father. For men they used "ap" meaning "son of" and for women they used "ferch" meaning "daughter of."

Illtyd ap Bicanys (*Ithl-tuhd app Bick-an-us*) - Often pronounced by English speakers as Ill-tud

Bicanys ap Aldwr (*Bick-an-us app Al-dure*) - Illtyd's father

Rheinwylydd ferch Amlawdd (*Rain-ooil-lith verch Am-lauth*) - Illtyd's mother

Gildas ap Caw (*Gill-das app Caoo*) – One of Illtyd's students

Kian (*Key-ann*) – A bard and druid and teacher of Illtyd

Scapilion (Skap-ill-eon) – A priest, scholar, and teacher of Illtyd

Myrddin ap Cynwal – (*Mur-then app Kin-ooal*) Illtyd's cousin

Arthwyr ap Meurig – (*Arth-ooer app May-oo-rig*) Illtyd's cousin

Brennus (*Bren-us*) - A warrior, battle chief, and teacher of Illtyd

Morgan, Llew (*Thloo* or Lou), Rhodri (*Rhod-ree*), and Cai (*Kah'ee*) - Warriors who served Bicanys and later Illtyd

Guielandus (*Gway-land-us*) - A blacksmith and friend to Illtyd

Trynihid (*Truh-ni-hid*) - Illtyd's wife

Catwg ap Gwynllyw (*Kat-oog app Gooen-thleoo*) - Illtyd's friend

Sadwrn ap Bicanys (*Sad-oorn app Bick-an-us*) - Illtyd's brother

Pawl ap Aurelian (*Paul app Aoo-rail-lee-an*) - One of Illtyd's students

Dewi (*Dehoo-we*) – One of Illtyd's students (later known as St. David)

LOCATIONS

(Also see maps at the front of the book)

- Glywysing (*Gleyoo-es-ing*) - A Brittonic (Silurian) kingdom in what is now South Wales split into sub-kingdoms including Gorfynydd (*Gore-veh-nuth*) and Penychen (*Pen-eh-chen*) and Gwynllywg (*Gooen-thleoog*).
- Rhegin (*Rheg-inn*) - A Brittonic kingdom in what is now South-Eastern England
- Armorica (*Are-more-eeka*) - A Brittonic kingdom in what is now Brittany in western France
- Liger River – The river in France later known as the Loire
- River Renk – In modern Brittany known as La Rance

HISTORICAL TIMELINE

Bolded events have broad historical affirmation. Events in *italics* are my inventions. All other events are judgement calls supported by evidence.

Date(s)	Events
44 AD	**Britannia becomes a Roman province**
100 AD	**Roman Villa founded in Llantwit Major**
360	**Picts attack from the north, Scoti (Irish) from the West**
367	**The Great Conspiracy – Picts, Scoti, and Saecsons (Angles, Jutes, and Saecsons) attack simultaneously**
368	**Picts, Scoti, and Saecsons defeated and driven out by Theodosius**
370-400	Deisi (an Irish tribe) move into Dyfed (South West Wales) – intermarrying with Britons – possibly invited as foederati (a common late Roman practice of settling foreign troops/mercenaries on the border to dissuade other potential invaders) possibly by Macsaen Wledig (Magnus Maximus)
382	Macsaen Wledig defeats Picts and Scoti again
383	Macsaen Wledig takes most of the troops and leaves for continent
370-400	**Martin of Tours in Gaul**
388	Macsaen Wledig dies on continent
394	Vitalinus born (later known as Vortigern)
404	Vitalinus marries Macsaen Wledig's daughter
406	**Mass Germanic Invasion over the Rhine**
407	Constantine III takes remainder of the Roman legions/British troops to Gaul. This is the end of the Roman military in Briton but many Roman government administrators (civitas) remained.
407	Vitalinus made Dux Britanniarum.
409	**Saecson Raids start – perhaps driven by Goths and others behind them**
410	**Rome sacked by the Goths**
410	**Honorius refuses to send aid to Britain in response to a letter from Romano-British leaders (civitas)**
410	Vitalinus appeals for troops from Brittany (trained and armed by the Romans)
410	Brittonic troops from Armorica come to the aid of Britannia, led by Custennin (Illtyd's uncle)
411	**Constantine III dies on the continent**

412-425	Internal struggles in Britain – political reorganization – tribal and civitas loyalties
423	Birth of St. Patrick in Britain
425	Vitalinus becomes Vortigern – High King (Self-declared/Pretender to the throne)
429	**St. Germanus visits Britain**
430	Vortigern invites the Saecsons to settle in Thanet (Hengest and Horsa) as foederati
433	Vortigern marries Hengest daughter Rowena and invites Saecsons to settle in Kent
434	Patrick taken to Ireland by raiders (Scoti) possibly from College of Theodosius (an early Christian settlement and training centre which was destroyed in what is now Llantwit Major)
440	Patrick escapes and returns to Britain
441	Saecson Foederoti revolt and break out
446	Vortigern seeks help from Soissons (the last directly Roman ruled province in Gaul). Aegidius refuses his request
447	Germanus returns to Britain, Vortigern flees from Germanus. Scoti and Picts defeated
450	**Hengest founds the Kingdom of Kent**
455	Hengest fight Vortigern at Aylesford.
455	**Vandals sack Rome**
456	**Patrick returns to Ireland as a missionary**
457	**Hengest massacres Britons in Kent**
460	**Night of the long knives – Saecsons kill nobles but leave Vortigern alive, Vortigern grants more land for his freedom**
465	St. Dyfrig born (Dyfrig was not included in our story, but may feature in future books)
468	*Arthwyr born*
469	Riothamus in Gaul from Britain – *Betrayed and went to Avallon in Burgundy*
470	**Brigid founds her monastery at Kildare**
470	Illtyd born
470	*Myrddin born*
470	Catwg born
474	Budic II born to Erich (brother of Budic I)
476	**Last Western Roman Emperor overthrown by Odoacer (a barbarian/Germanic military commander)**
477	**Aelle lands in Kent as Bretwalda, West Sussex slaughters locals**
477	*Myrddin arrives in Brittany*

480	St. Benedict born at Nursia
481	**Clovis chosen king of Franks at age 16, Clovis is founder of Merovingian dynasty of Frankish kings**
483	**Gundobad begins Lex Burgundionum**
484	**Euric, king of the Goths dies and Franks see this as an opportunity**
485	St. Samson born – Gildas born
484	*The Council of Brittany – Alliances formed – Scapilion and Illtyd go to Avallon* *Myrddin and Arthwyr go to Britannia*
486	Clovis captures Soissons – closes in on Brittany
485-489	Battles between the Saecsons and Britons in Britannia *(involving Arthwyr)*
489	*Bicanys killed by Saecson raiders. Illtyd rejects tonsure and returns to Brittany to fight – Further training with Brennus*
490	St David born – Paul Aurelian born
491	Hoel, son of Budic II born
491	Aelle takes Rhegin and kills all inhabitants *(including Arthwyr's father Meurig)*
491	*Myrddin turns to the dark, assisted by Kian*
492	*Illtyd goes to Britain, joins with Arthwyr and Myrddin*
492	*The first battle with Illtyd and Arthwyr at Battle of Bassas (Basingstoke)*
492	Battle at River Glein (near Water Newton/Peterborough)
492	Battles in Lincoln/Lindsey
493	**St. Patrick dies**
493	Battle at Guintguic (High Cross)
	Illtyd marries Trynihid and winters with Pawl
493 AD	**Clovis marries Clotilda, niece of King of Burgundy, and brings all Franks under one rule**
494	*Trynihid dies in childbirth - Illtyd moves to a western valley (later Llantwit Major)*
495	**Cerdic lands at Southampton kills local Britons – starts a new phase of the war**
	Paul Aurelian, David, and Samson arrive to learn from Illtyd
496 AD	**Clovis and 3000 Frankish soldiers accept Catholic religion, Clovis defeats Alemanni, Frankish border secured at Rhine, beginning of Middle Ages**
497	**Brittany allies itself with the newly-Christian Franks but retains self-rule**
500	Battle of Badon and 50 years of peace with Saecsons (settled in the East)
500	Gildas and Teilo born
500 AD	**Clovis Attacks Burgundians at Dijon**

500-540	**British civil wars – Squabbling between British kingdoms worsens, frequent wars**
507 AD	**Clovis Attacks Visigoths under Alaric at Vouille'**
508 AD	**Ostrogoths defeat Franks**
511 AD	**Clovis extends his rule to all of France and Western Germany, then Clovis dies**
520	Budic II of Brittany claims throne of Cornwall
521	St. Dyfrig appoints St. Samson as Bishop in Glamorgan
521	St. Samson founds monastery at Dol in Brittany and becomes Abbot
525	Teilo tries Kian and finds him guilty, Kian executed by Budic II
530	**St. Benedict founds monastery at Monte Casino**
530	*Illtyd dictates this book (to Gildas)*
531 AD	**Franks defeat Thuringian**
533 AD	**Franks defeat Burgundians, Burgundy absorbed by Franks**
535-36	Plague and famine
536-539	Extreme weather and famine from the lack of sunlight – crop failures
500-540	**Scoti conquer South Western Scotland**
537	Battle of Camlann – *Arthwyr wounded and taken to Avallon*
540 - 544	Gildas wrote during brief relative peace of this era
543	Benedict dies
547-9	**Plague strikes Britannia – spread from plague of Justinian (540)**

Printed in Great Britain
by Amazon